The Geneva Connection

"Thriller readers are hooked, barbed and immediately reeled in. The narrative mesmerizes from the outset. The pace is swift and the action enough to make any reader's toes curl in frightening expectation."

—Art Cockerill, writer and journalist

"I couldn't put *The Geneva Connection* down. The intricate plot, laced with just enough background information to make it realistic and understandable, takes twist after turn until you reach the final destination, white-knuckling it all the way. An intense thrill ride through the world of investment banking, drug cartels, and money laundering."

—Long and Short Reviews

"With this page-turner, Bodenham aspires to do for fund managers what John Grisham has done for lawyers."

—*Corporate Financier Magazine*

"Bodenham, a dealmaker who made his name in the cut and thrust world of turnarounds, is a fine writer of thriller fiction."

—*Real Deals Magazine*

THE GENEVA CONNECTION

ALSO BY MARTIN BODENHAM

Shakedown
Once a Killer (*)

(*) – coming soon from Down & Out Books

MARTIN BODENHAM

THE GENEVA CONNECTION

Down & Out Books Edition: March 2018

Down & Out Books
3959 Van Dyke Rd, Ste. 265
Lutz, FL 33558
www.DownAndOutBooks.com

Cover design by Liam Sweeny

ISBN: 1-946502-67-7
ISBN-13: 978-1-946502-67-4

To Jules, my best friend

CHAPTER 1

The spatters of blood on his hands were not a problem, but the fleck on his jacket was. It stood out against the gray fabric, creating an obvious stain. A burst of contempt swept through Miguel Rios as he rubbed his sleeve, making it worse. *Shit! The damn suit's ruined.*

A thumping sound came from the trunk of the Mercedes. Rios leaned forward and shouted at his bull-necked driver, "Hit the fucking gas," then slid back against the leather seat when the car accelerated.

Moments later, a convoy of CEMEX trucks came from the opposite direction, kicking up dust clouds and blocking much of his view of this grubby industrial area south of Tijuana. When the dust cleared, a graffiti-cloaked iron foundry emerged on the right. Outside its gates stood the charred skeleton of a vintage Buick that looked like it was trying to shaft the rear of an equally burned-out Corolla. What was Rios doing here? Ten years as head of the Caruana cartel's enforcement team, and still he had to work in this shit-hole.

Soon after, they passed Plaza de Toros Monumental, and Rios chuckled to himself as he remembered how the locals liked to call it the Bullring by the Sea. Up ahead, the road sign for Lazaro Cardenas appeared, looking ready to topple at the slightest breeze—almost there.

When the driver swung the car into the dead-end road without hitting the brakes, Rios grabbed the handhold above the door. The car slowed, and he released his grip before looking out of the window again. Drooping power cables from a weed-shrouded substation across the street now lined the route. When they reached the rear of a derelict sawmill, the driver stood on the brakes. The Mercedes slewed to a stop, a haze of dust settling around it.

Rios struck a match and held it to the tip of a cigar while the driver and the guy hired as extra muscle for this job climbed out of the car and popped the trunk. Rios studied their every move in the side-mirror. They reached inside and, with a grunt, hoisted out their victim, a sucker in his late thirties, stripped down to his underwear and bound at his wrists and ankles. He tried to yell through the duct tape wound around his face then tumbled to the ground, his head striking the car. Rios pivoted in his seat. *That shut him up.*

Rios cracked open his window and pointed to the entrance of the building. "I'll see you in there." He sat back and dragged on the cigar, enjoying the air-conditioned comfort of the Mercedes now that the thumping had stopped.

They grabbed the man by his hair and pulled him up before dragging him backward by the arms, his bare heels scarring a line in the parched earth. Seconds later, they disappeared behind the metal sliding door.

Rios turned on the rear-seat radio and tuned it to his favorite country and western station from across the border. They were playing Shania Twain. He snapped his fingers to the beat and thought about the girls at the bar he'd be visiting that night. The only problem was he'd have to change his suit before they went out.

He took several minutes to finish the cigar before stepping out of the car. He scanned the area as he walked into the building. Shafts of sunlight penetrated through holes in the roof like spotlights illuminating a stage. Rios sauntered over to the bloodied man, using the beams of light to avoid placing his designer loafers in the pools of stale rainwater on the concrete floor. He pointed to the back of the building with his chin. The henchmen picked the man up, carried him to a wooden chair bolted to the back wall, and strapped him in. The man looked down at the pool of dried blood around his feet and began to shake. Rios glared at him but said nothing. He slipped on a pair of leather gloves before tearing off the duct tape from the man's head.

"Please, Miguel." Sweat poured down his swollen face, mixing with the blood running from the corner of his left eye.

"Tell me about Merriman," Rios said without a hint of emotion in his voice.

"I swear I know nothing, Miguel."

Rios struck the man hard across the face with the back of his gloved fist. "I want to hear everything you've told Merriman."

"I swear on the lives of my children, I've spoken to no one."

Rios smirked at his associates. "He thinks he's a hard case. He thinks he's going to hold out. He thinks I want to stand here and let him fuck with me."

"I don't know this Merriman. You have to believe me."

"He's lying." Rios nodded to his men. "Let's see what one hundred and twenty volts will do to change his mind."

The hired gorilla worked a pair of heavily insulated gloves onto his fat fingers then reached above the victim and pulled down two industrial electric cables. He threw the switch on the wall and brought the exposed ends of the wires closer together; they crackled.

"Please, God, no." Urine ran down the man's leg as the leads were moved closer to his groin.

Rios leaned over the man and smiled. "Still nothing for me?"

"I don't know anything. I swear." The man struggled against the bindings.

"Fry him."

The piercing screams echoed around the cavernous building. At one point, Rios heard footsteps, swung round, and raised his sunglasses. Two young boys stepped out from behind some rusting equipment at the far end of the building and sprinted out of the sliding door. He waited for a few moments before ordering the torture to continue. Still, the man yielded no information.

"Leave him," Rios said after five minutes.

He led his men outside into the bright sunlight. They leaned against the car and fired up cigarettes. They talked about the football match that night. Rios bragged how his team, the Chivas, would thrash Monterrey, no doubt about it.

"The drill," said Rios when he'd finished his cigarette.

One of the heavies reached into the front passenger footwell and retrieved an electric drill—a nice one, a Ryobi with an eighteen-volt power pack built into the handle. It had a half-inch wood drill still in the bit, stained black from the last time they'd used it.

"Please, have mercy," the victim said when they returned. The wooden chair rocked as his contorted body fought in vain to slip free of the leather straps. Blood seeped out where the straps had cut into his skin.

"Tell me about Merriman. It'll be easier that way," said Rios.

"I'd tell you if I knew anything. You've known me for years, Miguel." He was sobbing, and his voice was weak. "God knows I'd tell you."

Rios pointed to the hired muscle with the drill. He powered it up, revving the motor. The victim swung back and forth, his head banging against the wall. "Lord, save me," he roared.

"Only the knees," said Rios before walking outside. When he returned, there wasn't much blood, but smoke and the smell of burning bone hung in the air. He took a perfumed handkerchief from his jacket pocket and held it to his nose.

"This will go on all night. It makes no difference to me," Rios said, staring into the man's expressionless eyes. "We're going to do your ribs next."

The man said nothing; he had no fight left. Rios pointed to his upper body, and the accomplice with the drill moved it toward the middle of the man's ribcage. Before it made contact, the man passed out, his head falling forward onto his chest.

"No more," shouted Rios, and the drilling stopped. "He

knows nothing. If it isn't him, then who the fuck is it?" He pointed to the machete behind the wooden seat. "Finish it."

While one of them lifted the unconscious man up by his sweat-soaked hair, Rios turned to walk back to the car. He didn't need to witness the final, bloody act. He'd seen it many times before.

CHAPTER 2

It was an old financial model, but it still worked. John Kent had created it years ago when he worked at an investment bank in London and had used it hundreds of times since. He sat in his corner office on the outskirts of Cambridge, England, tinkering with the Excel spreadsheet and hammering at his calculator. Without looking up from his screen, he shouted, "Tara, can you ask Joanna and Adrian to pop in? A coffee would be nice, too."

"Sure," said Tara Sanderson, his PA sitting outside his open door.

Joanna Kirkland and Adrian Johnson walked into Kent's office five minutes later.

"Grab a seat," Kent said from behind his iMac, pointing to the two sofas opposite his desk. "I'll be with you in a sec. I've come up with a better financial structure on the Henderson Wright deal."

Kirkland sat on one of the sofas and crossed her arms. "What do you have in mind?" she asked. "Can't really see anything wrong with the one I came up with." At thirty-one, she was the youngest and only female partner in Kent's successful private equity firm. She was also the highest paid, after Kent. Kirkland was a moneymaker, and Kent always used her for his most important deals.

"Don't be so defensive. It's good, but this is better." Kent rolled his chair sideways so he could see his two partners. *They're going to like this.*

"I'm all ears." Kirkland looked as if she was sucking on a lemon. "Can't imagine what I've missed."

"I want to can the German business as soon as we complete the rescue financing."

"Doug Wright will go ballistic," Kirkland said. "That subsidiary is his baby. It'll never happen."

"He'll just have to suck it up if he wants our money. If he doesn't, he can watch his entire group go over the cliff. It's his choice."

"How does that improve the deal for us?" asked Johnson, sitting on the arm of the other sofa. He took a sip of tea from an oversized mug with The World's Greatest Investor printed on it.

"I'm coming to that," Kent said. "It's losing too much money. We can release a lot of cash by shutting it down. If we take a charge on the German assets, we'll get the proceeds when we flog them off, and none of it will be wasted on the creditors."

Johnson smiled. "I like it. Who said private equity houses were money-grabbing asset strippers?"

Kent laughed.

Kirkland kept a straight face. "Wright won't wear it."

She's only pissed off because she didn't come up with the idea herself, thought Kent.

"He's not calling the shots," he said. "This is our deal, not his. Anyway, he won't know. We'll only tell him once the investment's completed."

"Surely, we have to tell the CEO?" Kirkland asked.

"I'm with John," Johnson said, finishing his tea. "Wright doesn't need to know." He placed his empty mug down on a table next to the sofa. "Right, I can't sit about here all day chatting to you lot; got to get on with the drawdown notices."

"Don't send the one to Grampian Capital," Kent said. "If Paul's still stuck in New York, I'll ask him to take it over in person."

"I can email it just as easy."

"I don't want to give them any excuse to delay coughing up the money. Any idea why they were late last time?"

"I never did find out. It's not like them. Want me to have a word with their CFO?"

"No. Leave it to Paul."

"These big institutions are a bureaucratic nightmare. I'm sure it was just a cock-up at their end."

"I hope you're right. I hate being so reliant on Grampian."

"Three quarters of our fund. I'd say that counts as reliant," Johnson said as he left the office.

Kent turned to Kirkland. "Have you issued our formal offer letter to Wright yet, Joanna?"

"Did it yesterday, and I'm still waiting for him to sign it," she said. "First thing this morning, he said he just needs to stand down the other private equity firm he's been talking to and then he'll sign our offer."

"Don't give him any longer than five o'clock to have it back to us. I don't want him showing our terms to the competition. He's a smart-ass, so I wouldn't put anything past him. I've been shafted by people like him too many times before."

After the meeting, Kirkland returned to her own office.

"Tara, can you come in for a moment?" Kent shouted from his desk. She was wearing a thin white blouse, partially revealing her bra and the outline of her firm breasts. When she sat, unfortunately, her wavy brown hair obscured Kent's view.

"Is Paul back from New York yet?" he asked, trying not to make it obvious where he was looking.

"No. He's still struggling to find a flight. They said on TV last night that they think the air traffic controllers' strike could go on for days. He said he's thinking of catching a flight to mainland Europe then making his way to the UK by train."

"Actually, I'm glad he's still over there. I've got some work for him. Once Adrian has prepared Grampian's drawdown notice, email it to Paul and ask him to take it over there. He can pretend he's stopping by to talk them through the Henderson Wright deal, but really I want to make sure they come up with the money."

***

A silver Bentley collected the American executive from the underground garage of the lower Manhattan office tower.

"The apartment," he said as the driver held open the door.

The car drove onto West Street and pushed its way into the heavy traffic.

"Beautiful day, Mr. Schaeffer," said the driver, peering up at the clear blue sky.

"Is it?" Schaeffer did not look up from his papers. He pressed the button to close the privacy screen then flipped open his cell phone and hit one of his speed-dials.

"Tom Grannis," said the voice at the other end.

"It's Dan."

"Have you heard?"

"Yeah, about an hour ago. They won't help."

"Nothing at all?"

"Not a penny. Hard to see what options we have left."

"I was optimistic they'd do something. We're talking about Grampian Capital for God's sake, not some hick bank nobody's ever heard of."

"Do you guys know any other senior people over there?"

"I'm sorry, Dan. We've exhausted our best contacts."

"Figured as much." Schaeffer snapped the phone shut.

Fifteen minutes later, they pulled up outside the forty-story Pyramid building, Manhattan's most expensive apartment block, across the road from the Met on the Upper East Side.

Schaeffer climbed out of the car. "Wait here. I'll be back in half an hour."

Kirkland returned to Kent's office with Anton Henning, another partner in the firm. She looked more irritated than she had earlier. Even the normally relaxed Henning looked agitated, slumping his lanky frame onto one of Kent's sofas.

"We've just taken a call from Doug Wright," Henning said. "You're not going to like it."

"You didn't mention the German business?" asked Kent, leaning over a wastepaper bin under his desk, clipping his fingernails. "Don't tell me Wright knows about our scheme already."

"What scheme?"

"Forget it. What's the problem?"

"Wright says the other private equity firm is prepared to do the same deal as us, but with thirty percent for the management team compared to our twenty."

"Fucking hell!" Kent narrowly avoided severing the tip of his left index finger. "Wright's playing with fire. His business runs out of cash in three weeks. How easy does he think it is coming up with a billion pounds in a hurry?"

He shoved his chair back from the desk, walked to the large picture window behind it, and stared toward Cambridge. After inspecting his bleeding finger in the light, he placed it in his mouth.

"What do you want to do?" Henning asked, interrupting Kent's thoughts.

Kent turned. "He's bluffing. Did you ask him to email us the other firm's term sheet?"

Henning dropped his shoulders. "No, didn't think to."

Kent smiled at his partner, as if to say he should have done. "Let's get him on the phone right now. Tara, can you get hold of Doug Wright and put him through?" he shouted.

"I have Mr. Wright for you," Tara said through Kent's open office door a few moments later.

Kent leaned over his desk and hit the speakerphone but said nothing, leaving an awkward silence and deliberately piling pressure on Wright.

"John, how are you?" Wright asked after a few long seconds. "We're in the thick of it over here, as you can imagine."

"I understand from my team you have a better offer on the table."

"Yes, it's all a bit embarrassing really. We were just telling the other firm they'd lost the opportunity when they suggested they could improve their terms. We're not sure what to do about it."

"Did you show them our offer letter?"

"No, not at all. I wouldn't do that. They said they don't want to lose the deal and offered to sharpen their pencil. Took me by complete surprise."

"I can imagine. Email us their terms so we can take a look at them." Kent hit the mute button and turned to his colleagues. "That'll flush the bugger out. Let's see how he wriggles out of that."

There was another uncomfortable pause at the other end of the line. "That wouldn't be very professional," Wright said. "I'm sure they wouldn't thank me if I did."

"He's struggling to figure out what to do. The slimy bastard's lying to us. He doesn't have another deal." Kent turned off the mute button. "Tell you what, Doug. It's now four o'clock. I'll give you until ten past to accept our offer. There's no point leaving our deal on the table any longer when you have an obviously better proposal available."

"I will not be bullied or rushed into accepting your deal. You're not the only people interested—"

Kent ended the call. "He'd better sign our offer letter while he still has the chance. It's a great deal for us. The last thing I want is for that idiot to blow it for everyone."

"Do you still think he's bluffing?" asked Kirkland.

"Dead right he is. He's out for himself. His firm's at death's door, and he's fannying about with our investment terms. I've a good mind to jack our equity stake up to eighty-five percent."

"Can we do that?" Henning asked, his face taking on a glaze of incredulity.

"Sure. We can do anything we want before our offer letter is signed. It's our money."

At 4:08 p.m. Tara walked into Kent's office. "This email has just come in from Mr. Wright," she said, handing out copies.

"Is it the other firm's term sheet?" Kirkland asked.

"No. It's a scanned, signed copy of our offer letter. Mr. Wright telephoned me a moment ago very anxious to know that I had it. He seemed most upset."

"Unbelievable," said Henning, shaking his head.

Kent smiled at his colleagues. *Another great deal in the bag.*

"The River Café," said Schaeffer, climbing back into the Bentley. He let several calls on his cell phone ring out as he gazed out of the window while the driver followed the East River to the Brooklyn Bridge. When the car pulled into the restaurant parking lot at the eastern end of the bridge, the driver jumped out and opened the door for his passenger.

"Don't wait for me," Schaeffer said. "I'll find my own way back."

"Are you sure, sir? It's really no trouble."

"I'm fine."

"Enjoy your lunch, sir."

Schaeffer waited until the Bentley disappeared and then walked away from the restaurant, heading back along the bridge. The pedestrian walkway sat above the traffic. When he reached the midpoint of the bridge, he stopped and looked around. The nearest people were about a hundred yards away. Quickly, he dropped his attaché case on the ground, scrambled over the rusting metal safety fence, and climbed onto the outside girder. He struggled to keep his balance on the narrow beam. When he found his feet, he stared across at the Manhattan skyline and picked out Grampian Capital's offices, where he'd been sitting an hour or so earlier.

He raised his head. A slight breeze, but the sky was crystal clear.

"I guess it is a beautiful day."

CHAPTER 3

He couldn't sleep. When he heard the first birds singing in his yard, Mark Merriman looked at the digital alarm clock: 3:58 a.m. He slid out of bed, taking care not to wake his wife, Patti. He went downstairs, made himself a strong coffee, and took it through to the study tucked away at the back of the house.

He sat down to read a bunch of PowerPoint slides he'd printed out last night. *These guys better approve this today. If they don't, we're going nowhere.*

On such an important workday, Merriman could have done with an early start at the office, but it was also his birthday, and he couldn't let his girls down. He'd already promised he'd have breakfast with them—blueberry pancakes with Aunt Jemima's maple syrup, prepared by their two enthusiastic young daughters, and supervised by his wife. Patti had been his childhood sweetheart, and they married twelve years ago, not long after he joined the DEA. They'd always wanted a large family, but Patti's medical problems a few years back meant there'd be no more children.

On the twenty-minute drive in from their home at Herdman Park to the DEA's headquarters in Springfield, Virginia, he ran through the morning's presentation in his mind. What was the best way to play it? How were they likely to react?

When Merriman pulled up at the entrance gates, he flashed his ID at the bored-looking security guard.

"Morning, Doug," he said through his open car window.

"How are you today, sir? Heavy traffic this morning? Normally, I set my watch by you."

"The birthday boy got delayed. The kids couldn't wait for me to open their presents."

The guard threw a knowing smile and then raised the barrier. Merriman drove in and parked in his usual space under the main building before taking the elevator to the executive level on the sixth floor. Now thirty-five, he was still the DEA's youngest Head of Intelligence.

He stepped out of the elevator and bumped into one of his team. Frank Halloran had joined Merriman's unit a year earlier after a couple of years in the field with the DEA's Mexico Division. Halloran wore a cheap suit and looked disheveled. Well over six feet tall, he towered over Merriman's five-feet-seven inches. At twenty-four, he was still a little rough around the edges, but his boss could see potential in him. Merriman's young coworker's energy and dedication prompted memories of himself at that age.

"Good weekend, sir?" asked Halloran, tightening his tie.

"We were up in Maine visiting my parents. How about you?"

"Spent most of it here, preparing for the presentation. I've left hard copies on your desk, and the meeting room's all set. Let me know if there's anything else."

"Good work, Frank. Who else was in?"

"All of us at different times. We've got a lot to report this quarter."

Merriman made his way to his office, a twelve-foot square box with one small window looking over an internal courtyard. On the wall behind his desk hung photos of him shaking hands with a number of high-profile congressmen and senators, a daily reminder for his staff that his team's work was central to the war on drugs and in maintaining national security.

The mahogany credenza he used was once his father's. On it stood several precious photos of his wife and daughters. His girls had inherited Merriman's jet-black hair. He smiled as he thought about how Patti always said they got their good looks from her side of the family. Merriman straightened up the frames.

The cleaners never put them back in the right spot. He looked over to the metal filing cabinet in the corner of his room. On the top sat a handful of gift-wrapped packages.

"Just a few presents from the team," said his secretary, popping her head round the door.

"Morning, Gail. Have you been talking?"

"Maybe," she said, raising one eyebrow. "All set for today?"

"I think so. I read through it all this morning. I'd kill for a coffee, though."

Merriman had developed a taste for strong coffee during his postings to South America. He couldn't bring himself to drink the bland, sweet concoctions sold by the coffee chains in the U.S., so he'd invested in his own espresso machine, a top-of-the-range Gaggia Accademia, which Gail kept in full working order just outside his office.

"Double?"

He shrugged. "Does it come in any other size?"

"Happy birthday, by the way."

"Thanks." He smiled and pointed an accusing finger at her.

Merriman drained his coffee before collecting two of his senior team members, Karen Camplejohn and Bill Greenough, from the open-plan pods outside his office door. Together they walked over to the conference room to prepare for their quarterly presentation to the DEA leadership.

"I'll set the scene and wrap up at the end," Merriman said as they arrived. "I'd like you guys to handle most of this today. It'll be a good opportunity for you to raise your profile."

Half an hour later, the seven other members of the DEA leadership filed in, taking up their usual positions around the table, arranged in an arc shape facing a large screen. They were joined by two VIP visitors. Merriman and his team stood between the table and the screen.

Merriman opened up by reminding everyone of the increasing danger posed by the Mexican drug cartels. Noting the visitors from the defense intelligence committee sat at the table, a senator from Wisconsin and one from Ohio, he took some time to explain the historical background.

"In the late nineties, the Colombian cartels became much weaker as we succeeded in closing the cocaine trafficking route through Florida," he said before pulling up a slide of a portrait of a man with a shaved head. "This man, Felix Safuentes, known as 'Jivaro' in the criminal underworld, recognized the opportunity to develop alternative supply routes across the Mexico/U.S. land border. After a vicious turf war, his Caruana cartel emerged as the leading drug trafficking organization in Mexico. From ten cartels eight years ago, there are only two remaining, and his organization is by far the strongest, controlling virtually the whole of the North American criminal narcotics trade. As a result, Safuentes, at the age of thirty-eight, is the most powerful organized crime leader the world has known."

"Why do they call this Safuentes guy 'Jivaro'?" asked the Ohio senator.

"Because of his brutality," Merriman said.

"Still don't get it."

Merriman looked at his senior DEA colleagues for a moment. They nodded. "During the years of the Spanish Conquest, only one indigenous American tribe failed to be subjugated—the Jivaro warriors. They were fiercely independent and refused to bow to any external authority. They terrified their enemies by decapitating those they caught and collecting their shrunken heads."

The senator shook his head. "Jeez! Not sure I wanted to know that."

Camplejohn powered up the screen and pointed to the images that appeared. "What we have here are satellite shots of known cartel stash houses in the U.S. So far, we've identified almost fifty of them, mostly located along the southern states, but a number reaching up into the northwest and northeast coasts. We believe there are many more yet to be discovered."

She ran quickly through a number of slides demonstrating the successful drug seizures achieved through intelligence gathered by Merriman's team, before handing over to her colleague.

Greenough continued, "Last year, we shifted some of our attention to the cash generated from drug sales by the cartels. Last quarter, we reported increasing success in tracing their electronic fund transfers within the U.S. banking network. As a result, most cartel money is now being shuttled back to Mexico in physical form." He pressed the control in his hand, and, on the screen, images flashed up of aircraft, speedboats, and tunnels. "Besides hauling cash by road, these are some of the other methods used to transport the money through the border."

Greenough took several minutes to finish his session. "I'd now like to hand you back to Mark," he said before sitting next to Camplejohn.

Merriman thanked his colleagues and took the floor to wrap up the presentation. His heart rate increased as he paused to choose his words. "Sure, these are some great results, but I'm convinced we're going to lose this war." He looked around the room and collected the startled reactions from his audience. Even Camplejohn and Greenough looked surprised.

"We need to completely overhaul the way we work if we want to prevail. Our current approach won't cut it. Stash houses come and go, and cash shipment routes change all the time. We're wasting our time chasing the wrong things. We need a completely new strategy." He stopped to take a drink of water, allowing his audience to digest what he'd said.

"What are you thinking, Mark?" asked Bob Butler, Head of the DEA, looking confused.

"We're just scratching the surface right now, Bob. We've got to hit the cartels where it hurts most, by taking away the profit from their activities. We have to go after their assets—what they acquire once they've laundered their cash. That's where most of their wealth sits, and that's where they'll feel it most. But first, we've got to track down the key financial players: investment fund managers, lawyers, accountants, brokers, and so on. Without these intermediaries, the cartels can't deploy their capital. If we can do this, we'll begin to close down these criminal organizations for good. It won't be easy. We'll need many more specialist skills and have to work in a whole new way, but I'm determined to crack it."

"We're much better off pursuing the cash," said Jim Randell, the DEA's miserable Deputy Head and Merriman's predecessor as Head of Intelligence. "You'll never get the advisers to talk. That's if you can find them first."

Merriman shook his head. "One thing's for certain: if we keep doing more of the same, we're going to lose. We have to be more ambitious."

"Just tracking down their advisers will require a lot more manpower. We simply don't have the budget. I admire the sentiment, Mark, but we're better off sticking to our proven methods. I can't support a fundamental change."

"I didn't expect you would, Jim. What I'm arguing for means throwing out a lot of practices you established. I know it's hard for anyone to tear up their own ideas. I'm not trying to attack your work, but we need a new approach. The threat we face today from the cartels demands it."

"It'll never work, Bob," said Randell, turning to Butler for support.

A wave of frustration shot through Merriman. He sighed. "Let me spell this out. If we don't put an end to the cartels now, Mexico could soon become a failed state. With a population of a hundred million, the potential is there for a massive influx of refugees across the border." He looked at the two senators. "Are we prepared to accept that? I know I'm not."

"He's right," said the Wisconsin senator. "If Mexico fails, the repercussions for the U.S. are unimaginable."

Merriman stared at Randell. "Give me a year. If I don't deliver tangible results in that time, I'll stand down." *That ought to silence him.*

After a half hour of heated discussion, Merriman won approval for his new strategy and a large increase in his intelligence budget. At the end of the presentation, he asked his two team members to leave the meeting. Then he turned to his senior colleagues.

"I've just one more confidential thing to add. We've been trying to infiltrate the Caruana cartel for some considerable time, without success. The good news is we've had one of our agents successfully embedded for two years now. The great news is we're beginning to collect some promising intelligence from deep within this organization. It's a real breakthrough, and it should help us start identifying their main financial advisers and investment managers around the world. I'm confident we'll be able to report substantive progress on this at our next quarterly presentation."

Butler pulled Merriman to one side when the meeting broke up. "Excellent work, Mark. It's great to see the progress you're making. Don't listen to Randell. He never supports anything he didn't invent."

"Thanks. He thinks I'm after your job. He sees me as his competition."

Butler laughed. "Let me know if there's anything else you need."

"Safuentes is the key to this. I'm going after his assets first."

"I'm with you there, but don't push it too far. This guy's a ruthless son of a bitch."

"That's exactly what my dad said over the weekend. I told him someone has to stand up to him."

"Do you really have to go after him first?"

Merriman ignored the question. *What's the point of chasing the small players?* he thought. "By the way, Dad asked me to say hello."

"Send him my best. He was a real loss to the service when he retired."

"Big shoes to fill."

"You're not doing too badly." Butler slapped Merriman on the back as they left the room. "I mean it, Mark. Don't take any unnecessary risks with Safuentes. That guy's an animal."

Merriman grinned. "Don't worry about me. I'll be careful."

By the time he walked back to his office, Merriman was hungry, so he offered to buy his team lunch. "It's my treat. You guys did a great job today."

"You have to open your presents first," said Greenough, beaming from ear to ear.

"If you insist," Merriman said. "Gail, could you book us a table at Carlino's, say for one-fifteen?"

His team crowded around as he began opening the gift-wrapped boxes on his cabinet. The first package was a pen from Gail, then, from Halloran, a joke book instructing the reader how to turn off a cell phone. Merriman had a reputation for never switching off his smartphone, and it would often go off in meetings, much to everyone's amusement.

Merriman laughed. "Very funny, Frank."

The next gift he picked up felt heavy. "There's no label on this one to say who it's from. Is it another windup?" he asked, looking over to Halloran.

Halloran raised his palms. "Not from me."

Merriman shook the box, trying to guess what it was. "Can't figure this one out." Quickly, he tore off the wrapping paper then flipped open the cardboard lid. As he peered inside, Merriman collapsed back against his desk, dropping the package. "Please, no."

A bloodied human ear and a man's left hand fell onto the carpet.

CHAPTER 4

Kent was having a wonderful recession. He was starting to make serious, life-changing money—the kind of money he'd always dreamed about.

Back in the boom years, the banks were all over companies like a rash, throwing cash at anyone with a pulse, but now, in the middle of the worst credit crisis in history, they were running scared. They'd turned off the taps, stopping all new lending, and were demanding their old loans back, and fast. Every week, Kent bore witness to their irrational behavior: pulling in lending lines; hiking up interest rates for no good reason; and depriving businesses, even great ones, of vital financial support. In the middle of all this madness, Kent was cleaning up. CBC, the private equity firm he'd founded a few years back, had cash, and plenty of it. Deals were flooding in, and Kent's firm was completing as many of them as it could. Like the man with the only water in a desert, Kent could name his price on any deal he chose to do—just the way he liked things.

The quiet purr of the engine brought a smile to Kent's face as he depressed the ignition button. He'd bought the top-of-the-line BMW a few months back, but there was still a strong smell of new leather. He slid the gearshift into drive, and the car crunched across the gravel, triggering the automatic opening of the wrought-iron gates in front of him. Not bad for someone brought up by a divorced mother on a Leicester council estate.

He glanced at his wrist. The Polar watch showed a steady sixty beats per minute as it picked up his heart rate from the chest band he was wearing. Kent had risen at four-thirty and was on the treadmill in his home gym a quarter of an hour later. Five miles in forty-five minutes, every day, kept him in excellent condition. The exercise and his meticulous low-fat/low-carb diet made him appear much younger than his forty-eight years. He'd seen many of his contemporaries in the private equity industry let themselves go; too many business lunches and dinners, alcohol every day, and no exercise. They'd become flabby. That would never happen to him.

In his rearview mirror, the security lights reflected across the yellow limestone of the Old Hall. *Worth at least ten million pounds on a bad day.* He'd acquired the private estate from a failed dotcom entrepreneur seven years ago in a typical Kent deal. The vendor had to get out before he went bust, which meant only one thing: Kent could buy the Rutland property at a massive discount to its real value because he was a cash buyer and able to move quickly.

He drove up the access ramp onto the A1 motorway then turned on his car radio to listen to the BBC's regular six-fifteen business news slot, a favorite program he'd guested on several times himself as an expert on investment matters.

Thirty minutes later, he exited the A14 dual carriageway and pulled into the Science Park on the northern outskirts of Cambridge. The city was an unusual location for Kent's leveraged buyout firm. Most were in London, some sixty miles to the south. When he'd founded the firm ten years ago, he saw no reason to follow the herd. He didn't have to. His reputation and moneymaking track record in the buyout market were so strong he could afford to be unconventional.

He drove into his parking space outside CBC's building a little after seven and looked up at the four-story glass structure. He smiled. Most of the office lights were on, but he made a mental note of who wasn't in so he could raise it with the people concerned later on.

The office building made a statement. It said serious money to management teams applying for investment capital, but it didn't look too flashy to CBC's investors who, after all, were paying for it through the exorbitant fees they paid to the firm. Kent thought he'd struck the right balance. He could have afforded to spend a lot more on the offices if he'd wanted. CBC was collecting three hundred million pounds a year in management fees. With bonuses, the partners were taking home six to eight million each on average, with Kent taking out twice as much.

"Morning, Mr. Kent," said Bill Chapman, the security guard who was seated at the front desk. Chapman was an ex-army staff sergeant now in his sixties. He'd spent most of his career in the SAS and some time in military intelligence. Not much happened at CBC without Chapman knowing about it.

"Morning, Bill. What's the gossip?"

"Haven't seen Mr. Prentis yet. Not like him."

"He's stuck in New York. Anything else?"

Chapman looked disappointed that this wasn't news to his boss. "Not really. Do you want your car doing today?"

"Sounds good." Kent threw over his car keys. Every Tuesday, CBC would have a car valeting firm spend a day at the office giving the partners' cars a thorough clean.

Kent bounded up the four flights of stairs. The elevator was for others. Most of his forty-five staff members were in, though their employment contracts stipulated a nine o'clock start time. None of them watched the clock. If they did, they didn't last long at CBC.

He walked into his corner office, put down his briefcase, and went over to the window. The morning sunlight lit up the old stone buildings in the center of Cambridge three miles away. He never tired of this view. It was the main reason he chose to locate the firm there in the first place. When he'd been a university student at Cambridge many years before, he'd grown to love the centuries-old architecture and the sense of permanence. Unlike most buildings in London, he knew the stone buildings in town would still be there in a few hundred years' time.

Kent sat at his desk, automatically reaching out for his mug of coffee with his right hand. No coffee. *Where's Tara?*

An hour later, she rushed into his office. "Sorry I'm late, John."

Kent looked up from his screen. "You look flustered."

"I had problems with my mum again this morning."

"How's she doing?"

"It's an awful disease. I told you she lives with me now?"

Kent nodded. "Does your sister still look after her during the day?"

"Normally, but she was delayed getting over to my place this morning. That's why I'm late. I'm really sorry."

"Don't worry about it. I'd like you to look into some professional help for your mum in the mornings so you're not worried about what time your sister arrives. CBC will pay. Would that be okay?"

"I really don't know what to say."

"You don't have to say anything. I know how difficult it can be living with Alzheimer's. My grandmother had it. Dreadful experience."

"Thanks, John." Tara's eyes started to well up.

She returned to her desk and printed off a bundle of pages, then took them through to Kent. "Here are your papers for the investment committee meeting."

"Thanks."

Kent picked up the papers and sank into one of the sofas. Tara came over to sit next to him. Every morning, he'd reel off a list of tasks for her before he became tied up in meetings and phone calls. She had the notepad ready.

Kent's eyes drifted from his papers. Tara was twenty-eight with olive skin and a perfect figure and, as she sat next to him, he admired her long, smooth legs under a short skirt.

"Besides Paul, are all the partners here for today's committee?" he asked, forcing himself to focus on the business in hand.

"Yes. I've checked their electronic diaries."

The Tuesday investment committee meetings started promptly at 9 a.m. Kent knew this would mean Prentis having to call in from New York at 4 a.m. his time, but he was certain he'd participate. All of the partners understood what Kent expected of them.

Shortly before the conference, Kent walked into the boardroom and sat at the head of the table. His colleagues were already seated. There were six partners, including Kent. Any new deal commitment required a majority to vote in favor, with Kent having the casting vote should he choose to use it. He never had. He made it clear during these meetings where he stood on any particular deal, and his partners were bright enough to pick up on his signals without putting a transaction to the vote.

Kent had surrounded himself with ambitious partners in their thirties and forties. He paid them well, but there was no misunderstanding. This was his firm, and he made all the big decisions. He owned eighty percent of CBC with the remaining twenty percent split evenly across the other five partners.

"Paul's still not back," said Kirkland.

"Says he can't get a flight," said Johnson, who'd been Kent's first senior hire shortly after starting the firm. They'd worked together at Kent's previous company. "I'm not so sure. I heard he spent most of last weekend socializing with the Grampian team. He says he's going to charge the entertainment cost to my investor relations budget. I think not."

Johnson had a big smile on his face, but Kent knew he was serious. Only Johnson's own costs were going to eat into his bonus calculation. For Kent, all that mattered when allocating bonuses each year was how much money each partner made for the firm. It was a transparent system, and he made sure peer pressure kept all the partners focused on making as much money as possible.

As the meeting got underway, Kent's mind drifted. He'd been

waiting for the economic storm clouds to arrive and had raised the latest fund so as to have plenty of dry powder ahead of the downturn. He'd seen it coming and knew it would create an excellent buying opportunity. Such smart thinking meant he was on his way to making his first one hundred million pounds. He could see the day rapidly approaching when he'd become the UK's richest private equity investor.

CHAPTER 5

The convoy of vehicles pulled off the highway at Mazatlan, Mexico and drove through the security gates. At the end of the half-mile private road stood the white, twenty-bedroom summer residence. Felix Safuentes smiled. This was the favorite of all his homes. He never tired of its sweeping view of the Gulf of California, providing a blue backdrop to the property. He liked how the house was not visible at all from the highway. He felt safe there and could relax and unwind in its privacy. Like the CEOs of many large multinational organizations, he had huge responsibilities, and there were many demands on his time. He took every opportunity he could to visit his Mazatlan home to recover from the stress of his hectic schedule.

He spent much of his time away on business. Three weeks out of four he visited overseas subsidiaries, key suppliers, and major customers. He'd founded the business twelve years ago. Now, it employed over fifteen thousand people across six countries and had annual revenues approaching fifty billion dollars.

Safuentes ran the Caruana drug cartel. Throughout his empire, he was known as "Jivaro." Only close friends and family called him Felix. A giant of a man at six feet eight inches tall, he had the physique of a honed bodybuilder. The shaved head made his bushy jet-black eyebrows the most prominent feature of his face, giving him a frightening intensity whenever he frowned, which was often.

Profit margins were high in the Caruana business. After allowing for raw materials and the cost of production, and then deducting overheads such as transportation, bribes, and seizures,

Jivaro's chief financial officer calculated that sixty percent of revenues dropped through to the bottom line. There was no other business like it. With net cash flows of thirty billion dollars a year and rising rapidly, Jivaro and his top lieutenants were billionaires, and with their wealth they bought influence and power in all the right places.

As a result, Jivaro did not fear the authorities. His only fear was being assassinated by a rival cartel. After all, he'd achieved his position by taking out his main competitors. He'd shown extraordinary brutality toward his adversaries over the years, always leaving his calling card; their mutilated, decapitated bodies would be left on show so as to discourage others from challenging him.

By now, he had many enemies and so employed an army of paramilitary enforcers for his personal protection. Jivaro even had staff on the payroll to taste his food in case it was poisoned. He rarely shook hands with, or came physically close to, strangers for fear of attack.

When the convoy pulled up outside the summer home, Jivaro waited with his young son inside the armored Mercedes S class. His guards climbed out of the other vehicles, and only when they indicated that the area was completely secure did he leave the car. He gripped his son's hand until they were safely inside the house.

He was there to meet a close friend, Salvador Garcia, a Colombian producer of cocaine. Like Jivaro, Garcia had foreseen the decline of the Colombian cartels and forged an early relationship with the Caruana organization. This had paid off handsomely; Garcia was now, by far, Colombia's largest grower and exporter of cocaine. He had only one customer, Jivaro, who for many years had taken his entire production. As a rule, Jivaro did not invite business contacts to Mazatlan, but he'd known Garcia for many years and their families had grown close. He was regarded as a good friend, a man who could be trusted.

Garcia was already at the house when Jivaro arrived. They greeted each other like brothers and briefly shared stories about their families.

Jivaro snapped his fingers, and the surrounding entourage left the room, moving outside onto the terrace overlooking the ocean. An armed guard remained standing in the corner.

"Jose, come join us," said Jivaro as he beckoned his eight-year-old son to sit next to him on the leather sofa.

"He's grown so quickly," said Garcia, looking at the young boy from his armchair. "I remember him as a baby not that long ago. You must be very proud of him."

"Yes, I like to involve him more now he's growing up." Jivaro smiled at his son then turned to Garcia. "Would you like another drink before we discuss business?"

"I'm okay." Garcia held up his large brandy.

Jivaro settled into the sofa, crossing his legs. "Tell me, how's the crop this year, Salvador?"

"Much the same as last year, perhaps a little poorer. We've suffered some pest damage at two locations, and this is bound to affect yields. I'm hoping this won't prevent us from meeting your demand."

"Pest damage?"

"Yes. You will understand this will impact prices next year."

Jivaro frowned.

"I'll do my best to contain the increase, of course," said Garcia before his host could say anything.

Jivaro stared out of the window for a while then shrugged his shoulders. "Actually, I'm relaxed about prices going up next year."

"That's a first." Garcia smiled.

"It won't affect my operation."

"I don't follow." Garcia's smile began to melt.

"I've decided not to buy your product next year."

Garcia said nothing for a few seconds as he processed the news. "Felix, you can't mean that, surely? You know all of my production goes to supplying your organization."

"It's already decided."

"Have I offended you?"

"You've done nothing wrong. You've been a good supplier."

"Then what is it? We've done business with each other for many years."

"I've no longer any need to purchase your crop."

"You're not getting out of the business?"

"No, far from it." Jivaro laughed. "And when I do, Jose here will take over from me." He rubbed his son's head.

"If it's a problem with the quality, I can fix this. I only mentioned the pest damage because—"

"The quality is acceptable."

"Have you found another supplier? I'll beat any price. Nobody beats me on price."

"There's no alternative supplier."

"Then I don't understand?" The stress showed on Garcia's face.

"Papa?" said the young boy at Garcia's obvious distress.

"Jose!" Jivaro placed his index finger to his lips, and the boy looked down.

Jivaro walked over to a cabinet and retrieved an envelope. "I intend to buy your plantations." He smiled at Garcia as though he was the bearer of great news.

"But my business is not for sale. What made you think it was, my friend?"

"It is now." He handed the envelope to Garcia. "Here's the number my brother has calculated I should pay you. More than fair, you will find."

Garcia opened it, his fingers trembling. "But this is less than half..."

"Think about it, Salvador. All of your hard work will now become part of an expanding, successful organization. You should be proud of your achievement." He knew he was stealing the plantations from Garcia, but he also understood that without the demand from the Caruana cartel, Garcia would have no business.

Having wiped out most of the competing cartels in Mexico, Jivaro was expanding vertically into production. He was intent upon capturing the grower's margin and, in order to acquire this at the right price, a little lost friendship wasn't going to stop him. He now controlled the largest cocaine grower in the world.

"Come, Salvador, let's join the others outside for a celebratory drink."

Jivaro grabbed hold of his son's hand and led him out to the terrace. Garcia followed. He was not about to put up a fight. He'd seen many Caruana suppliers wiped out so the cartel could take over their operations. He was one of the lucky ones. At least, he'd been paid for his business and was still alive.

CHAPTER 6

At 7 p.m. the traffic leaving Cambridge was heavy, and most of the cars seemed to be heading toward the access ramp for the A14 West. It was pouring with rain, three lanes were merging into two, and the roadworks ahead were causing bumper-to-bumper chaos. Kent was cocooned in his BMW, listening to Classic FM and running through the new deals in the firm's pipeline. One, in particular, was dominating his thoughts: Henderson Wright.

Kirkland had found the opportunity a few days back, and they'd already signed it in exclusivity. They now had a clear run at it. Kirkland had been ecstatic when she first described the deal to him. "This recession is throwing up some great opportunities for us, and Henderson Wright is the best deal I've seen. There's no way we could buy control of one of the Big Four global accounting firms in normal times. We stand to make a shed-load of money on this deal."

If Kirkland was so excited by the transaction, it was bound to be a good one. She'd been with the firm just two years. After graduating from the London School of Economics, she took an MBA from Harvard, coming first in her class. Kent hired her from Gain, the leading global firm of strategy consultants. It was a major coup for CBC; she had offers from all the other major private equity firms, but chose Kent's firm.

Kent was salivating over the prospect of buying the business on the cheap, then, while it was a private company, taking a scalpel to the cost base, selling off surplus assets and increasing its efficiency and bottom-line profits. Like a lot of the major accounting firms, it had become bloated with unnecessary overheads and stifling bureaucracy. If CBC bought the firm, it would be held for a number of years until the return of better economic times, when it would be floated on the stock market for a lot more money than the original acquisition cost. Any cash generated during CBC's period of ownership would be used to reduce the bank debt taken on to finance the deal and to pay dividends to Kent's fund. It was a well-trodden path to making money.

The traffic came to a standstill at roadworks, and Kent leaned across to the passenger seat, retrieved Kirkland's deal note from his briefcase, and started reading it. Henderson Wright had started as a small London-based accounting firm called Hendersons in 1910. It grew steadily until 1997, after which its growth rocketed when the now senior partner, Doug Wright, took the helm, shortly after his own firm merged with Hendersons. He renamed the group to include his name. Wright was an aggressive Scot who wasn't cut out to be an accountant. He was a buccaneering deal-doer with a shrewd sense for a sweet transaction. Shortly after taking over as senior partner, he acquired a number of consulting businesses and other accounting firms worldwide, often by merging with them or paying in cash. However, since becoming a publicly-listed professional services firm three years ago, Henderson Wright plc. had borrowed to make recent acquisitions. Its latest acquisition, the largest accounting firm in Germany, was tanking, and it was starting to bleed the rest of the group dry.

Just after it was acquired, the new German subsidiary suffered from the departure of many of its best partners who set up in competition, taking a large number of key clients with them. Wright had not protected the German firm with strong enough non-compete agreements, a basic business mistake that was now threatening to bring the whole firm to its knees.

Henderson Wright was already in breach of its banking covenants. A fundraising exercise for new capital on the stock market was a non-starter in the middle of a recession. A global accounting firm was about to fold, something which would have massive economic repercussions. The firm was auditor to a third of the world's largest one hundred public companies. If it failed, there was not enough capacity to spread this work across the remaining Big Four accounting firms. It would cause a systemic loss of confidence in the markets.

"Wanker!" shouted a driver through his open window as he pulled around the BMW. Kent had been immersed in the file note and had missed the traffic moving again. He was causing mayhem. He raised his middle finger at the irate driver then slipped the gearshift into drive. *Prat.*

As the road cleared, his thoughts returned to the deal. "We can name our terms on this one," Kirkland had said. "With the lead bank withdrawing a substantial part of its facilities in three weeks, Henderson Wright will go over the cliff without new capital. We stand to make a money multiple of ten to fifteen times our original investment. The deal's agreed in principle with the bank, and I've negotiated with Doug Wright that CBC will have an eighty percent stake in his firm in return. He'll sign anything to avoid failure." Kirkland had been ecstatic about the transaction, and Kent could understand why. The perfect distressed deal—a great business in need of cash and a desperate owner. *This really is shaping up to be a very nice recession.*

Kent was shaken from his moneymaking thoughts by the shrill ring of his car phone.

"Hi, John. You haven't forgotten we're having dinner with Allison and David tonight?"

He had forgotten, and he knew his wife was calling to remind him. "No, I'm on my way now, Sarah. Please don't let it drag on all night. You know I can't stand him."

Sarah had met Allison on a Rutland charitable committee and they got on well. Shortly afterward, they were invited to dinner at the Bryants' home in a nearby village a couple of years ago. They were now stuck in an awful merry-go-round of reciprocal invitations. Kent had asked Sarah to stop inviting them back, but Sarah said this was rude. As usual, she won.

David Bryant was a partner at a leading corporate law firm in Birmingham. When he'd learned what Kent did for a living, he'd been all over him like a tramp round a bag of chips. He kept pushing for some of CBC's legal work on their investment transactions. Kent couldn't blame him. After all, CBC spent almost twenty million pounds a year on legal fees. He'd tried Bryant out on a small deal a while back, but it went wrong, so he vowed never to use him again. The problem was Bryant didn't take the hint and continued to push for more work on the back of what he thought was a successful precedent transaction. No doubt, winning CBC as a client was a real trophy for Bryant's provincial law firm.

"They'll be here at eight thirty. Have you left the office yet?"

"Yes. I'm not that far from home." Kent slowed the car down to a steady fifty miles an hour; he was in no hurry now.

"I've heard that before. Please don't be late, John."

Kent knew this was not a request from his wife. He sensed she'd been half expecting him to say he'd been delayed at the office. If he'd remembered the Bryants were coming round, he would certainly have found an excuse to be held at the office. He smiled as he thought how well Sarah knew him.

For the rest of his slow drive home, he called Kirkland to discuss the planning for the deal.

Driving through the gates of his estate, he saw the Bryants' car. *What a waste of an evening.*

"Here's John now," Sarah announced to the Bryants as Kent walked through the door.

"Sorry, darling. The traffic was bad, and I had to take a couple of telephone calls," he shouted so their guests could hear. Sarah poured him a glass of chilled Viognier, his favorite white wine, to sweeten him up for the evening.

Just as Kent sat, David Bryant said, "Got any deals on at the moment, John? We'd be keen to help, you know."

"Nothing much right now." Kent took a large sip of the wine. "There's a recession out there, you know." *Never again.*

CHAPTER 7

Not many things triggered the memory, but when Merriman dropped the severed hand and ear onto the floor of his office, he was right there, his mind racing back twenty-five years. He was sat on the rear seat of his father's Honda Accord, on his way to the international school. He could feel the oppressive heat and humidity, the freshly brewed Colombian coffee from his father's flask filling the air.

Antonio, the gardener who'd tended the grounds of the DEA's residential compound since they'd lived there, slid open the metal entrance gates. As the car drove through, ten-year-old Merriman smiled at him through the open back window, but Antonio looked away.

"He's not very happy today," said Merriman.

"You never know what might be troubling him," his father said.

"At least he could smile."

"Try not to judge people, Mark. Life's hard for many here."

The Accord accelerated once they reached the freeway and then, as usual, Merriman's father turned on the radio.

"How long will we be here, Dad?"

"What do you mean?"

"In this country."

"Well, that depends. Why do you ask?"

"Mom says we've never been stationed anywhere longer than three years."

"That's right, son. The service likes to move us around. You're enjoying school here, aren't you?"

Merriman bit on his upper lip. "It's okay, I guess."

They left the freeway and joined the heavy traffic heading into downtown Bogota.

"Put your window up now, Mark."

Merriman closed his rear window. "Would be nice to try a different school," he said.

"Something troubling you?"

Merriman shook his head. "Not really. Some of the lessons are hard."

"Anyway, if I get the promotion I told you about, we'll be living back in the U.S. for a while. Wouldn't that be great?" He turned up the radio. "Here's the weather. All set?" They listened to the weather report in Spanish, a daily ritual. "Okay, what's it gonna be like?"

"Thunderstorms this afternoon and tomorrow morning. Ninety-five degrees will be the high," Merriman said.

"See? Your Spanish is improving all the time. The school can't be that bad. How many boys your age can speak English and Spanish back in the U.S.?"

The car came to a halt behind a line of vehicles at a traffic light. A truck had stopped in the middle of the intersection. Horns blared. Merriman looked out of the rear window. Fists were being waved out of car windows and voices raised.

"Here they go again," said his father.

Merriman felt something slam into the side of the car, tossing him sideways. When he sat back up, he heard his father screaming, "My God, close your eyes, Mark."

There was a loud smash against the windshield.

"Dad!" Merriman opened his eyes. A severed head had been thrown at the car, and it had come to rest between the wipers. The eyes were still open.

That was the day Merriman's father had the first of his heart attacks. In the days that followed, Merriman learned that a Colombian drug cartel had murdered one of his father's team. The severed head had been a warning to his father, who ran the

DEA's Colombian operations. Antonio, the gardener, was never seen again.

Merriman remembered his father never being the same after that; he became distant and lost much of his love of life. A few weeks later, they were transferred to the U.S., but his father never did receive the promotion. The episode ended his promising career, and he spent his remaining years, until retirement, in an administrative role back in Virginia.

CHAPTER 8

Motel Buena Vista, so called because of its view toward San Diego, was one of many Tijuana establishments where rooms were available by the hour. Sadly, it didn't live up to its name; with the tall U.S. border standing only five hundred feet away, there was nothing interesting to see. The white breeze block lower half was covered with graffiti, and the razor-wire top gave it a menacing appearance.

Next door to the motel stood the low-rise Esperanza apartment block. It was an unspectacular construction, with the only thing marking it out being the lime-green render, which added a bit of color to the street. Not that a lick of paint was going to improve the area much. This was a rough part of town where even the Rottweilers wandered around in pairs for their own protection. The block sat some distance from the busy road, allowing residents to park their cars in front of the building. That way, they could keep an eye on them from their apartment windows.

On the curb, at the entrance to the Esperanza's private parking lot, was a white hand-painted sign requesting visitors to the motel not to use the residents' spaces. Everyone ignored it. Cars were coming in and out all day and most of the night, making it difficult for the caretaker, Jesus Cortes, to monitor whether or not they belonged there.

Cortes did his best to keep the area tidy, but it was a never-ending task. Most days he'd have to pick up empty beer cans, discarded cigarette boxes, and other garbage from the block's kicked-over dustbins. What he hated most was clearing up the stomach-churning used condoms left by the prostitutes working outside the motel the night before. Not every client could afford the hourly room rate. It made him sick. He was a decent man who refused to be beaten by the poverty of his surroundings.

Cortes was in his fifties and walked with a stoop, making him look much older. Two divorces, and a life of living on the breadline, had taken their toll. He'd looked after the Esperanza since it was first built eight years ago. He lived alone in a cramped, two-bedroom caretaker's apartment in the basement of the building. There were no other units in the basement as there was no natural light down there. One of the reasons he spent his days tidying up outside so much was to enjoy the daylight. That and to keep out of the way of his daily visitors.

Every morning, except Sundays, four walking tattoos would arrive between eight and nine with a thump on his front door. He'd be waiting for them. He would let them in and move aside; there was no need for conversation. They had no interest in him, and they made it clear he was expected to keep out of their way. They weren't the sort of people you argued with. They'd never threatened him, but he knew what they were capable of doing.

The same four men would stay until sunset. They'd be joined by many others throughout the day, always following the same routine. The later callers would arrive in pairs by car so as not to draw too much attention in the parking lot. To a casual observer, they looked as though they were checking in and out of the motel next door. Each one would bring in with him two large canvas holdalls and would leave with two different bags a few minutes later.

During the day, when Cortes was out working, the second bedroom of his apartment was a hive of activity. The first men to arrive would follow the same pattern. They'd shove to one side the large wardrobe sitting against the back wall then switch on the lights and air-extraction pump. Cut into the wall behind the wardrobe was a full-height door, about the width of two men. Once the lights were on, the narrow-gauge rail was visible at the entrance to a tunnel. A small, hand-powered rail cart sat on the rail, just a few feet inside.

The men worked in two-man shifts, with the first team checking out the tunnel on the initial run of the day. Often, they'd have to carry out repairs to damaged sections caused by earth movements. The whole thing was lined with timber beams, and nailed into them were wooden panels running along the walls, serving as a barrier to keep out the soil and dust. About every hundred yards were small ventilation shafts rising the thirty feet or so to the surface. The men had to inspect these every morning to prevent the buildup of gas and to allow fresh air to enter.

The tunnel ran for almost a mile below the surface. It took the men around twenty minutes to push the rail cart the full length of the track. It was hot, exhausting work. Each two-man team made a return run then handed over to the other pair, alternating throughout the day.

The exit on the U.S. side of the border was in the basement of a single-story house off a quiet lane leading to International Park. The building was surrounded by woods and out of view from the road. The sign on the wall outside read: "Bed and Breakfast—No Vacancies." No one had ever seen any paying guests.

The holdalls brought into the Esperanza were stuffed with plastic-wrapped, two-kilo packages of pure cocaine. They were handed over to the men in the basement bedroom. The bags received in exchange were crammed full of U.S. dollars. The rail cart made between twenty and thirty round trips a day, delivering cocaine to the U.S. and returning with dollars to Mexico. The men ran a highly efficient shuttle service.

At the end of each week, Cortes would receive a hundred dollars in cash for his cooperation. Without this money, he struggled to make ends meet. He wasn't proud of this. He understood what was going on in his apartment but, like all the others in his situation, he knew it was best to turn a blind eye.

The Esperanza was one of many apartment blocks along the

border owned by the Caruana cartel. Jivaro had a strong preference for new builds and took a close interest in their construction, particularly at the foundation stage, when tunnels could be dug and earth taken away without attracting much attention.

Two years ago, the U.S. government invested in a new range of reconnaissance satellites. These latest units could, on a clear day, focus in on a six-inch area, creating crystal-clear imagery. All of the satellites were controlled by the DEA's intelligence center in El Paso, Texas. Special Agent Daniela Piechuta was one of a team of twenty agents attached to this division, which was responsible for the remote monitoring of drug cartel activities along the Mexico/U.S. border.

One hundred and fifty miles to the north of Tijuana sat a modern, detached home on a new development in the eastern suburbs of Los Angeles. The house looked much like all the other cookie-cutter houses on the street. These ordinary-looking homes were chosen precisely because they did not stand out. They were used by traffickers as stash houses for the local distribution of drugs and hoarding of cash generated from their criminal activities.

Just after lunch, two men came out of the house and stood talking on the drive right outside the garage. Recognizing a familiar pattern of movement, Special Agent Piechuta rotated the main dial of her console in a clockwise direction. In front of her was a high-resolution thirty-inch LCD screen. As she rotated the control, the image on the monitor became increasingly sharp. Six hundred miles above the earth, a telescope on board the three-hundred-million-dollar reconnaissance satellite adjusted its focus. The two men standing outside the garage appeared on the screen.

A pickup truck pulled onto the drive. Two men jumped out and shook hands with the others waiting outside the house. The four men went inside the garage and, moments later, reemerged carrying two large holdalls each, which they loaded onto the back of the vehicle. They returned to the garage and came out with eight more bags. When they'd finished, one of the men pulled over the truck's tarpaulin so the bags were no longer visible. The two men disappeared into the house as the truck drove away. Piechuta recorded the whole thing.

An hour and a half later, a black SUV pulled onto the San Diego Freeway at Carlsbad. Inside were three DEA agents. The agent in the front passenger seat was speaking on a two-way radio and giving instructions to the driver.

"We have visual. License number zero-two-one I-H-G on a gray pickup. Two suspects inside," he said over the radio.

"Copy that. They're all yours. Good luck," replied Piechuta.

She'd tracked the pickup by satellite from the LA stash house to Carlsbad on Interstate 5. As usual, it appeared to be heading toward the Mexican border at Tijuana, fifty miles further to the south. It was now the responsibility of the agents in the SUV to follow the truck.

Around four o'clock each afternoon, a small line began to develop at the border crossing into Mexico. The pickup was next in line, with the SUV two cars behind. When the agents were confident the pickup was blocked in, they jumped out of their vehicle, pistols in hand. They rushed over to the truck and pulled open its doors, catching the two Mexican bag carriers off guard. They were rarely any trouble. Bag carriers were expendable and not expected to put up much of a fight if caught.

"Step out of the truck and hit the floor," shouted one of the agents. The two Mexicans lay face down on the ground as they were being cuffed. Another agent climbed into the pickup and, after flashing his badge to the border guard, drove it over to a special holding area. After the Mexicans were put into a holding cell, the three agents spent the next few hours examining the holdalls, which, as expected, were found to contain U.S. currency, just over three million dollars in total.

CHAPTER 9

Sarah Kent was a consultant psychologist at a large teaching hospital in Nottingham. Like Kent, she came from a very modest background and was the first in her family to go to college. They met at Cambridge University, where they became close friends and fell in love. After college, Sarah returned to her home city of York, while he went off for a year to do his MBA at Harvard. They missed each other while he was away so, when he returned, she joined him in London, where he'd started training with the private equity arm of a U.S. investment bank.

Sarah had watched her husband's rise through the ranks, achieving this entirely on merit. Kent had a nose for a good investment and soon started making a lot of money for himself. Most years at the investment bank, he earned seven-figure bonuses. Money was important to him as a way of keeping score. He strove to be the best at everything he did; he had to win. His unspoken fear was that, if he ever stopped winning, his life could one day revert to the poverty of his childhood. He'd seen his mother struggle for years bringing up a family singlehandedly. He knew what life was like having to worry about where the next meal was coming from. While it was unlikely he'd face poverty again, the motivation to succeed was deeply ingrained in him. Sarah had often said she'd like to have him in her patients' chair so she could find out what it was that drove him to make more and more money. They'd never argued about it, but Kent knew it wasn't a compliment. She'd been telling him to slow down for years.

"How was your day?" Sarah asked when Kent arrived home from work.

"Great, and yours?"

"Oh, you know, the usual."

Kent didn't ask anything more. He admired the work Sarah did, and he knew how good she was at it, but he found many of the problems faced by her clients depressing and preferred not to hear about the details. He believed everyone had it within them to make a success of their lives no matter what their background. He found it difficult to understand how many of Sarah's patients remained mired in problems emanating from their past. After all, he'd escaped a poor childhood and didn't allow his past to weigh him down, so why couldn't they?

He changed the subject to the Henderson Wright deal and how it had the potential to become the best deal ever for CBC. He was in full swing when the phone rang. He picked it up.

"Hello."

"John, sorry to bother you at home like this. It's Paul."

Kent was surprised his partner was calling him at home. There was an unspoken rule at CBC that the partners did not trouble each other at home unless it was absolutely essential. Kent was not really that bothered about it. He never switched off from the business, but he knew Sarah objected to the intrusion of his work at home so he discouraged such calls.

"Paul, you still on holiday in New York? I've heard the Met's worth seeing."

"I wish it was a holiday. I need one after the day I've had."

"You'll get a flight soon."

"Look, something very important has come up."

Kent sensed concern in his partner's voice. He knew he was not one to exaggerate, and so braced himself for bad news. Paul Prentis had been in private equity for twelve years, most of it with CBC. Before coming into the industry, he'd been an army officer and had served in a number of armed conflicts. Now in his early forties, he was tough and not easily spooked.

"Go on. I'm listening."

"As soon as Tara sent over the Henderson Wright drawdown notice earlier today, I took it over to the CFO at Grampian Capital. What she said was alarming."

"What did she say?"

"She told me their CEO was dead."

"Dan Schaeffer's only my age. What happened?"

"He'd been missing since yesterday. They found his body in the East River this afternoon."

"That's awful. Shouldn't affect us, though, should it?"

"That's not all she told me, John."

"There's more?"

"She said Grampian doesn't have the money to meet our drawdown."

"Eh?"

"I know. This is an SEC-registered public company with a market value of one hundred billion dollars."

"They represent virtually our entire fund." Kent rubbed the crown of his head. "What do you mean, they don't have the money?"

"That's all she would tell me. I pushed her hard, but she wouldn't say any more."

"That's unbelievable. How can a reputable Wall Street institution struggle to meet its drawdown commitment? This is chicken feed for them." He slumped onto a kitchen stool.

Sarah stopped preparing dinner. "Are you okay?" she whispered. Kent shook his head no. She sat next to him.

"The only other thing she'd tell me was they'd be making a formal announcement to the market after it closes at four o'clock New York time," Prentis said.

"That's one hour from now. This sounds like a sack of shit is about to land on us. Who else have you told about this?"

"Nobody. I've only just left their offices. There were lawyers everywhere, John, and a real sense of panic around the building. I think they may be about to fail."

"That would be a disaster for us. I hope you're wrong about that."

"I hope I'm wrong, too, but it certainly felt like a sinking ship over there."

Kent knew the announcement would contain dreadful news. He could just sense it from Prentis's voice. If it had been any of his other partners, he'd have left it for a couple of days to see what happened, but Prentis was the last person in his team to hype a story and he usually had good instincts. Kent felt a tightening in his stomach as he contemplated the prospect of Grampian failing and what it would mean for CBC.

"Okay. I'm calling a partners' meeting for nine o'clock tonight. I want you to call into the meeting from your hotel. I'd like you to give the partners a blow-by-blow account of your conversation with the CFO."

"No problem. Speak to you in an hour's time."

Kent explained the situation to Sarah, who'd been waiting to hear the news. She insisted on coming to the office with him. He rang Tara and asked her to have all of the partners meet him in the boardroom just before nine. "Tell them to drop whatever they're doing. Tell them this is massively important. I want them all there," he said.

They jumped into the BMW, kicking up gravel as they sped away.

They reached CBC's building at eight-fifty. "Can I leave you to find Tara?" Kent asked as they jumped out of the car.

"Will she be in your office?"

"Yes. I need to go speak to the others."

Kent ran up the three flights of stairs to the boardroom while Sarah took the elevator to the fourth floor and sat in Kent's office.

Tara came rushing in. "What's this all about, Sarah?" She sat on the opposite sofa. "John didn't say much on the phone. He sounded really worried."

"I don't know that much about it myself, but John is going to brief everyone at nine. He said you should join them."

"Okay. I'd better get down there. Do you mind helping yourself to a drink?"

"Don't worry about me. How is your mother, by the way? John told me she's living with you now. I've just realized you must have left her on her own to come here tonight."

"Thanks for asking. It's no problem. I got my sister to come over to sit with her."

Tara made her way to the boardroom to find Kent. The other partners were already there and were grilling him on what had happened to require a meeting at such short notice. He told them what he knew, then asked Prentis, who was already participating in the meeting by phone, to tell everyone exactly what happened earlier in the day when he was at Grampian. As Prentis finished, Kent told them to watch the TV news report about to start. Tara turned up the volume.

"The financial crisis claims another major financial institution," announced the anchorwoman from the U.S. news channel. "This afternoon, Grampian Capital has filed for bankruptcy, blaming massive and unforeseen losses in its insurance division, which had been a major underwriter of mortgage-backed securities. A spokesman for the company said Grampian Capital had spent weeks in secret discussions with the Fed about a possible bailout, but no rescue offer had been received. In a dramatic twist to this breaking story, the body of Grampian's CEO, Dan Schaeffer, was found in New York's East River a few hours ago. Also making the news at this hour..."

Kent asked Tara to turn down the sound then he looked around the table at his partners. The room was silent. Kent assumed they were reaching the same conclusions as he was. Without Grampian, CBC would have no investment funds available. Grampian had committed seven-and-a-half billion pounds of the ten billion pound latest fund. Without their commitment, the remaining two-and-a-half billion pounds of commitments would have to be canceled as they'd been raised on the understanding that this capital would be invested alongside the Grampian cornerstone monies. CBC was about to go over a cliff.

CHAPTER 10

At the rear of the Monterrey branch of Banco del Comercio Internacional de México ran a quiet street which was used as a service entrance for the buildings fronting onto Avenue Colon. The bank closed at 4 p.m. on weekdays, later by appointment.

Just after four-thirty that afternoon, a gray, high-sided security truck drove into the service street and came to a halt behind the bank. Without prompting, the metal shutter doors at the back of the bank building were opened, and the truck reversed into the loading bay, filling the air with diesel fumes. The shutter doors closed. Three men jumped out of the truck's cab. One handed papers to the waiting bank official, another walked to the back of the vehicle and lowered the tail lift, while the third watched everything as he lit up a cigarette. There was no discussion; this was a daily procedure, and everyone knew his role.

Once the tail lift was down, the cigarette smoker raised an eyebrow to his two colleagues, who began unloading brown sacks. The printed label on the side of each bag read *Corolla Currency Exchange*—a Caruana cartel-controlled company, operating some six hundred currency exchanges all over Mexico. It was the largest money changer in the country and growing fast. Jivaro had bought the company when it operated just forty outlets, at a price that the vendor could not refuse.

There were exactly forty sacks, and it took the two men thirty minutes to finish unloading and placing them on the bank's industrial scales. Each one weighed exactly the same, just under seventy-five pounds, and contained seven hundred and fifty thousand dollars in identically mixed U.S. dollar notes.

The bank official did not look inside the sacks; he didn't need to. He signed the paperwork and handed a copy to the men before ringing a bell at the side of the loading bay. A group of bank employees came running through to the loading area and began hauling the sacks into a safe holding room. As soon as the paperwork was signed, the money became the bank's responsibility.

The cigarette smoker was Arturo Vargas, a man in his late thirties with a penchant for smart, Italian suits. He always wore a diamond stud in his left ear. Vargas joined Corolla Currency Exchange two years ago from the Mexican National Police. He'd been responsible for the arrest of a number of Caruana cartel senior lieutenants and soon after made it clear he was open to offers for their release. A month later, he was recruited by the cartel. The money he was now making made his seven hundred dollar a month police salary look like small change. Vargas still had good connections within the National Police which were vital to the cartel. He was very good with numbers and was soon promoted to run Corolla.

Vargas ran an operation with two thousand people on the payroll. He reported directly to the cartel's CFO as it was a critical position. His role was to oversee the collection of money from the currency exchange outlets and to combine this with the illicit drug proceeds coming over the border from the U.S. Then he'd arrange to deposit the combined monies in the cartel's three favored Mexican banks. He had to account for it all, so he took hands-on responsibility for the physical deposits at the banks. He liked to see the money arrive. Nothing had gone missing on his watch and that was the way it was going to stay.

Later that day, Vargas received a visit from his boss. His visits were always unannounced. The Caruana CFO was Raul Safuentes, Jivaro's younger brother. While Vargas had never met Jivaro, he thought his brother lacked Jivaro's reputed charisma. While Jivaro was a big man, Raul was short and skinny. While Jivaro was concerned with strategy, Raul was more comfortable immersed in the detail and, like Vargas, nothing made him happier than well-kept records and books that balanced.

The surprise visit to Corolla that day yielded no unusual or suspicious transactions. Vargas ran a slick operation; it was rare for any errors to be discovered. After reviewing the accounting records with his boss, Vargas took Safuentes to dinner at his favorite restaurant in the San Pedro district of Monterrey. It was an Italian restaurant tucked away on a side street, just as his boss preferred.

"Good evening, Mr. Vargas. I have you in this quiet corner," said the hostess. Vargas always sat away from the window. He ordered cocktails and tried to make conversation, but Safuentes was hard work and offered little in return. He lightened up as the meal came and the red wine began to flow.

"Jivaro has noticed you, Arturo. I've kept him informed of your good work at Corolla. He has plans for you," said Safuentes.

"I'm, of course, happy to help in any way I can. I still have much to do here, but if Jivaro would like me to take on other responsibilities, then I'm certain I wouldn't disappoint him."

"He wants you to join my team at head office."

"I don't know what to say."

"There's an increasing workload as our organization expands. You've seen the growth in deposits for yourself."

"The growth has been impressive. We had only two hundred branches when I joined two years back. Now look at us."

"Believe me, depositing the cash is just the start of our work. We need intelligent and loyal people like you to help us preserve the money we've worked so hard to make."

"What would my new work involve?"

"You'll be helping me transfer funds to our various investment managers around the world. But more importantly, we must monitor their investment performance, and you will be part of that process."

"Vital work."

"There's nothing more important than this. It's the final stage of converting our cash into legitimate assets. Jivaro himself takes an active interest in this area of our work. You will have many opportunities to impress him."

"It would be an honor to work at head office." Vargas began to absorb the consequences of his unexpected promotion. He'd be joining the inner circle. Not yet one of the fifteen lieutenants reporting directly to Jivaro, but just one step below. If his old police colleagues could see him now.

"Then it is settled. I'll make the arrangements."

"What will happen to my position at Corolla?"

"You'll be a hard man to replace."

"I have a few suggestions."

"We can discuss that later."

CHAPTER 11

For the first time in his life, Kent did not know what to say. He felt the weight of his partners' hopes that he'd come up with a plan. He'd always been the one to work out a clever way through difficult situations facing the firm. It was one of the things his partners valued in his leadership. No matter what the problem, Kent would always find a solution. But, this one time, he struggled to see a way out; he hadn't been here before. He felt like a champion boxer having just received his first knock-out punch and now he was on the ropes, gasping for breath.

"Doug Wright will go ballistic when he hears the news," said Kirkland, breaking the silence in the conference room. "He terminated his discussions with the other firm the moment he signed our offer letter today. He's bound to sue."

Kent stood up to leave. "Right now, I don't give a shit about that clown. We'll deal with Henderson Wright tomorrow. First, we need to assess what this means for us and how we're going to move on from here. Let's all sleep on it and meet up at eight tomorrow morning. Cancel any appointments you have."

He needed time to think this through on his own. There had to be a way forward. Maybe there could be something rescued out of the bankruptcy process. He wanted to sleep on things before making any snap decisions. The other partners stayed seated, staring at the images on the silent TV like blinded rabbits.

"There'll be a way through this," Kent said as he left the boardroom.

On the drive home, he was quiet as he contemplated the reality of losing his firm. A decade's work down the drain, and a lifetime's reputation torn to shreds. He might just have accepted this if CBC's investment performance had been poor, but it was one of the best in the industry. He couldn't accept the injustice of it all. What made it worse was losing CBC's investment firepower just when the recession was throwing off great buying opportunities. That morning, he had a large checkbook and an increasing choice of attractive investment deals in the middle of a recession—a buyer's paradise. He'd never be able to create these ideal conditions again. Grampian had ruined a once-in-a-lifetime situation. Had he been wrong to rely so heavily on them for investment capital? Should he have spent more time on the fundraising road for the third fund and spread the commitments across a wider group of institutional investors? It was too late now, anyway. He couldn't change that.

"How serious is this, John?" Sarah asked, breaking into his thoughts.

"It doesn't get any worse. The recession means the chances of replacing Grampian's commitment with other investors today are virtually zero."

"But CBC has a great track record."

"It doesn't matter. Most institutional investors are already overcommitted to private equity at the moment. They're looking to reduce those commitments, not add to them."

"I see."

"We're in trouble. This couldn't have happened at a worse time for us."

Kent bought all the main newspapers the next day. They were full of stories covering the failure of Grampian, the once-prestigious Wall Street financial institution. The company had collapsed without any prior warning. There was no hint of any disproportionate losses accumulating in its insurance division in its last quarterly SEC filing, and the share price had been stable in recent months. Press speculation ran wild with theories, ranging from fraud through to massive mismanagement. The commentators were unanimous in praising the Fed for not bailing out another risk-taking institution. Taxpayers would not accept any more. The fact that the whole market was taken by surprise didn't make Kent feel any better. He was still facing the almost certain failure of CBC.

The partners spent most of the morning discussing what options they had to rescue the firm. While they knew the market for fundraising was awful, Kent insisted they had to try to generate some new investor interest. He was not going to give up without a fight. He assigned the task to Johnson and Prentis as they had the most relationships in the institutional investor community. They'd know which institutions, if any, had an appetite to make new fund commitments. Although the thought turned his stomach, Kent decided they also had to investigate whether there was any merit in selling CBC to a competing private equity firm. He knew that was likely to be a waste of time; it would always be much cheaper for any competitor to hire those members of the CBC team they wanted rather than buy the whole firm. That's what he would do if he was in their shoes, but he owed it to all the staff to see if another firm would acquire CBC, even for pennies. He asked Henning to lead the search for possible buyers. If, through some miracle, he managed to hook any interest, Kent would take over the negotiations with the prospective buyer as it would be a messy fistfight.

The only live deal in the pipeline likely to be difficult to unwind was the Henderson Wright transaction being led by Kirkland. They could not continue with the deal now they had no investment funds available. Kent asked Kirkland to meet with Wright to see if there was an elegant exit from the transaction. Maybe they could suggest another private equity firm to replace CBC. Whatever help they offered Wright, Kent expected trouble. He'd just pushed him into accepting a hard deal for his management team, after all.

Kent spent the rest of the day fielding calls from the financial press and from existing investors. They all wanted to know the same thing: Did the failure of Grampian Capital mean CBC's future was in jeopardy? He did what he could to put out a strong, positive message, but he knew the failure of the firm was a real prospect, and the press sensed blood. CBC was losing its reputation as each hour passed. It was killing him, and there was little he could do besides stand back and watch it happen.

The following day, Kent picked up his *Financial Daily*. Right in the center of the front page of the Companies and Markets section was the headline "Grampian likely to bring down CBC." There followed a well-researched and intelligently written article on the massive reliance on Grampian Capital by CBC for its investment funds. It went on to address the difficulty of raising new funds in this recessionary climate, even with CBC's excellent investment track record. The article concluded, in the absence of a new cornerstone investor, CBC would fail in a matter of months.

Not far off the mark. A complete fucking disaster. The firm's demise was about to be played out in public, and Kent would become a laughing stock in the industry.

"Is there anything I can do to help?" asked Tara, stepping into her boss's office. She brought in his usual coffee and then sat on the arm of his sofa. She was dressed down for the somber occasion, but Kent couldn't help notice how her red lipstick stood out against the dark suit, making her lips fuller than usual.

"Thanks, Tara," he said. "There really isn't much you can do to help at the moment."

"I don't understand all the technical issues, but it looks pretty bad."

"It's bad, all right. Without Grampian, we have no money to invest. If we don't find a replacement investor quickly, we'll have to start winding down the firm soon."

Kent's phone rang. He picked it up.

"John, it's Joanna."

"How's it going?" he asked. She'd been down at Henderson Wright all morning and he had been waiting for her call. "I bet Wright didn't say, 'thanks for letting me know, maybe next time.'"

"Not quite. Let's just say, it's not going well at all."

"So we're off his Christmas card list?" Kent didn't care. His firm was going over the cliff. If Wright's firm went with them, so be it.

"I'm sorry to pile on more pressure, but he said he's coming up from London this afternoon to sort this mess out with you face to face. He was livid when I told him we were unable to complete his deal."

"Just what I need."

"I know. I've just left Henderson Wright's offices and I'm on my way back to the office now. I thought I ought to give you as much advance notice as possible."

"Thanks. I'll alert Chapman to load up his machine gun on the security desk. See you here later."

Kent was used to being in control, but for the first time in his life, he sensed events were in control of him. He couldn't just stand by and watch this slow car crash. He needed to do something. There had to be a way out of this mess. He gazed out of his window toward Cambridge.

His phone rang again. "Mr. Kent, this is Chapman. I'm sorry to trouble you, but we have a camera crew here at the front desk. They say they're from the BBC and are asking for an interview. I've refused to let them in. Is that okay?"

"Don't worry. I'll come down." Kent stood up and made his way downstairs.

He showed the camera crew and the BBC's business editor into a meeting room on the ground floor and prepared for a mauling. He gave convincing answers to most of their questions, which were mainly about CBC's ability to survive and what would happen to CBC's existing portfolio of companies should the firm not make it. For a man with few real answers to these questions, Kent performed well. He gave the impression there were many alternative investors lining up to take the place of Grampian Capital; he wasn't worried by this inconvenient setback. He knew if he looked as though he'd given up, there'd be no hope of attracting new investors.

After an hour, he was saved by Tara. "Mr. Wright is in one of the top-floor meeting rooms, waiting to see you," she said, interrupting the interview. Kent made his apologies and returned to his office.

"Is Joanna back yet?" he asked.

"Yes. Shall I ask her to join you in your office?"

"Please."

Moments later, Kirkland walked into his office. "I have to tell you, Wright is manic. It's clear he's a man who likes to get his own way. From what I've seen, all of his senior staff members are afraid to stand up to him. I'd say he's a classic bully."

"I'm not surprised to hear that. I already knew he wasn't liked much within his own firm as I know a number of his partners. They've told me the same thing."

"How are we going to deal with him?"

"Leave most of the talking to me," said Kent, taking off his tie. "I'll handle him."

They left his office and walked over to the meeting room where Wright was waiting. His face was red, and he was pacing up and down the room like a trapped animal. He had his lawyer with him, a senior partner from one of the top international law firms in London.

Kent had not even sat down when the Henderson Wright lawyer fired the first salvo. "Mr. Kent, your colleague, Ms. Kirkland, has informed my client that you're unable to complete the transaction set out in your offer letter of two days ago."

Kent had plenty of experience in handling condescending lawyers. "Good afternoon to you too," he said.

"I have informed my client they'll be entitled to recover considerable damages from CBC, in the event they suffer loss as a result of your failure to meet your obligations under this contract."

"Are you interested at all in hearing why we have a problem?"

"I don't give a damn about your problems. You made a formal written offer, which we accepted," spat Wright. He was leaning against the window, his arms crossed.

Kent wanted to shove him through it; he'd heard enough. "Our offer letter said the financing was subject to us being satisfied with our due diligence."

"And?" asked Wright, placing his hands on his hips, as if to say, "Is that the best you have?"

"Well, we're not satisfied."

"What the hell are you talking about? You haven't carried out any due diligence yet." Wright shook his head.

"We've done enough."

"My client would know if you had," said the lawyer.

"We started it today, Doug, when you walked into our offices. I decided I don't like your judgment."

"What?" Wright's face looked as though it was about to explode.

"Turning up here with your mad-dog lawyer and acting all belligerent shows very poor judgment in my view. It's not how we expect a CEO of one of our investee companies to act when he's under pressure."

"I object to that, Mr. Kent," said the lawyer. Kent ignored him. *An irrelevant stuffed shirt.*

"If we can't trust your judgment, there's no point carrying on with further due diligence. It would be a complete waste of our time and your money. You've fallen at the first hurdle, I'm afraid." Kent smiled.

"That's not due diligence," said the lawyer.

"We decide what to assess when considering an investment. That's why we're investors and you're just a lawyer. Now, gentlemen, we're busy here. I think we've completed our business."

Kent stood, offered no handshake, and left the meeting room. Kirkland followed, her jaw still wide open in awe.

***

One week after the BBC interview, Kent was sitting in his office reviewing his firm's latest quarterly return for the FCA, the industry regulator. The draft return had been prepared by Kevin Long, the most junior CBC partner and compliance officer. Long had suggested Kent might want to write a covering letter to update the FCA on the financial state of CBC. He'd reminded Kent that the FCA's rules required an open and transparent dialogue with the regulator. Kent thought this was a good idea; the market was now alert to CBC's situation so it would be wrong not to explain the details to the FCA. It was also right that Kent, as the CEO, should write the letter.

His phone rang. It was Tara. "I have a Mr. Baumgart for you. He wants to talk to you about our fundraising plans," she said.

"Thanks. Put him through," he replied.

Kent was now becoming pissed off with these inquiries. In normal circumstances, CBC might have expected one or two calls a month from potential investors. Since CBC's troubles had hit the press, however, the firm had received several calls a day. The problem was all of them had been secondary investors looking for a bargain. Kent had seen these vultures rise in prominence during the recession. They waited for large institutional investors, like Grampian, to run into financial difficulty so they could buy their fund investments at a large discount. For easing the existing investor's liquidity pain, secondary investors would normally enjoy discounts of between fifty and seventy percent on the assets they were able to buy. He quietly admired these opportunists, but they were of little direct value to him. CBC's stock response was to request them to call Grampian Capital directly, as the dialogue needed to be between buyer and seller and not CBC as fund manager.

Kent dropped his shoulders and prepared for another waste of time. "Good afternoon. John Kent speaking."

"Good afternoon, Mr. Kent. My name is Dieter Baumgart and I'm calling from Geneva, Switzerland. I understand you are fundraising."

"Yes. That's correct. We're in the market for new investment capital."

"I represent a multifamily investment office called Tritona. I'd appreciate a meeting to explore a potential investment commitment on our part."

"I'd be delighted to meet you."

This doesn't sound like a secondary investor, Kent thought.

"How much are you looking to raise?" Baumgart asked.

"Between five and seven and a half billion pounds." Kent was making this up as he went along. He had nothing to lose, so he decided to go for the full amount CBC had lost from Grampian.

"Okay. Those amounts are well within our investment parameters. I'll ask my assistant to liaise with your PA to arrange a meeting. I assume you're happy to come over here for our initial meeting?"

"Yes, of course." Kent realized the fundraising was unlikely to succeed, but he had to exhaust all options; his firm's survival was on the line. "In the meantime, I'll have our fundraising document emailed over to you. I look forward to meeting you."

"Perfect. I shall look forward to the meeting. I'll have my assistant join me to capture some notes of our discussion. I trust you'll do the same?"

"Of course," said Kent automatically, but immediately thinking it was a slightly odd request. *Must be a cultural difference.*

"Good-bye, Mr. Kent."

Tara brought in Kent's coffee, and he took a sip. "Any good?" she asked.

"The coffee?" He smiled.

"No. The investor. He called a couple of times this morning and seemed keen. I offered to take a message or put him on to one of the other partners, but he didn't want to. He insisted he would only speak to you."

"He seemed interested enough in our fundraising, but I don't hold much hope. Anyway, you'll be able to judge for yourself."

Tara slanted her head to one side. "How's that?"

"You'll be coming with me to Geneva to meet them."

"That's unusual, isn't it?"

"It is, but he seemed keen to have personal assistants attend the meeting to take notes. I'm not quite sure why it's necessary. All seems a bit over the top to me."

"At least I'll get to see Switzerland. I've not been there before."

CHAPTER 12

Jivaro chose Mexico's Isla Tiburon for his head office location because of its isolation in the middle of the Gulf of California. There were no roads to speak of, and the only practical way into the interior of the island was by helicopter. It took two years to build the underground fortress, complete with its own power supply, sleeping quarters, and water desalination plant. The total build cost came in at one-point-two billion dollars.

Everything happened underground. The only thing visible from the air was a cream-colored, concrete-block hut about the size of a basketball court. There was nothing to indicate what sat beneath the earth. No cars, no people; in fact, no signs of human life for miles around. Only red desert, sparsely punctuated by green clumps of gorse.

Sand flew everywhere when the helicopter came in to land, shrouding the four men as they climbed out. They ran into the building, passing three other men coming out on their way to the aircraft. Jivaro did not allow the helicopters to hang around as they risked drawing unnecessary attention.

Once inside, the four men took an elevator down into the main building. The one dressed in the smart suit got off at the third floor. The doors opened up into what looked like a NASA control room with at least thirty men and women at computer terminals. The pace of work was intense with little conversation between the employees. The dominant sound was of clicking keyboards. He scanned the room as though he was looking for someone.

"Welcome to head office, Arturo. I'll have your bags taken

to your room. Please leave them here," said Raul Safuentes as he came over to greet Vargas. Safuentes broke into one of his rare smiles when they shook hands. "I trust you had a good flight?"

Vargas had taken one of the cartel's private jets for the two-hour flight from Monterrey to Hermosillo and from there he flew by helicopter to Isla Tiburon. The cartel owned a helicopter charter business in Hermosillo. Its main function was to ferry cartel members back and forward to the island. Jivaro decided long ago it was a small price to pay for the isolation and protection afforded by the remote location.

"A relaxing journey, thanks. Now I'm keen to get started."

"Good. Let me show you around." Safuentes led Vargas over to one of the computer terminals.

"This floor is the financial heart of the organization. Each one of these screens gives the operator access to certain limited aspects of our business. For example, one operator might be monitoring our cash movements over the U.S. border. Someone else may be handling the bank deposit records you have been sending in from Corolla, while another, more senior, operator will be reconciling these amounts and accounting for any differences on a daily basis."

Vargas struggled to take it all in. The operation was much larger and more sophisticated than he'd imagined. "How many people are based here at head office?" he asked.

"It varies, but, generally, we have between three and four hundred people here at any one time. All of the living quarters are on the first two floors. I'll show you those later. As a senior member of staff, you will have your own room."

"As we entered the building at the ground level, I noticed there were many armed guards."

"Yes. My brother takes these matters seriously. We have at least twenty security personnel on each floor. You never know when we might be attacked."

"By the authorities?"

"I'm pleased to say that, so far, we've had no trouble from the authorities. We make it our business to take care of the right politicians and police chiefs." Safuentes smiled again.

"I understand. Then the threat must be from the other cartels?"

"That's right, but our location makes it extremely difficult for our enemies to attack us by surprise." Safuentes led Vargas down a flight of stairs to another level and through a security-coded metal door. "Now it gets interesting. In these offices are our most senior accounting staff members. You will be based on this floor. I work over there." He pointed to a corner office.

"It's good to know I'll be working so closely with you. What happens on this level?"

"From here we have electronic control of all of our bank accounts."

"I know from my work at Corolla how much we deposit with the banks each day. It must take some supervision."

"We settle our raw material purchases and overheads out of our physical cash resources first in order to minimize the trail. However, once we have deposited cash with our chosen banks, we move those monies around the globe and into other assets as quickly as possible. All of those instructions are issued from here using our encrypted communications network. As I mentioned, you will be involved in this work."

"I noticed the restricted access to this floor."

"That's right. Other than our senior accounting staff, only the fifteen lieutenants have access to this area. Everyone has individual access codes for the doors, so we know exactly who is coming in and out, and at what time."

"I'm looking forward to meeting the lieutenants. I've heard so much about them."

Safuentes nodded. "Now, follow me. You will see where they work in a moment."

Vargas was led down one more floor and through a fingerprint-scanning security door. He looked up at the CCTV cameras following their every move.

"The cameras run all day. Everything is recorded," said

Safuentes.

They entered a long corridor with a number of doors leading off it. One of the doors was open as Vargas walked by. He stopped at the doorway and looked inside the office. A large electronic screen was mounted on the wall facing a mahogany desk. There was no one sitting at the desk, but in the corner of the room was a smaller desk, where a young female assistant was working at a PC. She didn't look up from her screen and seemed immersed in her work.

"These are the offices used by the lieutenants when they're not in the field." Safuentes held Vargas by his shoulder, preventing him from walking into the office. He pulled the door closed as they moved on.

"How long do the lieutenants spend at head office?"

"It depends on their role, but I'd estimate they're here only one week in four on average. They are Jivaro's eyes and ears in the field, so it's important they're out managing our operations on the ground. Come, we must hurry; we're running a little late."

At the end of the long corridor, they took a sharp right turn leading to a much longer passageway, punctuated only by fluorescent lighting. Eventually, they passed through an automatic sliding glass door and into a large room, about one hundred and fifty feet by one hundred feet. It was full of natural light, unlike the dark corridors they'd just left behind. Vargas had to squint to regain his focus. At the opposite end of the room stood a floor-to-ceiling glass wall with a view over the ocean. He could now see the fortress had been dug into the side of a hill overlooking the sea. He estimated the window was some six hundred feet above sea level.

"This is amazing," said Vargas. "Absolutely amazing."

"Arturo," boomed a deep voice, resonating around the room. "Good to meet you. Raul tells me good things about your work." It was Jivaro, and this was his domain.

"Mr. Safuentes. It is an honor to meet you, sir." Vargas had to raise his head to make eye contact when Jivaro reached them.

There was no shaking of hands. Vargas had already heard about Jivaro's peculiar habits.

"Come. Sit down." Jivaro gestured to three leather sofas close to the window. On the side table next to Vargas were several photographs of Jivaro and his wife and only son.

"What an impressive view. It must be a great place to work."

"Yes, although I spend little time here."

A young woman came into the room from a separate entrance and poured coffee for the three men.

"How much time do you spend here?"

"Not much. Now, let's discuss your new role here on the island."

Vargas took the hint. The small talk was over.

The three men spent half an hour going over the key responsibilities of his new position. He'd be reporting directly to Jivaro's brother and would be spending most of his time at head office. As with all other senior staff members, he'd be permitted to leave the island one week in every four.

When the meeting was over, Jivaro stood, signaling to Vargas it was time for him to leave. "I know you will do well here, Arturo. Raul will keep me informed of your progress."

As they reached the exit, Jivaro pulled his brother to one side and whispered into his ear. Vargas could not hear what the great man was saying, but he looked irritated with his brother.

CHAPTER 13

The flight time from Heathrow to Geneva was just under two hours, long enough for Kent to show off to Tara his extensive knowledge of Switzerland and to read the briefing papers sent over by Tritona. Baumgart was the CEO of this multifamily investment office. The three families mentioned were well known ultra-high net worth Europeans, all with well-documented business backgrounds. Kent was impressed by their names and was not surprised to learn they'd set up their own combined family office. In recent years, he'd seen many very wealthy families do the same thing. Rather than pay many different outside managers to run their affairs, by setting up their own office, with their own professional staff, these families could retain greater control over their assets and ensure their financial interests were handled with the utmost discretion. Given the names involved, Kent was hopeful the trip was not going to be a complete waste of time.

Their plane landed at two-thirty in the afternoon, right on schedule. They left the terminal building fifteen minutes later and walked toward the waiting limousine.

Tritona's headquarters were in a small village called Bellerive on the southern shore of Lake Geneva, some ten miles from the airport. As the limousine rolled into the parking lot, Kent gazed out of the window at the building. It was nondescript, but not untypical of the low-profile style preferred by family offices he'd come across before. After all, they were spending their own money. They had no one they needed to impress.

It was two-fifty-five, just in time for their three o'clock appointment. In reception, they were greeted by a friendly young woman. "Good afternoon. Mr. Baumgart is expecting you both. Please follow me and I'll show you to the meeting room," she said.

Kent looked around as they walked. The décor on the inside of the building—austere with very few frills—gave no hint of the amount of wealth managed by Tritona. *Funny how the fanciest investor offices are occupied by managers spending other peoples' monies and not their own.*

"Would you like some coffee? Or, perhaps you might prefer tea?" asked the receptionist as the visitors took their seats in the meeting room.

"Coffee would be fine for both of us, thank you," Tara said.

Moments later, Dieter Baumgart entered the room. Kent nudged Tara's arm with his elbow. Baumgart weighed at least two hundred and eighty pounds, and Kent estimated he was some six or seven inches taller than his own six feet. He was so large coming through the door that he didn't notice Baumgart's assistant, a gaunt, weedy-looking man with bifocal glasses. They made an odd couple.

The Swiss gorilla smiled and extended his hand. "Dieter Baumgart. Very pleased to meet you, Mr. Kent. And who is this delightful young lady?" he asked, crunching Kent's hand in a viselike grip.

"This is Tara Sanderson, my executive assistant."

"And this is Franz Kulpman," Baumgart said, introducing the puny, little man who'd already begun taking notes.

What on earth could he be writing at this early stage in the meeting?

Baumgart sat at the head of the meeting room table, his chair creaking as it took the weight. The lower buttons of his tightly stretched shirt looked about to explode. "Mr. Kent, I've read your fundraising document with great interest. As you can imagine, I have a number of detailed questions for you. Would it help if I told you a little more about Tritona first?"

"That would be very helpful. Obviously, I've read the papers you sent, but there's nothing like hearing it firsthand."

Kent always preferred to hear a little more about a prospective investor before launching into his own presentation. That way, he could judge whether or not the investor was a tire kicker, and adjust the length of his presentation accordingly. He never ceased to be amazed by how many investors were happy to waste time in meetings with private equity firms, and yet had no intention of making a commitment. He assumed they did it to pick up market gossip, but he found it irritating.

They were interrupted by the coffees being brought in. "Laura, would you please make the dinner reservation for eight o'clock?" said Baumgart. He turned to Kent. "As you know, I've reserved two rooms for you at Hotel Morgana in Geneva tonight. I hope you don't mind if we continue our discussion over dinner at the hotel?"

"That would be great," said Kent, thinking that a first meeting would not normally need more than two hours. He was okay with this, however, as their flight was not scheduled to leave until 9 a.m. the following day.

"Excellent. Now, let me tell you more about our organization."

Kent noticed Baumgart's fat fingers and heavy breathing as he spoke. He was probably around the same age as Kent but in very poor shape. He assumed from Baumgart's size that he took every chance he could get to enjoy a meal out at a fancy restaurant.

Baumgart's assistant continued to scribble notes on his legal pad. Kent stared across at Tara, worried what their Swiss hosts might be thinking as she'd not yet taken any notes. Not that there was anything worth noting so far.

Baumgart hardly stopped for air. "Tritona was established four years ago when the Deutchman, Needmeier, and Kvarnback families merged their individual family investment offices into a multifamily office. Before the merger, I managed the assets of the Kvarnback family. Back then, we had a team of eight, which has now grown to thirty-five. Our growth has come from taking on the management of virtually all of the three families' wealth. And from good investment returns, of course! Today, we have over four hundred and fifty billion dollars in assets under management."

"That's impressive," said Kent. Tritona was a much bigger player than he'd first thought. Their assets under management meant they would rank as a top-ten global player. *Strange we haven't come across them before.*

"Our assets are located in most major markets with a heavy weighting in cash, real estate, and bonds. Most of the real estate portfolio has been acquired in the last few months. Now that markets are at a low point, we're interested in committing an increasing portion of our funds to equities, including private equity, where we are particularly underweight. We have a few direct private equity investments, but nothing with fund managers like CBC. Most of our assets are handled directly by our team here."

Baumgart's much smarter than he looks. Getting into real estate just after the market crashed, and now buying into equities at their low point, shows real investment judgment. CBC's fundraising needs are nothing for this lot.

"Impressive timing. Warren Buffett says an investor should be greedy when others are fearful, but most don't have the courage to follow the rule," said Kent. He could see from his beaming smile that Baumgart was flattered by the comparison with Warren Buffett.

The meeting continued with Kent's presentation and a series of detailed questions from Baumgart concerning CBC's strategy, investment performance record, deal-flow, and the background of each key team member. Baumgart was thorough and demonstrated deep knowledge of the private equity market. He appeared to be satisfied by Kent's answers. The CBC story was a strong one, after all.

Baumgart brought the meeting to a close at five-thirty and

suggested they meet in the bar of Hotel Morgana at seven-forty-five.

Maybe, just maybe, this is going somewhere, thought Kent as he and Tara drove off in the waiting limo.

CHAPTER 14

Merriman knew the DEA was the career he wanted from a very young age. He learned from his father how important it was and saw how it made a real difference to the lives of many Americans, even if most of them never witnessed the work being carried out in their name.

The problem was his father had to pull a few strings to get him accepted into the service, because of Merriman's poor academic record. But he'd made up for this by aiming high, taking risks, and being more tenacious than his more intellectual peers. Merriman was streetwise and understood what motivated people. If he was told something was not possible, or that it had been tried before and failed, he'd stick at it until he found a solution. This dogged determination, and his ability to get the best out of those who worked for him, meant he had a strong history of achievement in the job.

He was still a young man, full of ambition, and the poor academic record had left a lasting chip on his shoulder. It was not enough to have become the youngest Head of Intelligence; he wanted to leave a legacy, something by which he'd be remembered. And now that he'd persuaded the DEA leadership to focus intelligence resources on cartel assets, he knew this could be it: winning the war on drugs. Success here would enable him to close down entire criminal networks and hit the cartel leaders where it hurt most. The enormity of the challenge did not deter Merriman; it inspired him.

His primary target was the Caruana cartel, the biggest and most powerful. Others had tried to bring down this narcotic powerhouse, but they'd failed. Merriman would be the man who brought down Jivaro's empire, whatever it took.

"Got a moment, Mark?" asked Bill Greenough, standing at the doorway to Merriman's office.

"Sure, grab a seat." Merriman cleared a space on his desk so Greenough could rest the file he'd brought with him. "How can I help?"

Greenough pulled up a chair and opened the file. "You know I've been trying to track what happens to some of the Caruana cash once it's transferred overseas by their Mexican banks?"

"Sure. Was my contact at the Mexican central bank any help?"

"Extremely helpful. Without him, we'd be nowhere."

"Good. He owed me a favor." Merriman's cell phone went off in his hand. "Sorry, let me kill this." He looked at the screen of the phone, thought about taking the call for a split second, then hit the cancel button before turning it onto silent mode. "What have you got for me?"

"Well, I've concentrated my work on one bank in Monterrey and only for a six-month period so far." Greenough turned to some analyses on his file. "You can see here that the cartel is moving massive funds overseas. If I'm right in what I've extrapolated, then this whole thing's much bigger than any of us imagined."

Merriman leaned forward onto his elbows to read the data in front of him. "Let me take a look." He turned over a couple of pages of the file, read them twice, then looked up at Greenough.

"That's incredible. You think they might be shifting twenty to thirty billion dollars out of Mexico each year? Our earlier estimates were less than half this."

"I'm pretty sure I've got a good handle on the amounts."

Merriman sat back in his chair and steepled his hands as he thought. "Where the hell's it all going, Bill?"

"That's what I'm working on now. We've got some of our best people helping on this, but unpicking the corporate structures used by the cartel ain't easy."

"I know. What more do you need? We have to crack this."

"Does the name 'Oakham' mean anything to you?"

Merriman chewed on the question a moment. "Not really. Why?"

"It's just it keeps cropping up in our tracing results, but I can't connect the dots at the moment. Thought it might mean something to you. Long shot, I know."

"Sorry, I can't help. What or who do you think Oakham might be?"

"Difficult to be certain, but I think it's where a lot of this money ends up. The trail goes cold each time we come across this Oakham name. Sure would help to have an insider's help on this."

"We're working on that. In the meantime, how can I help you move this forward?"

"Can I have your approval to move a few more people onto this? I'm optimistic it's not a dead end."

"How many do you need?"

"Three if I can have them."

"If I find you ten, can you use them?"

Greenough's eyes lit up. "Easily."

"Leave it with me. There's no greater priority than this investigation."

"Thanks. I appreciate the help." Greenough stood up to leave.

"As soon as you learn more about Oakham, I want you to let me know. Good job, Bill."

Merriman shut his office door behind Greenough and sat to check his voicemail. Then he rang his contact at the Mexican central bank to thank him for his help. No doubt, his contact would have bent a few rules to gain access to the information. At last, this investigation is going somewhere. No one's traced an endpoint for Caruana's fund transfers before.

"Oakham, Oakham," he said quietly. *Don't know what it is, but we're sure gonna find out.*

CHAPTER 15

Hotel Morgana sat on the edge of Lake Geneva on Quai des Bergues. Built in 1820, it had accommodated Europe's glitterati and power brokers for decades. It was the finest hotel in Geneva and looked across the water to the Alps beyond. Tritona had reserved two adjacent suites on the fifteenth floor. Kent wondered who was selling to whom when he saw the hotel.

"It's six-fifteen now. Shall we meet in the lounge bar at, say, seven-forty?" he said to Tara as they stepped out of the elevator.

"Okay. This place is amazing," she replied. He was reminded that this was all very new to Tara. He'd long taken for granted international travel at the highest level. Sarah had often said he lived in a bubble, far removed from the real-world experience of most people.

Kent unlocked his door, placed his overnight bag on the king-size bed, then walked over to the large window to take in the view. It was getting dark, and the lights of the city hugged the lake. Snow covered some of the higher peaks in the distance. He was reminded of some of the recent ski holidays he'd taken with Sarah. There would be fewer of those luxuries if CBC failed. *Is Tritona really considering making an investment commitment? They sounded interested at the meeting and seemed satisfied with my answers. They certainly have the financial capacity with their massive resources.*

If nothing else, Kent was a realist. After a few minutes enjoying the dream, he remembered he'd been here before. He knew from experience that an investor meeting could go well, only to find no commitment is made, and then again he'd known situations where the opposite was true. He sat on the corner of the bed, grabbed a pen, and noted down a list of institutional investors his team had approached since the Grampian Capital disaster had hit. The list ran to more than forty names, and not one of them had made a commitment. Many of them had known CBC for years and knew of its excellent investment record but, as a result of the recession, most had the same problem: they were overweight in private equity and needed to reduce commitments, not increase them. No—Kent knew in his heart Tritona was likely to decline a commitment, particularly in the absence of an existing cornerstone investor.

He rang Sarah.

"How's it going?" she asked.

"Okay, I think." He didn't want to share his pessimism with her.

"Did they say whether they're interested?"

"No, but we haven't finished yet. They want to continue over dinner."

"That sounds promising."

"It does, but we've been here before, remember."

"I understand. I know you'll give it your best shot."

"I should know more when tonight's over."

"Whatever happens, John, we'll be okay you know. CBC isn't everything. Keep that in mind."

In spite of his effort to sound upbeat, Sarah must have realized from his tone that he was expecting this to be another wasted trip. *CBC is everything*, he thought; everything he'd worked for and the physical manifestation of his success. If it failed, he'd make his fortune again, no matter how difficult the challenge. Anything else was unthinkable.

"The hotel's good." He didn't want to discuss his company failing right now.

"Where is it?"

"On the edge of the lake. They've put us in suites on the top floor. Great views. It's a shame you're not here with me."

"Sounds lovely. Don't enjoy it too much without me."

"I'll try. Well, I'd better get ready. I still need to shower and change before dinner. I love you."

"I love you, too. Good luck."

Kent made a quick call to the office to check in with Johnson. He was always the last to leave the office. Since his divorce a few years back, Johnson had struggled to find another partner, which Kent thought was strange given he was such a sociable animal. Johnson spent most evenings sat at his desk. On the few occasions when Kent had to work very late, he'd insist on throwing Johnson out of the office to make sure he didn't become a complete hermit.

"Have we set up any more potential investor meetings?" asked Kent.

"A couple, but we've had a load more polite rejections today. It's not looking good," said Johnson.

"Grampian couldn't have failed at a worse time."

"How's it going with the Swiss?"

"Hard to tell, really. They've got plenty of money. Whether they want to use it is another matter. We should learn more tonight as we're seeing them again for dinner."

"Sounds good. Who's paying?"

"They are."

"Make sure you order something expensive. At least get something out of the trip. Good luck."

"Thanks. I'd rather come back with a big commitment, but don't hold your breath."

Kent jumped in the shower, had a quick shave, then caught a few minutes of the news on CNN before making his way to the lounge bar next to the main restaurant. It was seven-forty, and he was the first to arrive. He sat in an armchair facing the entrance so he could spot Baumgart and his weird assistant coming in. He scanned the room. The usual bunch of international business people. He could be sitting in a luxury hotel anywhere in the world and he'd see the same collection of people. In one corner was the usual group of loud Americans. There was always at least one group of them. *Why do they always need to shout at each other so the whole room can hear their conversation?* He gave them a sneering glance, but it made no difference. They were oblivious to him and everyone else in the room.

How do you get a drink in this place? At that moment, Baumgart entered the lounge. His assistant was tucked in behind him. Kent waved so Baumgart could see him, and he came trundling over, taking up the most of a three-seat sofa. Kulpman sat upright on a hardback chair. Kent couldn't understand why he didn't choose to sit in one of the many empty armchairs.

"Is the hotel satisfactory, Mr. Kent?" asked Baumgart.

"Wonderful, thanks," replied Kent. "Such great views."

"We always entertain our visitors here. I don't think any of them have been disappointed. The food is good, too."

Tara walked in, and Baumgart smiled. "Over here, Ms. Sanderson," he said, patting the cushion next to him on the sofa. Tara duly obliged by sitting next to him.

Bright girl, but you'll struggle to squeeze on.

The headwaiter came over. "*Gut, Sie wiederzusehen, Herr Baumgart. Was kann ich für Sie und Ihre Gäste zu bringen?*" Baumgart must be a German Swiss, thought Kent.

"*Ich würde sehr gerne einen Kir Royale haben, wenn das möglich ist, bitte,*" replied Tara.

"You speak German?" said Baumgart. He looked astonished.

"Yes. Also Spanish and French."

Bull's-eye! Kent was reminded of how many men saw only Tara's beauty and underestimated her as a result. He'd lost count of how many times he'd seen this happen. She was his secret weapon. A smart hire.

Baumgart placed the drinks order. "I want you to make the best Kir Royale possible for Ms. Sanderson."

He's smitten. Now he's flirting with Tara. Maybe she'll be able to coax an investment commitment out of him.

"Please, Mr. Baumgart, call me Tara."

"Then I insist you call me Dieter."

"Let's all use first names," said Kent, breaking up the love-in.

At eight o'clock, they were shown to their table. Kent looked around the dining room as he sat. *Baumgart must have some pull in this place. We're in the best hotel in Geneva and now we have by far the best table in the restaurant.* The waiters fussed over Baumgart and his guests as though they were the only table in the room.

Baumgart was slow moving the conversation back to the business in hand. Kent couldn't work out why. They talked about the economy, politics, and even the weather; anything but a potential investment commitment to CBC. Kent tried several times in vain to steer the conversation round to his firm and its search for new investors. By the time they were halfway through dessert, the night was almost over, and Kent was dismissing the whole trip as a waste of time.

Why is Baumgart still flirting with Tara? Was he always out just to have a good time with no real intention of making a commitment? Does he understand how critical this is to CBC?

There was another possible explanation: Kent had seen other investors place a lot of store on whether or not they liked the CBC team as people. *Maybe that's Baumgart's style.*

Every now and then, Kent glanced at Kulpman. Baumgart's assistant had continued to scribble notes all evening. *There's been no discussion worth noting. He hasn't uttered a single word; what's the point of him being here?*

"What's your own professional background, Dieter?" Kent thought he'd try one last time to turn the conversation over to a business level, although he'd pretty much written off the evening by now.

"My career was based around international law for twenty years."

Finally, Baumgart is actually prepared to talk business.

"How did you find yourself managing Tritona with that background?" asked Tara. Kent smiled at her, grateful for the help.

"One of my clients was the Kvarnback family. As we got to know each other better, I became the Kvarnback family counsel on a full-time basis. When they established their family investment office, I was asked to run that, and so it was natural for me to end up running the multifamily office when they linked up with the other families four years ago."

The waiter came and took their coffee order. Baumgart suggested they all move into the lounge to continue the conversation in comfort. *Just as the conversation gets interesting, the bloody waiter ruins the moment. It's going to be difficult to move the conversation back on track. Besides, it's probably too late. The night's virtually over.*

They found a quiet corner in the lounge. Baumgart waited to see where Tara sat then deposited his hulk next to her. *The man's a limpet.* Kent watched as Baumgart loosened his collar, relieving the pressure from his three chins.

"If you had your time over again, John, would you have raised your third fund being so dependent upon Grampian Capital? As you know, it's most unusual to be reliant on one investor," Baumgart said.

Kent hadn't seen that one coming. "We didn't set out that way. It just happened. We approached all of the usual institutional investors at the same time and expected it would take six to twelve months to raise the third fund. As you know from our fundraising document, our first two funds produced great returns, so we had a good story to tell."

"CBC has an excellent investment record."

"About three weeks into the process, Grampian contacted us to say they'd like to put up seven-and-a-half billion of the ten billion total target. We knew they were good for the money being one of the highest credit-rated institutions on Wall Street at that time."

"I understand they were the cornerstone investor in both of your earlier funds."

"Yes, that's right. As we knew them so well, we decided to accept their large commitment; it meant we could focus our efforts back onto doing deals, rather than fundraising. I prefer deal-making to raising new capital."

"Would you do it again?"

Kent took a moment before answering the question. A tricky one. "Knowing what subsequently happened to Grampian, it would be easy to say no, but, if the exact same fundraising circumstances happened again, then I think we would. Nobody could foresee, at the time, how hard Grampian would be hit by the collapse of the U.S. mortgage market."

"I see." Baumgart paused and took a sip of his double espresso.

"Do you think it was a mistake, Dieter?"

"I think it was a brave decision, but the right one in the circumstances. Now, remind me what you're looking to raise at the moment."

"Without Grampian in place as our cornerstone, we've had to cancel the two-and-a-half billion pound commitments from our other investors. Today we have no investment firepower at all. We've not been in this position before, so I can't be too prescriptive as to what we need to achieve. Ideally, we'd be looking to replace the lost seven-and-a-half billion Grampian commitment from a handful of investors. If we achieved this, then I'm pretty confident our other investors would recommit their original amounts, taking us back up to ten billion. I'm sorry it's a long answer."

"So you're looking for ten billion pounds in an ideal world?" Another sip of coffee.

"Yes. That's right. I should've just said ten billion." Kent smiled. *Is he actually going to make us an offer?*

"One further question, if I may."

"Of course. What is it?"

"We're keen to invest directly in certain situations, rather than solely through funds managed by investment managers such as CBC. If we make a commitment to CBC, would there be an opportunity to co-invest directly in transactions? That way, we could put more capital to work without incurring further management fees."

With this question, Kent was reminded how shrewd Baumgart was. CBC's smartest investors liked to have co-investment rights as these served to dilute the impact of fund management fees, which were only charged on commitments to the fund and not on the co-invested capital.

"Of course." Kent had nothing to lose. Besides, CBC often came across much larger deals than they could handle on their own and needed to bring in other investors alongside them to make up the required capital.

"Excellent. Then let me share with you where we are as far as your fundraising is concerned."

Hallelujah! "I'd be keen to hear your initial views." It was eleven o'clock, and the lounge was already thinning out. There were only two other groups in the whole room.

"After we completed our discussion this afternoon, I spoke to our investment committee members. As you know, I chair that committee. We've agreed we will make a commitment to CBC. We've been impressed by your track record, and we believe your investment strategy, focusing as you do on distressed investment opportunities, is right for this difficult market." Baumgart paused.

"That's good to hear. What level of commitment did you have in mind?" *Please make it big. Anything less than a billion will be of no use in getting CBC back on the road.*

"We'll commit twenty billion pounds."

Kent looked at Tara and wondered whether she'd heard the same number as he did. Clearly, she had; her mouth was wide open. *Did Baumgart really just say he wants to commit Tritona to more than twice the level committed by Grampian Capital? Fucking hell.* Kent put down his coffee cup. *There's got to be a sting in the tail? What pound of flesh will they want in exchange?* He couldn't be choosy and, within reason, he'd have to accept any conditions. It was hardly as though other investors were lining up to support CBC.

Before he could finish collecting his thoughts, Baumgart added, "However, there are conditions. First, we'd like to have first right to provide any co-investment capital CBC requires for larger deals. Second, in exchange for such a large commitment, we'd want a twenty-five percent shareholding in CBC itself."

Kent quickly did the math. This would still leave him, personally, with a controlling stake in CBC. It would still be his show; he'd still be calling the shots. With twenty billion pounds, he'd be back on the road with a vengeance. With twenty billion pounds, his ambition to make one hundred million pounds personally would become a reality again. Hell, it might even become two hundred million pounds. He could no longer pretend he was giving the offer serious thought. It was obvious to everyone the Tritona proposal was a great one.

"Dieter, CBC would be absolutely delighted to accept your commitment and the associated conditions. I know we can build a substantial portfolio of fund investments with your backing. Thank you for your confidence in our team. We'll reward it with excellent investment returns." Kent reached out and shook Baumgart's hand. No knuckle-crunching pain this time.

"That's good to hear. We can settle the legal formalities over the next week or so. These need not take long; we don't want you to be out of the market for too long. In these difficult economic times, you need to be busy tucking deals away for us."

"I'll make the legal documentation our top priority so we don't risk losing deals. Thank you, again, for your faith in CBC."

"Now, I'm afraid we must leave you as it's getting quite late," said Baumgart as he and his assistant stood up. Kulpman had not said a single word all night, but this no longer bothered Kent. He had a result. He could have kissed them both.

Kent and Tara walked with Baumgart to his waiting car and said their good-byes. Baumgart shook Kent's hand again, gave Tara a kiss on both cheeks, and then left.

As the car moved out of sight, Kent yelled out loudly, "Fantastic! Absolutely, bloody fantastic!" His British reserve quickly kicked in when he realized they were drawing attention from people outside the hotel entrance. "Let's go back inside for a celebratory drink," he said.

"Great idea," said Tara.

They made their way back to the lounge and sat in two comfortable armchairs, furthest away from the group of noisy Americans, who'd returned. Kent ordered a bottle of expensive champagne.

"You were wonderful tonight, Tara." Kent clinked their glasses together.

"You did all the hard work. I was watching Baumgart as you answered his questions. I couldn't follow all of the conversation, but he was clearly impressed. I think he decided he's backing you. Supported by the team, of course."

Kent knew Tara was right, but could not openly agree. He allowed himself to absorb the moment as the champagne began to increase his sense of elation. He'd rescued his firm from near-certain death and had come back even stronger. With a fund of twenty billion pounds, not only was he back in the game, but now CBC would rank among the top global firms in the private equity industry. In fact, if Baumgart was intent on putting up co-investment monies, then CBC may even be the largest global player in terms of investment firepower. It felt good to be back. He'd dodged the bullets and come back stronger.

"Let's have another one," he said, already filling up their empty glasses.

Kent could feel the alcohol going straight to his head. He enjoyed the feeling. He deserved it. The last few weeks of uncertainty had been hell.

Just before midnight, he suggested they make their way back to their rooms. He could easily have ordered another bottle, but it was late, and they had a flight to catch next morning.

As they stepped out of the elevator on the fifteenth floor,

Kent tripped and went crashing to the ground. He got to his feet quickly, and the two of them burst into howls of laughter. He held Tara's hand for steadiness as they made their way to their rooms along the wide corridor.

Just before they reached Tara's door, she dropped her card-swipe key. Kent picked it up and placed the card into the door for her, and the door opened.

"Thanks, John. Good night." Tara began to walk into her room.

"Tara."

She turned back round. Quickly, he put his left hand behind her neck and pulled her toward him. He kissed her for several seconds; his nostrils filled with her perfume. She put both hands around his lower back and pulled him closer. He kissed her lips and neck as she leaned against the wall next to the bed.

Kent placed his left hand under the short hem of her black dress. She guided his hand between her legs. Immediately, he felt her warmth and, as she placed her tongue into his mouth, he followed by sliding his fingers inside her. She was excited.

After a few moments, he unzipped her dress and let it fall to the floor. *She's beautiful.* He began to kiss her shoulders and breasts. Tara dropped onto her knees and unzipped Kent's suit trousers. She took him into her warm mouth, slowly at first and then a little faster.

Suddenly, she stopped. "John, I'm sorry. I can't do this." She pulled away. "It's not right."

He left the room and returned to his suite. *You bloody fool.* An overwhelming guilt washed over him. The night was ruined.

CHAPTER 16

The following morning, Kent was down first for breakfast. He avoided eye contact when Tara came over to join him.

"I don't know what to say," said Kent. "I'm so sorry."

"There's nothing to say. We were both drunk."

"We won't discuss this again. It never happened."

"That's right. It never happened."

Breakfast seemed to last for hours, and the conversation was punctuated with awkward silences. When they'd finished eating, Kent made some excuse about having to make a number of important calls in his room and suggested they meet in the lobby when the limo was scheduled to take them back to the airport.

They were back at CBC by 2 p.m. By the time they arrived, they'd reconciled themselves to the previous night's events and had agreed to concentrate on the business success of the trip. They were both mature adults. They could move on from this.

Kent immediately called a partners' meeting and briefed everyone on the discussions with Tritona. It was clear from their relief they'd been expecting the worst. They wanted to hear all of the details. He gave a blow-by-blow account, but they still wanted to hear more, particularly the part about their new investor's enormous investment appetite. They couldn't hear enough about the size of their new checkbook. Tara filled in any gaps from the notes she took during the trip.

"There are a number of action points which flow from yesterday," said Kent, bringing the euphoria to a close. "First, we need to cover off the usual compliance checks on Tritona." He looked at Kevin Long. "Kevin, I'd like you to deal with these.

You'll need to involve Tara in the process. She has all the details on Tritona's corporate structure and the families behind them."

"Sure. I'll get right onto it. Tara, let's have a few minutes straight after the meeting, please?" said Long. Tara nodded.

"Can you also draft a letter for me to send to the FCA? We need to inform them of these important developments," Kent said.

"Will do."

"Second, I'd like a strong message to go out to our other investors, telling them we're back. It would be great if they decided to recommit their two-and-a-half billion. Adrian, can you pick this up and let me see a draft announcement tomorrow?"

"No problem," said Johnson, smiling from ear to ear. At last, he had some good news to share with his investor contacts. "I can't wait to tell them."

"Finally, we need to get the PR message out quickly. The market needs to know we now have a much fatter investment checkbook. We've had a lot of negative press lately—especially from that lunatic at the *Financial Post.* I want to rub his nose in it." Kent stopped to take a sip of his coffee. "It's essential we make a big splash about our ability to do deals again. We really need to ramp up the deal flow. I want us to show Tritona some early results." Kent would normally wait for the compliance checks to be completed before announcing to the market that CBC had signed up another investor. But this was different. The compliance checks were not going to throw up any issues, and he couldn't wait for the market to learn he'd rescued his firm and come back even stronger.

"You can bet our competitors have been exploiting our difficulty," said Kirkland.

"Dead right. I'll handle the PR aspects with Paul." Kent nodded toward Prentis.

Kent turned to Kirkland and Henning. "I think it's worth contacting Doug Wright to see if we can get back into that deal. It was a great one, after all."

"I'm pretty certain the deal's not completed yet. Let's put a call in right after this meeting," replied Kirkland. "You never know."

"It won't be an easy conversation," said Henning.

"Don't look so worried, Anton. We've nothing to lose," replied Kent.

They moved on to discuss new deal inquiries. Although the flow of new business opportunities had fallen off a cliff after CBC lost the backing of Grampian, there were still a couple of new deals to consider and terms to kick around. Business as usual for Kent.

At five o'clock, Kent, Kirkland, and Henning went back to Kent's office to make the call to Henderson Wright. "I'll make it on the speakerphone. Tara, could you get hold of Doug Wright for us?" Kent shouted through his open door.

"Sure." She called their offices. "Putting Mr. Wright through to you."

"What the hell do you want?" asked Wright.

"Doug, as you know, we lost our cornerstone investor just as we committed to do your deal a few weeks back. We'd really like to take another shot at it, now we have the checkbook back."

"We don't need your money and, even if we did, we wouldn't take it. Now fuck off!" Wright slammed down the phone.

"That went well," Kirkland said.

"Shit! He must've found the backing elsewhere," said Kent. "Let's track the deal as their backers might still pull out. You never know." A deal was never done until it was signed at the closing meeting. Kent had seen many situations where a private equity firm had pulled out of a deal close to the finish line. In fact, some of his best deals had been completed in just these circumstances, where he could step in and rescue the investment at the last minute. The best part was, at the eleventh hour, he could always name his terms.

Kent made it home that night by seven o'clock. He'd only

had time to send Sarah a brief text that morning. Now he could spell out how he'd reeled in the giant investor and saved his firm.

"It's wonderful news, John. I'm really proud of you."

He hugged her. "It's a huge relief. Feels great to be back."

"How do you feel about Tritona as a shareholder in your firm?"

"It's a small price to pay for such a huge commitment. I'll still have majority control. We're going to be rich on the back of this, Sarah."

"Tell me all about the bit when they said yes. I want to hear everything."

Kent was delighted to share all the details, except one. The guilt was eating him up inside.

CHAPTER 17

Jonathan Gateley took the north exit from St Paul's tube station and darted into Caffé Zero at the end of Cheapside as it was beginning to rain.

"Strong white Americano?" asked the server. Gateley just smiled. The server was already making it before he could answer.

"That's great, thanks." He placed the exact money on the counter, grabbed the coffee, and doubled back across Cheapside and into Paternoster Square, heading for his offices on the north side. He kept close to the buildings to avoid the drizzle.

Gateley took the express elevator to the nineteenth floor, taking care as he rushed not to spill his hot coffee. The modern glass sign, to the left of the reception area as he walked in, read, "Oakham Fiduciary Services—Wealth Management for high net worth individuals and multinational corporations, with offices in London, Guernsey, Nassau, Singapore, and Hong Kong."

He was in a hurry. Due to meet a client at 6 p.m., Gateley was cutting it fine when he'd left his previous meeting in Chelsea at five-fifteen. He could have saved some time by going straight to the office, but the coffee from Caffé Zero was superior to the brown liquid served in the office, so he'd taken the risk. It was the right call. He made it to the meeting room with five minutes to spare.

Gateley was the CEO at Oakham and was well-known in investment circles for his big tax brain. Today's meeting was with a new client and his accountant. The client had just sold his IT business for two hundred and forty million pounds and wanted Gateley's advice on where best to hold the proceeds pending the client's later investment instructions. Bread and butter work for Oakham.

After the meeting, Gateley returned to his corner office. On one side was a view of the London Stock Exchange and on the other St Paul's Cathedral.

"Do you have a minute?" asked Gordon Thompson, one of Gateley's senior team members, as he walked through the door.

"Sure," Gateley said.

"We've received another investment instruction from our friends in Geneva. They want us to invest three hundred and fifty million pounds of the cash we hold for them in Nassau in these FTSE 100 companies." Thompson handed over a list of six of the largest one hundred companies listed on the London Stock Exchange. "As with last month's instructions, the client is not really concerned about the price we pay for the stock, but doesn't want the market to think they're building up a significant holding. They don't want the attention."

"I know they like a low profile."

Thompson laughed. "That's one way of putting it. I've never come across a firm more secretive than Tritona."

"As long as they keep paying our fees, we'll do what they want. I assume they'd like us to spread the purchases across a number of their holding companies as before?"

"That's right. I need your advice on which vehicles to use and in which jurisdictions."

"No problem. How quickly do they want us to build up these holdings?"

"Over two weeks, three at the outside. They said they'll have a similar amount to invest next month."

Gateley mapped out on a sheet of paper where the cash should first be transferred, which of the client's existing trust arrangements should be used, and which brokers should be used to effect the stock purchases in each jurisdiction.

"Can you have a copy of this typed up and put on the Tritona file, as usual?"

"Will do, Jonathan. Thanks for the help."

***

It was a crisp, late March morning. The outside temperature was just below zero but didn't feel like it due to the unbroken blue sky. Kent had parked his BMW in the four-car garage at The Old Hall the night before. He couldn't be bothered with scraping ice from the windscreen so he rarely left the car outside during the cold months. This morning, he was a little later than usual as he wasn't going to the office. This gave him a chance to have breakfast with Sarah, something he was trying to make more time for these days. He still hadn't forgiven himself for his indiscretion with Tara. While spending more time with his wife would hardly absolve him, at least it made him feel a little better.

He was due in Leeds at eleven-thirty for a regular board meeting at one of CBC's investee companies. Each of the partners took primary responsibility for a number of portfolio companies. This involved sitting on the company's board as a director and working with its management team to maximize the value of the business. While it wasn't his favorite part of the job, the right focus on investee companies created increased realization values when the businesses were eventually sold.

On the drive to Leeds, he made several calls on his mobile phone. The first was to Kevin Long.

"Where are we up to on the Tritona compliance checks, Kevin?"

All regulated financial services companies were under strict legal requirements to check out the identity of new investors and to ensure they didn't appear on the Bank of England's blacklist before accepting capital from them.

"We're in pretty good shape, but there's been quite a lot of paperwork to wade through. I'd expect to have it all signed off pretty soon."

"I know it's a pain. They have a complex structure."

"The time-consuming bit is building the file in case the FCA chooses us for an audit."

"That's tedious. The real criminals will always find a way around the rules. In the meantime, it's us poor suckers that have to jump through hoops."

As CEO of CBC, Kent had ultimate responsibility for compliance as far as the FCA was concerned, so he had to take these compliance checks seriously. Not that they changed the way he did business. It was in CBC's own interest to do things properly. It took years to build up a good business reputation and this could be shattered in moments if there was any hint of illegal activity.

"Will you let me know when everything's been completed? I want to get on investing Tritona's money. It would be good to show them some early results."

"Certainly will. My guess is it'll all be done by tomorrow evening."

"Good man."

CHAPTER 18

Two days later, Kent was sitting in his office when he took a call from Baumgart.

"How are you, Dieter?"

"Very well, thank you," said Baumgart. Kent held the handset slightly away from his ear. Baumgart was loud enough in person. Hearing his voice booming down the line was almost unbearable. "I'm calling from Singapore. I've had to come over here on an unexpected business trip. I was hoping to be in London tomorrow for a deal closing, but that's not possible any longer. It would have been a good opportunity for us to meet up and see where we are on everything."

"I'm sorry we can't meet up. Maybe next time."

"There's something you guys could do for us, however."

"Always happy to help."

"Good. As you know, before committing to your fund, all of our private equity investments were handled by us directly and not through fund managers."

"I remember you saying that."

"Well, we have another direct deal completing tomorrow."

"Oh."

"Don't worry. It's one we started before we committed to CBC."

Kent forced a laugh. "That's a relief."

"It involves us putting one billion pounds into the transaction. All of the legal documentation is ready, and the due diligence is complete, but there are the usual last-minute matters which need to be dealt with at the meeting in London tomorrow."

"We'd be happy to take care of that for you."

"That's exactly what I was hoping. It would be good for you to see how we do things, anyway."

"Can you email over the draft investment documents and a power of attorney so we can sign on your behalf?"

"I'll ask Franz Kulpman to send over everything you need today. When you're happy everything's in order tomorrow, all you need to do is contact Gordon Thompson at a firm called Oakham Fiduciary Services in London, and he'll transfer the money electronically. They hold some of our cash. I'll get him to call you with his details."

"I'll let you know when it's completed. Have a safe trip back from Singapore."

"Thanks. One more thing."

"What's that?"

"We'd like you to manage this investment on our behalf, once it's done. Of course, the monthly monitoring fees will go to CBC, and we can discuss a performance fee linked to the exit value when we next meet."

This relationship's getting even better, thought Kent when the call was over. It made sense for Tritona to use CBC to manage any companies bought directly by them. After all, managing portfolio companies was what CBC was good at.

An hour later, Tara came into Kent's office with the email from Kulpman and the print-out of the draft investment agreement he'd sent.

Kent grabbed the stack of papers. "Thanks, Tara. Could you ask Joanna to join me so we can review these together?"

"I think you'll find the deal an interesting read," she said with a hint of mischief in her voice.

"Why do you say that? You can't have read them already. Even you're not that quick."

"Take a look at the name of the target company on the second page."

He looked down at the papers. There it was on page two,

highlighted in yellow by Tara. Tritona had agreed to invest one billion pounds in Henderson Wright.

Kent shook his head. "Wow! Those guys in Geneva are smart. Wait until Joanna hears about this."

Kirkland came in a few minutes later. "I gather we have a deal to complete for Tritona already," she said. "They don't hang about."

Kent tried to suppress a grin. "That's right. You and I need to go down to London tomorrow to complete a direct investment for them. I've got the paperwork here. There's a copy for you." He slid a bundle of papers across the desk. "I suggest we look at them for a few minutes together first before both of us digest them overnight."

Kirkland sat on one of Kent's armchairs and began flicking through the documents. "You're never going to believe this," she said, raising her head, mouth wide open.

"I know. Tara pointed it out to me a moment ago. I wanted to leave the surprise for you. We're going to have some fun with Wright tomorrow," he said, now grinning.

Kirkland flicked through the pages then stopped. "It gets better. I see Tritona has offered the exact same deal as we did—an eighty/twenty percent split of the equity."

"I told you they were shrewd investors."

"It should be an interesting day."

"I can't wait to see Wright's face when we turn up."

CHAPTER 19

Kent and Kirkland had one of the firm's drivers take them down from Cambridge to Henderson Wright's offices on the North Colonnade at Canary Wharf, a few miles east of the City of London. It was only a sixty-mile drive and so much easier than taking the train to London; getting out to Canary Wharf from the City was a pain in the neck as far as Kent was concerned.

They arrived early, so, rather than being dropped at the door, they walked from the parking lot over to the office building—fifty-two floors of concrete and steel. It reminded Kent why he'd chosen to locate CBC in Cambridge. *A city with real character with real buildings.* He stared at the hundreds of people going to work, like ants running backward and forward into the various tower blocks. *Modern-day factories.*

Joining the line for the security check was another thing Kent detested about these buildings. It always took ages to get through their inane procedures and up to the meeting floor.

"You don't know how much I'm looking forward to seeing our friend," said Kirkland, making a poor job of hiding her smile.

"Me, too," said Kent as they finally made it through the barrier.

They made their way up to the meeting room level on the fiftieth floor and announced themselves to the receptionist. "We're from Tritona for Mr. Wright," said Kent, winking at Kirkland.

"Mr. Wright's PA will be here to collect you in a few moments. Please take a seat," said the receptionist, pointing over to the waiting area.

What an absolute jerk, Kent thought. *Wright's soon-to-be eighty percent owners have just arrived and, rather than collect them himself, he expects us to wait while a PA comes along. The man's a fool.*

They waited five minutes, compelled to listen to the oversize flat-screen televisions in the waiting area. Why these giant screens were supposed to enhance the visitor's first impression of the firm was beyond Kent.

He pointed to the TV above his head then looked at Kirkland. "If I ever suggest putting in one of those bloody things at CBC, you have permission to shoot me."

"Mr. Wright will see you now," said the officious young woman who came to collect them.

Does she think Wright is doing us the favor? Kent thought.

They followed her through to an enormous meeting room, filled with lawyers and representatives from Henderson Wright's banks. Kent estimated there were fifty-five to sixty people in the room, running about, shuffling papers. Wright was holding court in the middle of the crowd, seemingly full of his own self-importance.

"You'd hardly suspect that is the same man who's brought his firm to the brink of collapse," whispered Kent into Kirkland's ear.

"What the hell are you doing here?" shouted Wright across the room when he saw Kent. The room fell silent.

Kent could see Wright was struggling to process the situation. "We're here to complete the deal, of course."

Wright looked as if he had a bad smell under his nose. "You're mistaken. We're doing the deal with Tritona."

"We manage Tritona's private equity investments." That was true, but Wright didn't need to know this was the first deal to be managed by CBC on Tritona's behalf. "Did no one tell you?"

"Over my dead body!" Wright's face reddened. "There's no way I'm going to sign this deal if CBC effectively controls eighty percent of Henderson Wright. The deal's off." He looked across at a group of bankers, who did not jump to his support.

Kent shrugged his shoulders. "Then we'll leave." He put some papers back into his briefcase and sauntered toward the exit.

"Please," said one of the senior bankers seated at the conference table. "Can we persuade you to stay for a moment?"

Wright threw the banker a shit-look, but he ignored it.

"We represent most of the banking lines extended to Henderson Wright. If this deal doesn't happen today, then early next week we'll be appointing an administrative receiver to sell off this firm bit by bit." He turned to Wright. "Is that what you want, Doug?" Wright looked down at the table. "You'll be spelling the end of Henderson Wright."

All eyes in the room focused on Wright. "I will not work with CBC. It's that simple," he said.

This confirmed what Kent already knew. Henderson Wright was up against the wall with no real choice but to do this deal, and working with Wright would be impossible. He was too much of a hothead who managed by the seat of his pants. After all, it was Wright's impulsive decision to do the German deal with insufficient non-compete protection that caused all of this mess in the first place. Wright was an expendable commodity, and this was Kent's chance to remove him. What he didn't want to happen now was for the banker to persuade Wright to work with CBC for the sake of the deal.

"Our position has changed," Kent announced to the room. "We will only complete this deal if Mr. Wright is no longer part of it. After all, he's made it abundantly clear he won't work with us as controlling shareholder. That's obviously an untenable position."

Wright, fists clenched and eyes narrowed, looked ready to jump out of his seat and lunge at Kent.

"Could you please let us have a few minutes, Mr. Kent?" asked the banker.

"Of course. Joanna and I will go out for a coffee. We'll be back in half an hour."

Kent and Kirkland went down to the ground floor, where

they found a big-brand coffee retailing concession that took up most of that level of the Henderson Wright building. "This will be one of the first things to go," Kent said, looking round at all the wasted space. "I counted three coffee shops in the two hundred yards we walked from the parking lot. I cannot understand why they need to waste a whole floor on another."

"Do you think Wright will fall on his sword?" asked Kirkland.

"I'm certain of it. It's really a decision for the banks at this stage, anyway. They're calling the shots. They'll be up there now squeezing him hard. He has nowhere else to go. Of course, he'll say he resigned, but he's just been fired."

They finished their coffee and returned to the meeting room. Wright was no longer there.

"Mr. Wright has decided to step down from the firm as senior partner with immediate effect," said the banker. "I trust this will now allow us to proceed?"

"Just one more thing," said Kent.

"What's that?"

"Our equity stake has gone up from eighty percent to eighty-five." The papers Kent had read overnight said that Wright was going to have five percent of the equity for himself, with the other seven senior partners sharing the remaining fifteen percent. At a stroke, Kent had just increased the attraction of the deal for Tritona without taking away anything from the remaining management team members, with whom he would have to work. Indeed, the other partners were likely to have as much antipathy toward Wright as Kent had. No doubt, they'd be delighted to see Wright's departure.

"Very well. Let's get this deal done," the banker said.

CHAPTER 20

The spring and early summer months were busy for the team at CBC. Since completing the Henderson Wright deal, the firm had been flooded with new deal inquiries. That transaction had raised CBC's profile and proved that the firm was back in business. The market's reaction to CBC's new, expanded checkbook was phenomenal. Kent was back on the map and now regarded as a major player, with investment banks bringing him ever-larger deals to consider. The deepening recession was throwing up more and more great deals, and his team could pick and choose the transactions they wanted. In the space of just three months, they'd completed twelve buyout transactions across the globe, investing ten billion of the twenty billion pound new fund. They were making a lot of money for Tritona and for themselves. Life was good, very good. Kent was like a dog with two dicks, strutting around the investment market as if he owned it.

Baumgart was delighted with the way Kent had sweetened the Henderson Wright deal at the last moment. On top of this, the accounting firm was hitting all of its numbers and was flourishing under the new CEO Kent had appointed after firing Wright. Baumgart demonstrated his absolute confidence in CBC's judgment by co-investing in every one of their deals, moving a further eighteen billion pounds of Tritona's monies, in addition to the amounts invested via the CBC fund.

In late June, Baumgart asked Kent to join him in Geneva for a general catch-up meeting and dinner. This time, Kent traveled alone. The last thing he wanted was a repeat of the hotel episode. To Tara's credit, she'd never once mentioned it and had been a complete professional. *Why would she? Nothing really happened.*

"Great to see you, John," said Baumgart as he met Kent in Tritona's reception area. "Where's Tara? Is she not with you on this trip?"

"Sadly, she wasn't able to make it, but she looks forward to seeing you when you're next in the UK," said Kent, thinking on his feet. Tara never talked about Baumgart, but he didn't want to disappoint his main investor. Baumgart was besotted with Tara, and it suited Kent to keep him that way.

Baumgart dropped his shoulders. "That is disappointing. Maybe next time." They walked through to Baumgart's office. Kulpman was in there, already taking notes.

What the hell do they do with all those notes? Kent wondered.

He ran through his presentation on CBC's investment activity. Then he compared the actual financial performance of each acquired company with the projections for each one compiled by CBC when the deal was completed. Every company in the rapidly growing portfolio was trading on or above target. The early indicators were this was going to be a superb fund, vindicating Kent's judgment that having plenty of investment firepower in a downturn was the route to great returns.

"I've been keeping our investors up to date with your performance at CBC. They're very pleased," said Baumgart.

"That's good to hear. We've been working hard to put away some great deals for you, but that's only half the story."

"How so, John?"

"Our aim now is to keep up the momentum. Having bought well, we plan to be good owners of each company so we make the most of each investment. After all, we want the best exit price when we come to sell them."

"Actually, that's one of the reasons I wanted this meeting. You know we manage a number of different assets from these offices, including a small number of direct private equity investments we made before we came into your fund."

"Yes. We talked before about you making direct investments.

But that was before we teamed up."

"That is not quite correct."

Kent frowned. "It's not?"

"Since we made our initial commitment to CBC, we've made many more direct investments ourselves as the market conditions have been right."

"You mean the co-investments with us, surely?"

"Not exactly. We have done many others, too."

"You've been busy, Dieter." Kent had no idea Tritona had still been investing in other private equity deals on their own in addition to the monies they'd been putting to work through CBC. *How much money do these people have?*

"We see this as the right time to be making new investments while acquisition prices are low."

"I couldn't agree more. In years to come, we'll look back at this time and see it as a golden buying opportunity."

Baumgart was indeed a kindred spirit as far as investment timing was concerned. It had always baffled Kent how most investors reduced their investment rate during recessions and increased it again in the boom times. A savvy investor would do the opposite, buying cheaply in downturns and selling high in upturns. He couldn't understand why most investors didn't get this. Baumgart was a notable exception.

"We've been very impressed with your handling of Henderson Wright. That would have been another one within our direct portfolio, had you not been able to take on its management for us."

"We were delighted to help out on that one." Kent meant it. Not only did he enjoy completing a good deal, but also he'd taken great pleasure in removing Wright. That was a real bonus.

"As you can imagine, these direct investments take up a lot of our management time, and we're not really set up to do this properly, attending monthly board meetings, dealing with consent matters and so on."

"I know how much time they take up. More than people

imagine if the job is being done properly." *Where's Baumgart going with this?*

"We'd like to hand over the management of all our existing direct investments to the team at CBC. We know you're best placed to extract maximum value out of these companies on our behalf."

"That's great news." *More money.*

"Of course, CBC would receive the usual monitoring fee income and some form of performance-related reward linked to the increase in their value under your stewardship."

"How many companies are we talking about?"

"Currently, we own sixty-five companies directly, with a combined investment cost of almost two hundred billion dollars."

That's an incredible portfolio, Kent thought. It was many times the value he would have guessed. Taking it on would more than quadruple CBC's assets. The carried interest and monitoring fee income on the investments would be enormous. His team would have to expand; maybe even move into larger offices to accommodate the extra staff. *This achieves ten years' growth for CBC in a single move.*

"We'd be delighted to take on this portfolio for Tritona. With such a large number of investments, there'd need to be a transition period while we expanded our team, but this needn't take long. I'm sure we can handle it."

God knows where we're going to find enough good people quickly.

"I've already given this some thought, as you can imagine. The most effective way to deal with this is for CBC to acquire Oakham Fiduciary Services, which handles much of our group structuring and the administration of our holdings. You dealt with them briefly on the Henderson Wright deal. They could take over much of the additional admin work for you. In this way, CBC could continue to focus on what it does well, leaving the routine administration to Oakham."

"That makes sense. They came across to us as good people,

but is Oakham actually for sale and would the team be happy to join CBC?"

"There's no problem with Oakham. Tritona acquired that business last month. We'll simply transfer it to CBC. We can discuss the details over dinner this evening. I have another great restaurant to show you."

On the flight back to London the following morning, Kent pondered the events of the previous day. He thought how fine the line was between business success and failure. Just a few months earlier, he'd been facing the very real prospect of losing his business and having to let his staff go. Now, he was the CEO of what was about to become the largest private equity firm in the world by far. With the certainty that Tritona would invest as much as he could ever need, there was no deal too large for him to consider. He'd be able to go hunting for targets among the largest companies on the planet.

Kent smiled as he gazed out of the plane's window. This would be a poke in the eye for all of CBC's competitors and those who'd written him off after the Grampian disaster. Now he'd show them all how wrong they'd been underestimating him. He was about to become a truly global player and, just as important, he was on his way to becoming a billionaire. Of that, he was certain. He could almost taste it.

CHAPTER 21

The jet landed at Biggs Army Airfield, a few miles north of El Paso International Airport. Dressed in a black suit, Merriman felt the intense heat the moment he left the aircraft. Halloran and Camplejohn came down the steps behind him. A black SUV drove up to within fifty feet of the jet, and the three of them climbed in. There was little conversation during the one-hour drive north to Las Cruces in New Mexico.

Merriman gazed out of the window as the car turned onto a street off University Park. The houses were all single story with parched, brown lawns and pickup trucks parked on some of the drives. A small Catholic church sat at the end of the street, next door to a two-story motel that had seen better days. The paintwork on the white wooden balcony running along the length of the upper floor was peeling, and the driver had to take care to avoid the potholes as he pulled up in the motel parking lot. Merriman and his two colleagues walked across to the church where they joined the back of the line of people filing in. The place was packed with more than one hundred worshippers. Merriman's team stood out as the only white faces in a crowd of Hispanics as they made their way to the few remaining seats at the back.

It had been four months since they'd learned of the death of Special Agent Luis Santiago, who'd been known as Arturo Vargas when working undercover. Since receiving the package of body parts on Merriman's birthday, there had been no further contact with the agent. Merriman's other undercover agents had learned through their networks that Vargas had been killed shortly after he transferred from Corolla Currency Exchange in

Monterrey. None of them had actually seen a body, but the intelligence was clear. He'd been killed by the cartel. Merriman needed no further proof; the diamond stud earring in the bloodied ear had been the Caruana cartel's way of showing him they knew who he was. There was no information on how he'd been compromised, something that troubled Merriman since he had others still working undercover.

The memorial service lasted an hour. Santiago's father spoke about the family's move from Mexico before Luis was born and how he and his wife were so proud when their American son graduated from college. He recalled how excited Luis had been when he won a place at the DEA's Intelligence Center in El Paso. They'd watched his career develop with such pride.

Merriman spoke of the important work their son had been involved in, and how he was much respected by his colleagues. Luis had been a rising star and would be missed by all who knew him. He was one of the best. He meant every word. Merriman felt a strong sense of personal responsibility for Santiago's death. He'd trained him and assured him he was ready for the difficult and risky challenge of working undercover. Too many good people had paid a heavy price in the war against drugs.

"I promise you, your son's life was given for a noble cause. His sacrifice will not have been for nothing. I will do everything in my power to finish his important work," said Merriman before leaving the podium.

As he walked back to his seat, he made eye contact with Mr. Santiago. Merriman knew his words would never make up for the loss of his son. He promised himself he would not stop until he'd seized all of the cartel's assets and wiped them from the face of the earth. That would be the way he'd honor Luis and the others who'd made the ultimate sacrifice.

Merriman and his two colleagues stayed for an hour at the Santiagos' home after the service. It was difficult to share in any detail the work their son had been doing. They seemed to understand; they told Merriman they knew Luis was involved in sensitive work. Merriman found it hard to explain why there had been no body. He did his best to strike a balance between telling them enough without compromising security, but he found it challenging. As he talked to Mrs. Santiago, he could tell she was hanging on to a slim hope that Luis would return one day. She kept telling him that because there was no body, there was no certainty her son was dead. He had to tell her he was certain Luis was not coming back, but he hated himself for removing her last shred of hope.

"I give you my word, we'll stop at nothing to bring your son's killers to justice," he said, hugging Mrs. Santiago.

"You're a good man. Luis spoke about you all the time. He looked up to you, and I can see why," she said, wiping a tear from her eye.

Merriman met the local DEA team at the El Paso Intelligence Center later that afternoon. He knew most of them personally, and many had served with him on overseas missions. They shared stories about the past; there were plenty of them.

Eight years before his promotion to Head of Intelligence, Merriman had been assigned as the Country Attaché for Colombia, where he achieved a massive reduction in the availability of cocaine. From there, he'd been promoted to Country Director for the Mexico Division, where he was responsible for bringing down major drug trafficking organizations, including the Artis-Laramo and Castro-Estrada cartels. The DEA field teams respected his achievements and, even though he was now their ultimate boss, considered him one of them. More than anyone else on the DEA leadership team, Merriman understood the challenge of the work on the ground and how difficult it was to make sustained progress against the rising power of the cartels.

He gave them a presentation on the results achieved so far, particularly in seizing physical money movements using the satellite reconnaissance technology run from El Paso. He went on to share with them the DEA Leadership's agreed new strategy of focusing increasing resources on tracing the cartels' assets.

He told them this would involve sophisticated electronic monitoring combined with many more agents on the ground, pursuing the network of advisers and financial middlemen who were helping the cartels acquire assets and keep them hidden.

"I promise you, we will win this thing. Nothing is more important," he said, wrapping up his presentation. They gave him a standing ovation.

The three agents were back in the air by 5 p.m.

"That was a hell of a day," said Halloran soon after takeoff.

"You never get used to losing agents, Frank. They put their lives on the line every day, and the sad thing is the value of their work goes completely unrecognized. You saw today that not even the parents can fully appreciate the contribution they make," replied Merriman.

"I admire their courage. It takes a special type of person to do it," said Halloran.

"The toughest job we ever ask people to do."

Camplejohn turned in her seat to join the conversation. "I understand they're all volunteers," she said.

"That's right," said Merriman. "We never compel our agents to work undercover. It has to be something they choose to do."

"How many do we have working undercover?" asked Camplejohn.

"Outside of the leadership team, we never disclose the identities or numbers of agents in the field, but we have enough to achieve our goals." Merriman knew exactly how many agents he had working undercover; he had an army of them. It was dangerous and painstaking work, but he was confident that progress was being made. It was only a matter of time before a major breakthrough. *We'll get there.*

The three-hour flight back was quiet. There was little appetite for conversation. Merriman's mind was already working on how to step up the search for assets. Ideally, he needed to apprehend or turn a senior Caruana cartel insider. That way, he'd have a roadmap; he'd know where to look and could focus his resources. He didn't underestimate the scale of the challenge ahead, but he was confident of ultimate success.

If we need to cut a few corners, or bend a few rules, so be it. We owe it to the Santiagos.

CHAPTER 22

Route 41 was a much slower road than the E20 motorway but, at this time of year, the extra forty-minute journey time was well rewarded. Lucas Stromholm loved how the road changed from agricultural scenery, complete with red farmhouses and barns, one moment to stunning views of the rocky coast in another. Besides, he was in no hurry; he'd left in plenty of time. He had made this journey many times before, leaving his offices in Molndal and always arriving at Falkenberg at lunchtime for his client meeting. This special client preferred a working lunch session at his office complex on the outskirts of Falkenberg when discussing personal matters.

Stromholm was in his early forties and was the only son of a successful Swedish industrialist. After studying at the University of Gothenburg, he joined Sweden's largest firm of financial advisers in Stockholm. Five years later, with his father's financial backing and encouragement, he set up his own firm. The firm had grown to the second-largest financial adviser in the country, but its client base was the best by far. His father had introduced him to many successful entrepreneurs and industry executives over the years. Stromholm's firm now specialized in financial planning and wealth management advice for ultra-high net worth individuals and families. It was a goldmine of a client base.

The client in Falkenberg, Andreas Kvarnback, was Stromholm's firm's biggest fee earner, so he handled the account personally. Kvarnback had made his money in pharmaceuticals. His original factory was based in Falkenberg, but now the company had subsidiaries all over the world. It was listed on both the New York and Stockholm stock exchanges. Since its flotation twenty years ago, the share price had risen tenfold, ranking Kvarnback seventeenth in *Forbes*' list of the world's richest people. Though he could live anywhere in the world, Kvarnback preferred the relative obscurity and more normal life afforded to him by the west coast of Sweden.

Stromholm won Kvarnback as a client just after the company was floated. It was another of his father's introductions. Kvarnback needed advice on where to invest the proceeds from some of the stock he'd sold on the flotation, and Stromholm had provided it. Since then, Stromholm had been involved in all key decisions regarding the investment of the family's immense fortune. He'd guided the family well. Their capital had been preserved, and he'd taken them into real estate and equities at the right times, leading to healthy returns. The family trusted him and respected his judgment.

Stromholm parked his old Saab in the visitors' parking lot next to the main 1960s'-design office block. The building gave no hint of the family's fortune. Kvarnback was known for his aversion to ostentatious displays of wealth and preference for keeping a low profile.

After signing in, Stromholm went up to Kvarnback's office, where he was expected.

"Lucas, it's good to see you. How was the drive?" Kvarnback held out his hand to his visitor. "I've organized a light lunch. Would you like a coffee?"

"A coffee would be fine. The drive was wonderful, as ever."

Stromholm glanced around the room. As usual, there were none of the outward signs of wealth on display in the office. If anything, the place looked austere, and the furniture seemed as though it had been there from the days when the company was first founded. Even the view out of the window was toward the redbrick factory. The only thing of note in the room was a framed copy of Kvarnback's first pharmaceutical patent hanging at an angle on the wall behind his desk. It looked like it needed a good dust.

"Good. I assume you took the scenic route?" Kvarnback pointed to the corner of the room. "Come, sit down."

"I did," said Stromholm, taking a seat around the small meeting table. "My father asked me to say hello. Says he might come down one day and drag you out for lunch."

"Send him my best wishes. Is he any closer to retiring?"

"No. He's like you, Andreas. He'll go on forever. He loves his work too much."

They tucked into the open shrimp and smoked salmon sandwiches while Stromholm gave Kvarnback an overview of his personal portfolio and its recent performance. He suggested a few changes to the weighting of assets and gave some specific investment recommendations, all of which were accepted. Near the end of the lunch, Kvarnback asked his adviser to consider some suitable private equity fund investments for him.

"You've not been interested in private equity as an asset class before," said Stromholm.

"I know, but I've seen some of my friends committing to private equity over the years, and the returns have been good. I think the timing might be right to put some into our portfolio."

"I'll do some research and come back with a few recommendations."

"That's what I like about you, Lucas. You always do your homework first. Let's discuss your research next time we meet. There's no hurry."

When the meeting finished, the two men walked over to Stromholm's car. "Sorry it's such a long trip for an hour's meeting," said Kvarnback.

"You know me, Andreas. I like the drive. Any excuse to get out of the office." Stromholm pointed to the clear blue sky. "Particularly on a day like this."

"When are you going to get rid of this rust bucket?" Kvarnback patted Stromholm's aging Saab.

"Plenty more miles in it yet," said Stromholm with a beaming smile. Both men knew he could afford any car he wanted.

Stromholm arrived at his office just after three-thirty that afternoon. The drive back had given him time to think about private equity opportunities for his client. He knew an increasing number of high net worth investors were now making commitments to private equity funds, but these were in relatively small amounts compared to the commitments made by institutional investors. He'd also heard how difficult it was for individuals to obtain access to the best performing fund managers. Institutional interest was so strong for these funds that there was no need to take on lots of small commitments from individuals to hit fund-raising targets. He realized he needed advice from someone with more current knowledge of the market.

He stopped by his PA's desk to collect his telephone messages.

"Lena, could you please dig out the number for Anton Henning at a firm called Cambridge Buy-Out Capital in the UK?" he said.

Stromholm had gone to school in Gothenburg with Henning. They were good friends back then but had lost regular contact when they went off to different universities. When Henning made it back to Gothenburg to visit family every so often, they'd meet up for a drink. He'd be able to obtain a good current overview of the private equity market from Henning.

Lena brought the number in, and Stromholm picked up the phone. As he hit the numbers, he wondered whether or not to mention the name of his client during the call. He knew the inquiry would be taken more seriously if he did. Kvarnback was a well-known businessman, after all.

"Lucas, good to hear from you. How are things?" asked Henning.

"I'm well, thanks, and you? I read some of the coverage on CBC and Grampian Capital a few months back. That must've been tricky. Well done on getting the show back on the road. I keep reading in the financial press about all the deals you guys are doing."

"Thanks. Yes, that's all behind us now, I'm pleased to say. It was a very difficult time for this firm. Now we're focused on deal-making, which is lots more fun."

"Anton, I hope you don't mind, but I need a little help on the current state of the private equity market."

"I'd be glad to help. What do you need to know?"

"I have a client, an ultra-high net worth individual, who's thinking of investing in private equity for the first time. Before you say it, I know how difficult it can be for individuals to get into the best funds. I really need some advice on who the best funds are at the moment, and who might just be open to individuals."

Henning ran through the various top fund managers, most of whom were not out raising money due to the poor financial climate. He made one or two suggestions on the best people to contact.

"You didn't mention your own firm," Stromholm said. "Would CBC be open to a commitment from an individual?"

"In the past, we've been exclusively funded by institutions, but we do have substantial family office money behind us now, so it wouldn't be a huge leap to accept an individual investor. I guess it would depend on the size of the commitment to make it worthwhile."

"My client is Andreas Kvarnback, but that's obviously confidential."

"The Svensk Pharmaceuticals Kvarnback?" Henning's tone sounded confused.

"Yes. He's by far my largest client and would be able to make a sizeable investment commitment, at least as big as an institution."

There was a long pause, then, "He must have some private equity investments already. A man like that is bound to have."

"No. As I said, this would be his first time. He's very conservative in his investment style."

"Are you certain of that?"

"I manage the family's whole portfolio, so I'd know if they'd invested in the asset class before."

Another pause. "Yes, of course you'd know. I'm sorry. I didn't mean to be rude. Can you leave it with me, Lucas? I'll have a word with our CEO and come back to you."

"I'd be very grateful. I'll look out for your call once you've cleared it with your boss. Speak to you soon."

"Okay, leave it with me. 'Bye for now."

Henning raced over to Kent's office, where Kent was having a rare break at his desk. The last few weeks had been so hectic there'd been little time for anything else but work. He was sat back in his chair, catching up on the news in the *Financial Daily*.

"Do you have a moment, John?" said Henning as he stood at Kent's open office door. "It's just that I'm a little confused about something."

"Sure. Come on in," said Kent, pushing aside the newspaper. "What is it?"

"I've just taken a call from an old school friend of mine in Sweden. He and I go back a long way. He runs a successful financial advisory practice aimed at very high net worth individuals. Some of them are heavy hitters—well, at least in Sweden."

"Would you guys like a coffee?" shouted Tara from her desk through the open door.

"I'd love one," Kent said.

"Me, too, please," said Henning.

"As I said, Lucas is the financial adviser to many of the leading industrial families in Sweden. He's built up a great practice," continued Henning.

"Pity he's not over here. I could do with a good personal financial adviser." Kent was only half joking. He had little time to devote to the management of his own financial affairs at the moment. He was making a lot of money, but he knew it wasn't being put to work in the best way.

"He rang me to ask for advice on a suitable private equity fund investment for his biggest individual client. He asked if we'd consider a sizeable commitment from him."

"For the right level of investment, I think we would. The main reason we don't normally do it is the admin burden for small commitments from individuals. It can be a real pain in..." Kent stopped talking. Henning's grimacing face gave him the look of a man with the weight of the world's problems on his shoulders.

"I realize all that, John, but that's not what I wanted to discuss with you."

Tara brought in the coffees.

"Sorry; I interrupted," said Kent. *Henning can be a real worrier at times.*

"Lucas said the name of his client is Andreas Kvarnback."

"Did you tell him he's already an investor in our fund?"

"No, because he said his client had no prior exposure to private equity. I checked it was the Kvarnback family behind the listed pharmaceutical group, and it is."

"That's odd. How many Kvarnbacks are there in Sweden? It doesn't sound like a common name?"

"Not that many, and there can't be any more than one who's made a fortune in pharmaceuticals."

"Your friend must be mistaken. He probably just doesn't know his client is already invested in private equity. Why don't you go back to him and tell him in confidence that the Kvarnbacks are already invested with us through Tritona?"

"I'll do that, but Lucas seemed pretty certain his client was not currently exposed to private equity." Henning looked at his wristwatch. It was 6:30 p.m., which meant seven-thirty in Sweden. "I'll give him a call tomorrow morning; it's probably too late now. I'll leave you to finish your newspaper."

"Let me know how you get on. There's no point disturbing

Tritona over this. It's likely to be a screw-up with your pal in Sweden."

Kent picked his newspaper back up. *There'll be a perfectly sensible explanation. Why is Henning so worried?*

Henning left Kent's room, stopping at Tara's desk to thank her for the coffee before returning to his own office.

"Anton looks rattled," Tara shouted in to Kent.

"It's nothing. You know what he's like."

"I'll be setting off in five minutes. Do you need anything before I go?"

"No thanks. I'll see you in the morning." Maybe now there would be a few minutes peace to finish the newspaper. He'd started reading the same article three times.

CHAPTER 23

The elegant four-story Georgian townhouse stood on King's Parade, directly across from King's College and its famous gothic chapel. The moment Henning and his wife Nora saw the property four years ago, they knew they had to buy it, whatever the price. They'd been looking for a Georgian townhouse in the center of Cambridge for two years, but they were rare finds and usually sold within days to cash buyers. They snapped it up, paying well over the asking price. They spent the next eighteen months completely renovating the property, and now it was a source of great pride for them. They had received six unsolicited offers for the house in the short time they'd lived there. After lavishing so much love and attention on their home, there was no way they'd be selling up for many years. Having bought their little bit of England, the Swedes had fast become more British than the British. They loved living in their adopted country and could not ever see themselves returning to Sweden.

The Hennings were both in their forties, and had known each other since school, but had married only seven years ago. She'd always known they would marry eventually. It was obvious to her. Henning, however, was not an impulsive man. He liked to take his time over significant decisions, weighing up the pros and cons and how others would be affected by his actions, before deciding what to do. It was one of the things Nora loved about him. She knew he was a thoroughly decent man who didn't like to disappoint or offend anyone.

Nora taught at a senior school in the center of town. While she walked to work, Henning always cycled to CBC's offices.

He worked hard to keep fit and, like many Scandinavians, his favorite type of exercise was cycling. On the weekend, it was not unusual for him to cycle sixty miles in a morning. He was also a creature of habit. He'd carry his road bike up the basement steps of the townhouse and onto the pavement at six-thirty every weekday morning, preferring to be away early to avoid the heavy Cambridge traffic. His usual route meant he'd normally arrive at the office by six-fifty. By the time he'd showered, he'd be at his desk by seven-fifteen.

This morning it was raining heavily when he lifted the bike to the pavement. He put on his lightweight waterproof jacket over his cycling jersey before setting off. Normally, he'd pedal slowly up King's Parade and take in the view of the six-hundred-year-old buildings of King's College and Chapel, but today he was preoccupied.

Henning couldn't stop thinking about the conversation he was going to have with his friend, Lucas Stromholm. How was he going to let him know his client had already invested in CBC's fund through Tritona? He didn't want to breach Tritona's or Kvarnback's confidence, but he needed to clear the confusion. How would Lucas take the news? Would his friend be offended or embarrassed to learn he didn't know everything about his client's personal financial affairs? Lucas had seemed pretty clear that he dealt with all of the Kvarnback family's investment matters. After all, it was his biggest client so he'd know the family's business inside out, wouldn't he? No doubt it would become clearer after his telephone conversation later in the day. He needed to work out a strategy first.

As he cycled east on Newmarket Road, past the Grafton shopping center, the rain began to pelt down. It was not a cold rain, but Henning was getting soaked, and the rain was causing his goggles to mist up badly. At Elizabeth Way, the rain began to overflow the drains and run down the street. He increased his pace and moved over into the middle of the lane to avoid the running water. There were few cars around at this time of the morning, so he felt safe to be further into the road.

When he approached the roundabout on Milton Road, Henning slowed the pace. On most days, the absence of vehicles meant he could avoid stopping altogether and ride straight onto the circle. Just as he was turning right, his mobile phone rang in his breast pocket. For a moment, he lost concentration and didn't hear the white van racing up behind him. The vehicle smashed into his right side, throwing him twenty feet into the air. He landed against a steel lamppost. There was a loud crack as Henning's neck snapped. He was dead by the time he hit the road. The van raced on without stopping, leaving the mangled bike lying in the middle of the street.

CHAPTER 24

Tara came running into Kent's office. "The police are in reception asking to speak with you," she said.

"The police? And they're asking for me?" Kent asked.

"Yes. They said it was an important matter but wouldn't give any details."

"Okay. Bring them through into my office. It's bound to be some claptrap about a neighborhood watch scheme."

Kent looked at his watch: 3:30 p.m. *The squash court's booked for four-thirty*, he thought. *Can't spend long with these people; it's a league match.*

"Mr. John Kent?" asked the senior of the two police officers as they entered.

Kent was struck by the somber mood of the officers. *This is something serious.* "It's not Sarah, is it?"

"Who's Sarah?"

"My wife."

"No, this is not about your wife, sir."

"Thank God. I'm sorry. Please take a seat. What can I do for you?"

"Can we first confirm that Mr. Anton Henning works at these offices?"

"Yes. He's a partner here. What's this about?"

"I regret to inform you, Mr. Kent, that Mr. Henning was killed earlier today in a road traffic accident."

"What? I assumed he was out at a meeting today..." Kent stopped to digest the news for a few seconds. "I'm sorry. How did it happen?"

"I'm afraid we're unable to share any details at the moment. We found office papers in his rucksack. They pointed us to CBC. We'd like to contact any family he might have. We assume you have personal contact details for him?"

"You mean Nora doesn't know about this?"

"Is Nora his wife?"

"Yes. I'll get you her contact details." Kent walked over to his door. "Tara, can you dig out Anton's personnel file and bring it here for me right away?"

"Sure. Is everything okay? You look pale."

"I'll tell you in a moment."

Two minutes later, Tara returned with the file. "What's happened?" she asked.

"Anton's been killed in an accident."

"Oh my God! How? Was he on his bike?"

"I can tell you he was cycling this morning when the accident happened," said the officer. "But we can't release any further details until we have spoken with his wife."

"Nora doesn't know. The police need her contact details at work so they can get hold of her," said Kent.

"Of course. Let me write them down for you," said Tara. "Poor Nora. What awful news."

"Would you like me to come with you? It might help to have someone she knows with her when you tell her," said Kent.

"That would be very helpful, Mr. Kent, if you don't mind."

"Not at all. Nora doesn't have any family in this country. They're both from Sweden." Kent stood up and slipped on his suit jacket. "I still can't believe it. We were just talking last night in this office, and now he's dead."

The following Sunday morning, Kent woke up early. He was exhausted and couldn't stop thinking about the accident. He could only imagine the hell Nora was going through.

The worst point had been telling her the dreadful news of her husband's death. Kent had tried to find the right words to comfort her, but he'd struggled. He did everything else he could to help, arranging for her sister to come over from Sweden and taking care of the formalities regarding the identification of Henning's body. Thankfully, there were no children involved. He knew Nora would be comfortable financially, given CBC's group life assurance cover and her husband's vested stake in the carried interest scheme at the firm. But it was not about money or practical arrangements at that moment. She just needed emotional support. Sarah had been invaluable; she knew exactly what to say and what to do to meet Nora's needs, leaving him to focus on the more practical issues.

Had the police released the body, he would have offered to organize the repatriation to Sweden, too. But they were not ready to do so; they'd yet to complete their inquiries.

What's taking them so long? It's obvious how Henning died. Nora needs to organize a funeral.

He got out of bed and went downstairs to pick up the newspapers before making himself a coffee and going through to his study. He decided not to disturb Sarah as she was still asleep.

It's been a difficult few days for her, too, he thought. *She needs the rest.*

He searched through his newspaper for the business section, junking the sports and culture sections. As his eyes scanned the first page the words jumped out at him. "CBC Partner Killed in Hit and Run."

Hit and run! How could someone plough into a cyclist in broad daylight and then drive off?

Suddenly he understood why the police were withholding the body and continuing their investigation.

This isn't just an accident. It could go on for weeks, he realized. *How's Nora going to cope?*

CHAPTER 25

The following morning, Kent held a partners' meeting and updated everyone on the events of the last few days. All of them had read the *Sunday Post* story, and there was nothing Kent could add. He'd spoken with Nora on Sunday afternoon. She'd heard from the police but was struggling to take it all in. They told her they were looking for a white van or small truck, but didn't go into any more detail. Kent suggested they continue to pay Henning's salary to Nora until the firm's life assurance paid out. He didn't want her worrying over money. All of the partners agreed.

Kent returned to his office. He had a lot of work to catch up on; the previous week had been chaotic. He opened up the electronic diary on his PC and scanned the last couple of weeks to make sure there was nothing left unfinished.

He noticed the entry from the previous Monday where Tara had noted his meeting with Henning.

That was the last thing Henning did here.

As he replayed that last meeting with Henning in his mind, Kent remembered Henning was going to make some inquiries about Andreas Kvarnback's prior involvement in private equity.

"Could you dig out the compliance file on Tritona for me?" he shouted to Tara.

"Sure. Is there anything I can find for you in particular?"

"No. I just need to take a look at the file."

Tara came back with it a few minutes later. "I think what you're doing for Nora is very kind, by the way."

"Thanks. Anton was a friend. Still can't believe he's gone."

"It makes you value what you have."

"You're right. Easy to forget when we're rushing around."

"Let me know if I can help with the file. I put it together with Kevin."

"Thanks. Just leave it with me. I'm not sure what I'm looking for really."

He sat on one of the sofas and started to read the file. There were the usual CBC checklists on the front setting out the various compliance checks that had been carried out and who'd completed them. All the boxes were initialed either by his compliance partner, Kevin Long, or by Tara.

They'd taken copies of the various Tritona companies' key documents, certificates of incorporation, and so on. Further back were checks on the families behind Tritona, including copies of passports for each of the key family members. Tara had initialed the boxes, which confirmed that she'd compared the copy passports to the originals. Everything seemed in order.

Kent looked at the various supporting documents: the key verification papers and agreements, including the investment agreement between the three families behind Tritona. He flipped through the passport copies of Hans Deutchman, Franz Needmeier, and Andrees Kvarnback.

Something made him take a second look, and this time it jumped out at him. "A—N—D—R—E—E—S."

It's spelled wrong. It ought to say ANDREAS. He stared at the copy of the passport photo then walked over to his desk, reached for his keyboard, and powered up his search engine. He typed in "Andrees Kvarnback." The screen flashed up, "Your search—Andrees Kvarnback—did not match any documents."

This is weird.

He punched in "Andreas Kvarnback," and the search engine came back with more than three thousand results.

He scrolled down through the results. Most of them referred to "Andreas Kvarnback" and "Svensk Pharmaceuticals," the SEC listed pharmaceuticals group of companies. He clicked on a few links and tracked down a PDF copy of the latest published report and accounts for the group. He turned to the chairman's report and saw a large color photograph of the chairman, Andreas Kvarnback. Kent compared it to the passport photo on the compliance file. *Definitely the same person.*

Henning was right; his friend's client was the chairman and controlling shareholder in Svensk Pharmaceuticals and this client was, indeed, one of the investors in Tritona. *But why didn't Henning's friend know of his client's existing investment in Tritona?* Kent continued staring at the copy of the passport photo page and at the computer screen in front of him. The incorrect spelling in the passport makes no sense. *Surely, Andreas Kvarnback himself would have picked up a mistake in his own passport?*

What the hell is this all about? Was this why Henning was so worried? Had he taken the time to look at the compliance file and found the same thing? He'd always been a stickler for detail.

He stood, grabbed the file, and ran downstairs to the security reception to speak to Chapman.

"Do you have a moment, Bill?"

"Of course, Mr. Kent," replied Chapman from behind the desk.

"Good. Let's use this office for a moment."

They walked into a small office just across the hall from the security desk, and Kent closed the door behind them.

"Am I being fired?" asked Chapman. "Tell me straight."

"No. What makes you think that?"

"It's just we've never discussed anything before other than at my desk. Now we're standing in an office behind a closed door."

"No. Relax, Bill. I need your help. That's all. Grab a seat."

"Thank goodness for that."

They both sat at the small table. "What I'm about to share with you has to remain absolutely confidential. I mean no one can know about this," Kent said, lowering his voice.

"I can assure you it will remain only with me. Whatever it is."

"It's a delicate matter."

"How I can help? Is it a staff problem? Has someone been stealing?"

"No. Nothing like that."

"Oh." Chapman looked disappointed.

"Are you still in contact with any of your old army intelligence colleagues?"

"Tell me what you need, and I'll let you know if I can help."

Kent opened the file in his hand and placed it in front of them. "You see this passport photo page? Does anything jump out at you?"

Chapman studied the copy for a few moments. "Can I take it off the file?"

"Sure."

Chapman held the document up to the light, turned it around, then upside down, narrowing his eyes as he did so.

"Anything?" asked Kent.

"No. Not really."

"I need to know if there's something not right about it." He decided not to mention the spelling of the passport holder's name.

"It's obviously not a British passport."

"Yes, but I mean anything else besides that."

"Do you have something in mind? Can you give me a clue what you're looking for?"

"I just need to know there's nothing wrong with it. That's all. Call it, in-depth verification, if you like."

"There are a couple of retired contacts I have who know a thing or two about identification papers. You know, driving licenses, work permits, passports, and so on. I'd be happy to run this by them."

"I'd really appreciate that. Let me make a few good quality photocopies for you." Kent stood up and grabbed the file. "I'd prefer you not to say anything about CBC when you speak to your contacts."

"There's no reason for me to say anything to them about the

firm. I'll just give them copies of the page and ask if anything appears unusual to them. They don't need to know who's interested or why."

"I owe you one for this."

"Don't mention it. I'm happy to help. It's nice to start using the old gray matter again."

"Thanks, Bill."

"Give me a few days, and I'll let you know what turns up."

CHAPTER 26

A week later, as Kent arrived at work, Chapman suggested it would be a good idea if they could meet at some point in the day. Kent arranged to meet him midmorning; he was already scheduled to meet with a management team who were coming in at 9 a.m. to discuss a potential transaction with him and George Townsend, another of Kent's partners. He thought about canceling the meeting as he wanted to hear what Chapman had to say, but it could wait another couple of hours. He'd thought about little else over the past few days, trying to rationalize the passport and why Henning's friend knew nothing about his client's involvement in private equity. None of it made sense.

The meeting with the management team dragged on, and Kent found it difficult to concentrate on the potential deal. He was anxious to find out what Chapman had learned. He hoped it would put his mind at rest or, at least, provide some answers. In the end, he made his excuses and left Townsend to finish off the meeting on his own.

Just after eleven-thirty, he ran downstairs to see Chapman.

"I had a word with one of my contacts, as I said I would," said Chapman, closing the door behind him.

"Great. What did they say?"

"I don't know if it's good news or bad."

"Go on."

"It's a forgery."

Kent slumped in one of the chairs, exhaling loudly through his nose. He didn't say anything for a few moments as he digested the news.

Jesus, what the hell does this mean?

"And they could tell that from a photocopy?"

"There's no doubt about it."

"How?"

"Take a look at the passport." Chapman drew up a chair next to Kent and pointed to the photocopy. "It's only two years old. According to my contact, Sweden adopted the standard format of the European Union passport three years ago. Although unexpired, old-style passports would still be valid, all new passports had to follow the EU format."

"So what style is this one?"

"The old style, which means it can't be legit."

"Are you absolutely certain about this?"

"When this passport was made two years ago, no old-style passports were being issued by Sweden. Whoever created it did a great job at replicating the old format, but they screwed up by not following the new format."

"How confident are you that your contact is right about this, Bill? It's massively important."

"There's no doubt." Chapman smiled. "Let's just say counterfeit passports are his specialty, but I'd prefer to leave it at that."

Kent was not about to press Chapman any further. He was in enough trouble already. "I'm not sure I wanted to hear it's a forgery, but thanks for your help on this. I know you'll keep it to yourself."

Chapman nodded. "Is there anything else you want me to do on this?"

Kent shook his head no. "You've been a great help. I owe you one."

Kent spent the rest of the day in his office thinking about the counterfeit passport and Andreas Kvarnback.

What does it all mean? Does Tritona know the passport isn't authentic? Have they been misled by their Swedish investor, too? What if the Swede isn't an investor at all? What if Tritona are hiding the real source of their money? His mind ran wild with theories. Whatever the explanation, he knew it was suspicious and that he'd have to notify the UK's National Crime Agency.

The penalty for not filing a report of a well-founded suspicion was fourteen years in prison, and Kent wasn't about to risk that. He wanted to discuss the matter with Baumgart first, but that was a nonstarter. It was also a criminal offense to tip-off the party under suspicion. Kent knew Tritona may be as innocent as CBC but, under the law, he had no choice but to report what he knew.

Could there be a legitimate explanation for all this? Kent couldn't see one. *Either Kvarnback's up to something or Tritona is*, he thought. *Either way, it's bad for CBC.* He decided to sleep on things before taking any action. It was too important a matter to make a snap decision only to regret it later.

Early the following morning, after a restless night, Kent was sitting in his quiet office, before any staff had arrived. By now, he'd reached the conclusion that someone had tried to deceive him and that there was no credible innocent explanation. He realized this could even spell the end of his profitable relationship with Tritona. The implications of that for his firm were unimaginable.

This could be a complete fucking disaster.

Kent was certain of one thing: the law required him to notify the authorities. He took out a pad of paper and began drafting the letter he'd send to the NCA. He wondered how to start. His words needed to concentrate less on whom he suspected, as he was still not sure about that, and more on the details relating to the passport. There was no need to mention Chapman or his army intelligence contacts. None of that was relevant.

The authorities don't need to know how I found out about Swedish passports, he figured. *Keep it brief; stick to the facts.*

Kent told Tara to hold all his calls when she arrived for the day and then closed his office door. He wanted some peace to concentrate on the letter without interruptions. It took him most of the morning and several drafts.

It's got to be right, he thought. *This letter may be CBC's death warrant.*

He wasn't hungry at lunchtime, so he took a walk around Science Park to get some air and to chew over the letter in his mind. When he returned to the office, he read his draft one more time and decided it was ready.

Once I let this go, there's no going back.

He called Tara into his room. "I need you to type up a letter for me, but you need to keep the subject matter in strict confidence. You can't mention it to anyone."

"What's it about?" she asked.

"Listen, I don't want to talk about it right now." He handed Tara the letter. While she had no idea about the significance of the document she'd just received, Kent had no illusions as to the massive step he'd just taken. Now he'd involved someone else in his discovery.

"Okay. Do you want me to drop what I'm doing now to work on this?"

"Please. Do it straightaway. It'll be obvious why when you read it." Tara returned to her desk and began to read:

"Dear Sir/Madam,

"I am the CEO of Cambridge Buy-Out Capital (CBC). CBC is a private equity fund manager. The firm is authorized and regulated by the Financial Conduct Authority (FCA).

"More than ninety percent of the funds managed by this firm have come from one investor. This investor is a multifamily office called Tritona, based in Geneva. When CBC accepted Tritona as an investor a few months ago, we were informed that there were three families whose wealth is managed by Tritona. These families are the Needmeiers, Deutchmans, and the Kvarnbacks, all of whom are well known amongst the business community in Europe.

"As part of our due diligence and compliance procedures, we examined a number of documents to confirm the identity of Tritona and the families behind them. It is in this connection that I wish to file a suspicious activity report.

"It has come to our attention that Swedish passports changed in format three years ago, moving to the new EU format. However, one of the passports we have received to confirm the identity of Andreas Kvarnback, a Swedish national, is in the old format and yet it is only two years old. Furthermore, the spelling of his name on the attached photo page of Mr. Kvarnback's passport is incorrect.

"I confirm that I have not raised the matter with either Tritona or Andreas Kvarnback so as to avoid 'tipping off.'

"Please contact me should you require any further information.

"Yours faithfully,

"John Kent. Chief Executive Officer."

Kent held up his palms when Tara came back into the office. "I know. It's a bloody nightmare," he said before she could say anything.

"What does this mean for the firm?"

"I haven't thought that far ahead yet." He lied because it wasn't right for him to discuss with Tara what it meant for CBC before he'd sat down with his partners first.

"When do you want the letter to be dated?"

"Put tomorrow's date on it. I want to mull over the wording once more before it goes out. I'd like you to set up a partners' meeting for tomorrow afternoon, so I can brief everyone on this too."

"I'll set it up."

"Don't mention the letter. Just tell them an important matter has come up, but don't tell them what it is."

I need to work out how I'm going to break this to them, he thought.

That night, Kent again struggled to sleep. He kept searching for possible explanations for the suspect passport. The best theory he could come up with was that Andreas Kvarnback had supplied Tritona with a false passport to hide some form of personal embarrassment. The worst was that Tritona had knowingly supplied CBC with the forgery in order to mask the real identity of their investors. He suspected the worst.

What if none of the named investors behind Tritona is real? The money's real enough; it's coming from somewhere.

By the time he fell asleep it was 4 a.m. He slept through his alarm and only woke at seven-thirty when Sarah's alarm went off. He had breakfast with her but didn't mention anything about the previous day's events.

She'll be horrified, he thought. *I'll tell her when I get to the bottom of it all.*

Kent arrived at CBC midmorning. "You look tired. Can I bring you a coffee?" asked Tara as he walked by her, heading straight for his office.

"Make it a strong one. Did you arrange the meeting with the partners for me?" he asked, trying to force a smile.

"I did. I've set it up for 4 p.m. It's in your diary."

"Thanks. Can you print off copies of my draft letter ready for me to hand out at the meeting?"

"Sure. Did you have any further changes to make to it first?"

"No. I think it's pretty much there, subject to any comments from the other partners."

He sat staring at the screensaver on his PC. *What's the point of doing any work if the business is about to go off a cliff?*

Tara brought in his coffee. "By the way, this came for you by courier first thing this morning," she said, handing him a large brown envelope marked "Private and Confidential."

Kent sipped the coffee. "Thanks." Tara walked back to her desk while he ripped open the envelope. Inside he found a DVD case and a typed note. It read: "You may wish to reconsider sending your letter after watching this."

What the hell's this? He stared at the DVD on his desk and then reread the note. There was no signature, and the envelope gave no clues as to the identity of the sender. It took a few moments before his brain engaged. He stood up, shut his office door, and then inserted the DVD into the drive of his PC. His hands were shaking.

The machine whirred as it launched the disc. The PC screen turned black, and Kent could see the reflection of his face, wide-eyed and frightened. A moment later, the display lit up.

"Oh my God!" he said out loud. "How the..."

CHAPTER 27

On Kent's PC screen was a large room with a double bed in the middle of the shot. He recognized it immediately as Hotel Morgana. Then there were muffled voices of a man and a woman out of view. When they appeared, they were kissing each other. The DVD caught every last detail of Kent and Tara on the night that "never happened."

"Jesus Christ!" he said, covering his mouth with his hand.

Kent fumbled for the button then ejected the disc and threw it into his briefcase with trembling hands. His heart pounded the inside of his chest, and he shivered, the revelation hitting him like a brick wall. In that awful moment, he realized they were dealing with serious criminals; people who had the resources to set up cameras in the hotel.

They must have my office bugged, too. Other than Tara, no one knows about the draft letter to the NCA.

He sat motionless, staring at his PC. What the hell was he going to do? He held his face in his hands, elbows leaning on the desk. His shallow breath caught in his chest as a chilling thought jumped into his head. Could these people have been behind Anton's death? It was a hit and run, after all. Henning had been in Kent's office when they were discussing Andreas Kvarnback. The next day, he was dead.

This office has to be bugged, he thought. *Is Sarah at risk? This is a fucking nightmare.*

He stood, picked up his briefcase and rushed out of his office. "I'm going out for an hour," he said to Tara, without stopping.

Kent drove away from Cambridge as fast as he could. He

needed to place some distance between him and the office and whoever was watching him. He drove onto the M11 motorway and put his foot down. Could they be following him now? He kept looking in his rearview mirror. When he caught sight of his reflection, his face was white and his eyes were glazed. He took the car up to ninety before he realized he was going too fast and slowed down. Twenty miles south of Cambridge, he stopped at a motorway service station. He got out of the car and walked into the coffee shop, bought a strong coffee, and sat in a quiet corner looking out of the window. He was in a public space. *Surely, it's safe here?*

When he rang Sarah's mobile, it went to voicemail. He left a message asking her to call him. *I need to know she's safe*, he thought, though he knew she was probably with a patient.

He nursed his cold coffee for two hours, ignoring the cell phone calls from the office. For the first hour, Kent sat, numb, staring out of the window at the traffic rushing by on the motorway. With his mind blank, the people coming and going in the coffee shop seemed to be in another world, as though none of this was really happening.

As the shock began to fade, he took out a sheet of paper from his briefcase and began capturing his random thoughts on this nightmare: Who was he dealing with? What do they want now they've declared their hand? CBC must be of some ongoing value to them. After all, it would be just as easy to kill Kent as they did Henning. Somehow, his death had to have been a warning.

Seeing the whole thing on a sheet of paper helped him collect his thoughts. One thing was certain: he could no longer file his suspicious activity report with the NCA. He had to bury the letter. Going to the authorities now was out of the question. These people wouldn't hesitate to ruin his marriage or harm him or Sarah.

Kent rubbed his chin then closed his eyes for a moment. He couldn't mention this to Tara. They were bound to hear any conversation in the office. Besides, he couldn't burden her with this on top of the problems with her mother. What good would it do, anyway? There was nothing she could do about it.

He picked up his voicemails. Still nothing from Sarah. He rang her office and was told she was still in with patients. *Thank God.*

Tara had rung several times, so he called her back and said something had come up on the personal front. He asked her to leave the NCA letter face down on his desk and to cancel the partners' meeting arranged for this afternoon. "Just tell the partners something's come up and apologize on my behalf," he said.

Kent had to make sure the letter never saw the light of day.

CHAPTER 28

Doug Wright had developed a leathery tan, the kind you get from spending too much time on the golf course. He was a good ten pounds heavier, too. Since leaving Henderson Wright as senior partner, he'd taken on a couple of non-executive director positions: one with a major oil company and the other with a firm of management consultants, where he was now chairman. Both roles combined took up only one day a week, so he'd spent the last few months improving his golf swing and taking long vacations in the Mediterranean. The boredom was killing him. Apart from golf, he had no real interests or friends with whom he could spend time. Even other retired partners from the old firm found excuses to avoid him when he called them suggesting they meet up for lunch or dinner. His wife was anxious for him to find another challenging role so he'd be out of her hair. It was never part of the deal that she would have to spend sixteen hours a day listening to him rant on about this and that. He was becoming a pain, and he knew it.

When he received a call from a well-known headhunter asking if he'd consider taking on a part-time role as head of a new, high-profile division at the FCA, Wright took all of a nanosecond to decide he wanted it. He'd heard the FCA was beefing up its activities following the financial crisis and that part of this involved taking on senior figures from commerce and industry to head up some of its new units. It was the mention of "high profile" that turned his head. Wright didn't need the money, but he still missed the kudos that went with being the head of a Big Four global accounting firm. He missed his stage.

The headhunter laid it on thick. He'd already tried several other senior business people before calling Wright, but none of them would remotely consider taking on a quasi-government role; they had no desire to become a regulator and they saw the pay as pitifully low. By now, the headhunter was halfway down his B-list.

"My client is adamant that you're the perfect fit for this position, Mr. Wright. They're impressed with your track record at Henderson Wright and have asked me to do everything in my power to persuade you to consider taking on this pivotal role," he said. "They know you'll do a great job for them. In many ways, the role was designed for you."

Wright did not need persuading but tried to appear nonchalant. "I may have time to fit it in. It just depends on the position itself. Tell me more about the new division."

"The new team will take a proactive approach to investigating regulated financial services firms rather than simply waiting for regular reports to come in from those firms and reacting to problems. Since the demise of Lehman Brothers, the regulator has wanted to investigate actively those firms that don't appear to be in any trouble. They call it 'pro-active regulation,' and they recognize that they need a City heavy-hitter to set out this new strategy, build an appropriate team, and then head up these new investigations."

Wright couldn't contain the smug grin on his face. "Yes, I can certainly see how my background and experience would fit."

"They'd really like to meet up with you to explore this further, if you are interested, of course."

Wright was salivating over the role. "I see no harm meeting the people," he said, coolly. In his mind, the job was already his. He didn't care what they'd have to say about the money or any of the other details; the status was everything. Each time he found a firm up to no good, it would be all over the newspapers, and Wright would have his name right there in the middle of the story. He couldn't wait to start.

Immediately after the call, Wright rushed to tell his wife. "Do you really have to take it, Doug? I'll miss spending the time with you," she said, with as much conviction as she could muster.

A week later, Wright found himself back at Canary Wharf for the meeting at the FCA. He'd researched the background to the regulator and the history of regulation of financial services firms in the UK. He'd read all the articles he could find online relating to the challenges of financial services regulation. He'd even asked his wife to play the role of the interviewer most evenings so he could anticipate the questions and rehearse his answers. He was well prepared. Although he craved the position, his challenge was not to let it show.

He walked right past the Henderson Wright tower on his way to the FCA's headquarters. He still missed his time there and would never forgive John Kent and CBC for forcing him out. He smiled as he thought about how they'd come to regret making an enemy of him once he was in his new role. He'd do everything possible to use his new position to give CBC a good kicking, and he wouldn't be satisfied until Kent was ruined.

When Wright arrived at the regulator's office building, he was shown to a large meeting room on the twenty-second floor, where he faced a panel interview. The chief executive of the FCA led the meeting. Check. Wright had already decided if the position wasn't sufficiently senior to warrant the CEO handling the discussion, then it wouldn't be the right role for him. It was his test to see how senior the position really was.

The panel had the usual questions, all of which Wright had anticipated, and to which he gave eloquent, if verbose, answers. It was clear from the start they wanted him as much as he wanted the job. He had a number of questions of his own, mostly to enable him to confirm the power of the position: Would he be allowed to recruit his own team? Would he have complete unrestricted access to the resources of the FCA? Would he be able to select any firm for investigation, no matter its size or connections? Would he be the public face of this important new division? The answer was the same in all cases—yes.

They offered him the job, and Wright grabbed it with both hands. He couldn't wait to get started.

CHAPTER 29

For the next couple of weeks, Kent tried his best to get back to business as usual, but the DVD kept playing on his mind. Whoever sent it knew he'd been about to file a suspicious report with the NCA and had the video delivered just in time to stop him in his tracks. Ever since that moment, he'd been cautious about any discussion in his office. There was no doubt they were listening and monitoring his every move, whoever they were.

He immersed himself in new deals and meetings, but nothing could distract him completely. At night, he struggled to sleep and during the day, he had no energy or appetite. Sarah had commented on his weight loss. Even Tara had telephoned her to say that he was not his usual self and to ask if he was all right.

Behind all the tension was Kent's loss of control and a need to know who he was dealing with. Who the hell was Baumgart, really? And who did he represent? Kent decided to go and face Baumgart and to have it out with him. Even though that would be risky, he couldn't go on like this, not knowing what or whom he was up against.

"Tara, could you get hold of Dieter Baumgart and arrange for me to meet with him over the next few days?" he shouted through his open office door.

"Sure. What shall I tell him the meeting is about when I call?" replied Tara.

"Just tell him it's a regular catch-up session. Tell him I want to update him on the progress of their investments and what deals we have in the pipeline. Nothing unusual." Kent tried to make it all sound perfectly normal as the hidden microphones would be recording everything. *Christ! I feel like I'm going mad. Maybe I am?*

A few minutes later, Tara walked into his office. "Mr. Baumgart is actually going to be in London for a couple of meetings next week and has suggested you meet him at his hotel one evening while he's over here. Is that okay with you?"

"That's fine. Can you sort out the travel arrangements? I won't need to stay down there. I'll catch a late train home."

I don't want to spend any more time with that man than I have to, he thought.

Kent caught the 6:30 p.m. train from Peterborough to London the following week. The high-speed train arrived at King's Cross station fifty minutes later. He was early for his eight o'clock dinner appointment with Baumgart, so he walked the thirty minutes or so it took to reach the Langham Hotel at the southern end of Portland Place. Besides, it helped to calm his nerves and gave him time to think.

How should he play the meeting? He didn't know if he could trust Baumgart at all. The truth was he knew very little about the man. *He must know something.*

Kent arrived first at the hotel's restaurant, at a couple of minutes before eight. A condescending maître d' showed him to the table in a small alcove just off the main dining room. The table was visible from the main dining area but was private enough to hold a discreet conversation. Sitting with his back to the window, he could watch the room and see when Baumgart arrived. His heart rate was rapid, and his palms were sticky. He dried them on his suit trousers. The last thing he wanted was to appear nervous in front of Baumgart when they shook hands. That would ring alarm bells. How would he be able to explain such out-of-character behavior without giving away what he knew?

Scanning the room for anyone who might be watching him,

Kent played with the cutlery. The restaurant was almost full, and most of the suited diners appeared to be deep in conversation. But the two men who sat at the table in the opposite corner of the room appeared to be looking over at him. They averted their eyes as he looked directly back at them. *Are they watching me?*

The waiter came to take a drink order and Kent ordered mineral water; best to keep a clear head for the difficult meeting to come. He skimmed the menu, but he had no appetite; eating tonight would be purely for show. *This isn't a social meeting. It's not even a business meeting*, he thought.

What could he expect from this dinner with Baumgart? Would he just come out and admit he's a criminal? *What happens then?* Kent was no longer sure this was a great idea. Where would this lead, and did he really want to know everything?

He glanced at his watch; ten past eight and still no sign of them. *Maybe they're not coming.* Just as he was about to call Tara to check he had the right place and time, he heard, "John, very good to see you. So sorry to have kept you waiting." Baumgart and his sidekick, Kulpman, were making their way over to the table.

Baumgart beckoned over the waiter, ordered a large glass of Riesling, and started to read the menu. *He looks relaxed*, Kent thought. *What's his game?*

Baumgart made small talk as they waited for their food order. Though Kent joined in, he was boiling inside. *When's he going to drop the bloody façade?* he thought. *Stop fucking about. We all know why we're here.*

"So, John, what would you like to discuss?" Baumgart said as he scraped his fork on the last morsel of food on his plate.

Kent had hardly touched his meal. He pushed his plate aside and stared at the Swiss giant. Should he just come out with it? If Baumgart was going to play games, then maybe he'd have to be direct with him. What could he say, though? *I know all about the DVD, and I know you or your people were behind Anton's death?*

"Current progress on our portfolio and the deals that are coming through over the next couple of months," said Kent. He couldn't bring himself to do it. The whole thing had the potential to go horribly wrong and spin out of control. Instead, he ran through the performance of the main companies in the investment portfolio.

Baumgart was his usual self, praising the great work being done by CBC and Kent in particular. "Our investors are very pleased with your performance and would be delighted to make more capital available should you need it."

Kent looked down. "I think we're comfortable for the time being but, of course, I'll let you know if we can deploy more capital." That would never happen. If Kent had his way, he'd hand it all back tonight and call it quits.

"There's always plenty of money available for the right deals."

"Have you picked up any new investors recently, Dieter?" Kent said in the hopes of prompting a reaction from him.

"No. All of our capital still comes from the three families. Nothing's changed. Now, are we going to have a coffee? I know I will."

Incredible! Baumgart was still claiming Tritona's money came from the three founding families. What about Andreas Kvarnback? What about the fake passport? What about the bloody DVD?

Kent stared at the tablecloth. Was it possible Baumgart wasn't involved? He had to be. Nothing else made sense.

"We were horrified to learn about your partner being killed in that road accident," Baumgart said, breaking into Kent's thoughts.

Kent bolted upright. How could Baumgart casually drop this into the conversation? *You bastards killed him. I bet you were horrified.*

"We read about it in the newspapers. It must have been a shock to you all," continued Baumgart.

Kent felt his cheeks heating up. "Yes. It was a shock, all right."

He wanted to shout out that it couldn't have been a surprise to Tritona. He wanted to tell Baumgart to stop fucking about with his silly games. He wanted to know more about the DVD taken in the room Tritona had so carefully arranged for them. He wanted to grill Baumgart on the people behind his Swiss firm. Was it mafia money? It had to be. How long had he been on their payroll? How many other people had he been party to blackmailing and murdering? He wanted Baumgart to simply stop the pretense and tell him the truth, but something stopped him from blurting this all out.

As the coffees came and went, Kent remained in a daze, nodding politely as Baumgart continued to talk.

"Next time I'd like you to bring that delightful young lady, Tara, with you," Baumgart said as they walked to the hotel foyer at the end of the meal. Kent wondered whether that was Baumgart's way of saying he knew about the DVD.

While he was revolted by the thought, Kent shook hands with Baumgart and then jumped into one of the waiting taxis in front of the hotel. As the cab made its way along Euston Road, he ran over the evening in his mind. Could Baumgart actually be innocent in all this? Was that credible? He leaned forward and cupped his head in his hands. Who was pulling the strings? Who sent the DVD? Who killed Anton? He sighed. *I've learned nothing tonight. Nothing.*

Kent caught the ten-thirty train from King's Cross. His carriage was half empty. There were a few people who looked as though they'd been down for the theater or dinner, but nobody rowdy or drunk. It was too early for the late-night revelers to be making their way home. As the train pulled out, two men in business suits looked in Kent's direction from the other side of the aisle three rows away. He looked at them, trying not to make it obvious. They were not the same men from the restaurant, although they were dressed in similar suits. He glanced away when they looked directly back at him. They appeared to be discussing him. Kent felt his stomach tightening. *Am I being followed? Are these the people behind Tritona?*

The train stopped at Stevenage, but the two men stayed on. Kent thought of moving to another carriage to see what the two suits would do, but decided it was safer to stay put. At least there were other people in this carriage. *Surely they wouldn't attack me with witnesses around? But how am I going to get back to my car?* The men were staring at him now and making no effort to hide it. Kent looked away, thinking it best not to let them know he'd spotted them.

He left the train at Peterborough. A few people got off at the same time and made their way across the tracks via the pedestrian footbridge. He started walking to his car in the station parking lot then noticed the two men were only forty yards behind him leaving the station building. *They're definitely following me. Shit!*

There was no one else in the parking area, and it was not well lit. Kent did not look around but could hear the footsteps of the two men getting closer. He increased his pace a little, as imperceptibly as he could, then took his car keys out of his briefcase so he'd be ready to open the BMW without stopping. He could sense they were close now.

As he made his way under the rail bridge, he knew he would be out of their line of sight for a split second, so he started to run, slowly at first then a sprint. He pressed the key fob and jumped into his car, starting the engine before pulling the door closed. The tires squealed as he raced toward the exit. Kent fumbled with the ticket at the exit barrier. *I'll drive right through this fucking thing if it doesn't open.* He looked in his rearview mirror as the metal arm lifted. The men were gone.

CHAPTER 30

It was hot and sticky. The strong Gulf wind intensified the sandstorm blown up by the turbine engine. A desert cloud surrounded the building as the helicopter climbed into the air, buffeted by the gale.

Raul Safuentes was the only passenger on board. "How long before we're above this?" he shouted to the pilot.

"Not long, sir. It's all low-level turbulence," said the pilot. "Should only be a few more minutes before it smoothes out."

Safuentes gripped the sides of his seat and closed his eyes. *Infernal machines.* When the aircraft climbed, the wind dropped, and he began to relax. Isla Tiburon became smaller and smaller through his window as the helicopter continued its ascent. He'd installed the latest IT and communications systems at head office so he could avoid all unnecessary travel, but his role as the cartel's CFO demanded that he dealt with certain matters face-to-face. His brother expected no less of him.

Forty-five minutes later, the town of Hermosillo came into sight. Safuentes closed his eyes again when they came in to land, taking deep breaths as he counted down the seconds until he felt firm ground.

Six hundred miles above his head, a DEA reconnaissance satellite was monitoring every inch of the helicopter's flight. The special agent controlling the satellite from El Paso noted when the aircraft loaded up at the island, that there was only one passenger on board. He increased the focus when the helicopter came in to land at the small airstrip on the edge of Hermosillo. Then he leaned in toward the microphone next to his control screen.

The encrypted radio crackled as he spoke into the microphone. "Only one passenger, and I'm pretty sure it's Safuentes. Do you have visual?"

A quarter of a mile away from the airstrip, a DEA agent answered from his hideout in a disused water tower. "I have visual." He concentrated on the passenger leaving the helicopter. The Leviathan high-powered telescope on a slim pedestal picked up all the close detail he needed. "I can confirm the passenger is Raul Safuentes. It's affirmative, Raul Safuentes."

"Copy that. Will continue to monitor," replied the agent in El Paso.

As soon as Safuentes was on board the waiting Hawker 750 private jet, the pilot started the engines and took off in an easterly direction. A slim, young cabin attendant brought Safuentes his favorite drink, bourbon with a little ice, while he reclined in his leather seat. Besides the pilot and crew, he was the only passenger on board. He finished his drink before taking out a stack of papers from his briefcase, occasionally reaching for his calculator to check some of the figures.

Two hours later they stopped to refuel at Monterrey, but Safuentes didn't leave the jet. The aircraft headed out across the Gulf of Mexico, eventually landing at Nassau, the capital of the Bahamas.

After clearing immigration at Lynden Pindling International Airport, ten miles west of Nassau, Safuentes was picked up by two muscle-heads in a black Mercedes. They drove him downtown and dropped him off outside a bland office building on East Hill Street. The brass plate on the entrance door gave only a hint at what went on inside. It read, "Oakham Fiduciary Services—Nassau Branch."

Safuentes walked into the building, straight past reception, and up a flight of steps to a small, wood-paneled office with no windows. Already waiting there for him were Baumgart and Kulpman.

"Good afternoon, Raul. Good trip?" asked Baumgart.

"I've had worse. I assume you arrived yesterday?" Safuentes replied.

"Yes, so we could make sure the files were in good order for today's meeting. Can I get you a drink?"

"Coffee. Let's get on with it."

Baumgart poured a coffee for the three of them while Kulpman looked on. "We have a lot to cover with you. It's been an active year."

Safuentes unpacked the papers from his briefcase. "I'm listening."

"In the last twelve months, we have received transfers from your Mexican bank accounts amounting to twenty-seven billion dollars."

"That agrees with my records."

"Good." Baumgart feigned relief. "Those funds were transmitted to our various accounts in Geneva then transferred immediately to the established list of holding companies and trusts administered by Oakham Fiduciary Services. At our latest count, these were located in sixteen different countries, all selected by Oakham for their low tax status and guaranteed discretion."

Baumgart handed over a list to Safuentes. Against the name of each holding company or SPV was a dollar amount detailing the distribution of the twenty-seven billion dollars. The analysis went on for six pages. Safuentes took a few moments to review the list before nodding his approval.

"Another coffee," said Safuentes. It wasn't a request.

Baumgart looked at Kulpman, who didn't move, so Baumgart placed his notes on the table and grabbed the flask of coffee. He refilled their cups.

"Go on," said Safuentes.

"The monies set out on that list have been added to funds already held by those vehicles. As in previous years, we have drawn down on those combined funds as and when appropriate investment opportunities have emerged."

Baumgart handed over another sheet of paper. "On this report, we have shown the assets acquired during the year. It's been a busy period for investment. We've made investments totaling some forty-three billion dollars. We have added to our real estate and quoted securities portfolios, and these additions came to a total of twenty-one billion dollars. Furthermore, we've invested heavily in an asset class where we have historically had only a small exposure."

"Private equity," said Safuentes.

"Exactly. We deployed a total of twenty-two billion dollars in private equity, and most of this has been through CBC."

"CBC's returns are encouraging." Safuentes broke into a half-smile before stopping himself.

"They've been a very good find. Since compiling this report, we have invested much more through them. I believe we'll be able to deploy a lot more of your capital through CBC in the coming years."

"What about the problem you mentioned a few weeks ago?"

"The problem—"

Kulpman raised his hand, stopping Baumgart in mid-flow. He sat forward in his chair and turned to Safuentes.

"There will be no more difficulty with CBC." Kulpman's tone was slow and deliberate. "We took immediate action and now have enough insurance in place to guarantee their continued cooperation. Problem solved."

Safuentes's mouth creased into a thin smile, but this time he allowed it to show. If something was guaranteed by Kulpman, then he could rely on the information without question. Safuentes himself had trained Kulpman before he joined the senior enforcement team within the cartel. Because of his intellect, absolute discretion, and complete loyalty, Safuentes had placed him close to the assets at Tritona some years ago. It had been a shrewd decision; he was the cartel's eyes and ears on the ground where it mattered most.

"Very good, Franz. I will speak no more of this," Safuentes said.

In the three hours that followed, Safuentes grilled Baumgart on everything, taking nothing on trust. He couldn't afford to; later on, he'd have to answer to his brother. He wanted to know the details of the assets being acquired with the cartel's funds and the returns being generated. He also demanded chapter and verse on the legal structures being set up by Oakham Fiduciary Services. These esoteric corporate arrangements made it difficult for the authorities to trace the cartel's assets and thus represented a legal firewall, almost impossible to penetrate without an insider's knowledge.

Across the street, in a large colonial-period property, somebody was watching. The house was leased to a Mr. and Mrs. Ragula from Cleveland, Ohio. It was acquired as their holiday home, but they'd never visited. The couple didn't exist. The whole lease arrangement was a front for the DEA's intelligence team. Merriman's intelligence reports, and the investigation work carried out by his subordinate, Bill Greenough, had suggested there was an important connection between Oakham and the Caruana cartel. He had teams on standby at all known Oakham locations ready to monitor any visits by senior cartel personnel.

Safuentes's entire flight from Hermosillo had been monitored by El Paso via the reconnaissance satellite. Three DEA agents in Nassau had taken over the surveillance once the jet landed and Safuentes was on the ground. They'd followed him from the airport and were now holed up in the house, where they'd set up microwave listening and sound recording equipment. Early on in Baumgart's presentation, the three agents had contacted Merriman to inform him of the high-quality intelligence being gathered. Merriman had requested them to patch through the conversation, and he'd heard most of it live.

Once Baumgart had finished delivering his annual report to Safuentes, Merriman came on the phone and spoke to his men in the house. "Great work, guys. This is a major breakthrough for us. We're finally starting to understand the cartel's financial network."

"And we've got the whole thing on tape, sir," replied one of the agents.

"Besides Baumgart and Kulpman, is Safuentes alone? We know he was the only one on the flight over."

"Looks that way, sir."

"No one else from the cartel is there with him?"

"That's right. He arrived by car from the airport accompanied by two minders. They're already parked around the corner waiting to collect him. We're assuming they'll take him right back to the airport in a moment."

Merriman thought for a moment. This was an opportunity to capture a senior cartel figure. Safuentes was thinly guarded and exposed. They could wait a long time for another chance like this. The intelligence they could get from someone like Safuentes would save years of undercover work and save the lives of many agents. But his agents were in another sovereign country, so things could get messy.

"Do you think you guys could apprehend him with his two guards there?"

"I'm certain we could, sir. We'd have the advantage of surprise on our side."

There was another pause while Merriman weighed up the risk and reward. Safuentes was a potential goldmine of intelligence. This could bring down the entire Caruana cartel once and for all. "Then, before he reaches the airport, go ahead and grab him. We'll have a helicopter collection crew on standby, awaiting your signal the moment he's in your hands."

"We'll let you know as soon as we have him."

"I'll continue the satellite tracking so we know where to find you. Good luck, guys."

It was starting to get dark by the time Safuentes left Oakham's offices. His Mercedes was waiting outside the front door. One bodyguard was driving while the other sat in the front passenger seat. When it pulled away, the three DEA agents, now in a dark gray Range Rover with tinted windows, pulled out about a hundred yards behind. They kept a safe distance behind Safuentes and his men so as not to arouse suspicion.

The Mercedes drove along Harrold Road toward Cable Beach Golf Course then took a left onto John F. Kennedy Drive, following the south bank of Lake Cunningham. Moments later, when there were few other vehicles around, the Range Rover came up close behind the Mercedes for the first time. As the Mercedes slowed down to take a left turn onto Coral Harbor Road, which led to the airport, the Range Rover sped up. It ploughed into the back of the car, spinning it around ninety degrees before it came to a halt. Safuentes was thrown forward and then whipped back into his seat.

By the time the two guards realized what was happening, the three agents were already out of their vehicle, pistols drawn. One agent ran to the driver's door and pointed his weapon through the smashed window.

"Put your hands in the air or I'll blow your fucking brains out," he yelled to the bleeding driver.

When the two other agents went to grab the handle of the rear passenger door, the bodyguard in the front passenger seat lifted his AK-47 assault rifle from the footwell and rolled out of the car, crouching low. He held the trigger and sprayed them with automatic fire. The two agents let off a few rounds before falling to the ground.

The agent who was standing at the driver's door took his eye off the driver for a moment, aimed his pistol through the car and shot the bodyguard holding the assault rifle.

The driver pulled out a gun from his breast pocket and shot the agent in his neck. The agent's head flew back, and he was dead before his body hit the ground.

The whole firefight was over within fifteen seconds. The three DEA agents were dead, and the guard with the AK-47 lay dying on the road, taking his last few breaths as he bled out.

Safuentes was lying limp in his seat, blood pouring from a small bullet hole in the back of his head. He was dead. The driver hit the gas pedal and sped away, with Safuentes still slumped in the back seat.

The reconnaissance satellite caught the whole incident. On his screen, Merriman struggled to make out exactly what had happened, as the poor light made the details hard to see. What *was* clear to Merriman, though, was that the Mercedes managed to escape after the shoot-out, and the DEA vehicle was motionless. Through the speaker, he could hear his team in El Paso struggling to make radio contact with the three agents. They had to be dead.

How could I have been so stupid? he thought.

CHAPTER 31

The single-family homes on Sea Street backed onto the small harbor, filling up with sailboats taking overnight cover from the winds running through West Penobscot Bay. An elderly couple was sitting in the garden of their pretty white cottage, sipping wine and enjoying the wonderful view across the inlet toward the town of Camden. Theirs was one of a number of houses built around the port during the nineteenth century on the back of wealth created by the fishing industry. As usual, they stayed out on the rear deck until the large schooners had returned. The days when the boats served a commercial fishing purpose were long gone, but they remained a magnet for tourists enjoying day-trips out on the water. By the end of each day, the visitors would be gone, and the locals would reclaim their town for a few hours.

A classical music evening performance was taking place at Camden's impressive open-air auditorium next to the public library. This part of Maine drew many high-ranking diplomats and senior military service personnel as a place to retire, due as much to the area's cultural attractions as its stunning, rocky coastline.

The couple rarely missed the orchestral shows. They arrived early to grab the best seats; the right positions gave a view of both the musicians and the water beyond. Their faces lit up when the violin began playing the famous opening bars from "The Lark Ascending."

The concert, a performance of the music of Ralph Vaughn Williams, lasted just under two hours. By 7:30 p.m., they were seated at their favorite table and deciding on dinner at Francine's on Chestnut Street.

"The concert was a real treat," said the man. "Shall we order some champagne?"

"Well, it is a special occasion, after all," said the woman, glancing down the short menu.

"Hard to believe we've been retired ten years to the day. Where did that go?"

"I know, and almost eight years living here. Can you believe that?"

"I'm going for the fluke again tonight. It was so good last time."

It was dark when they left the restaurant around nine, but the streets were well-lit and they'd made the ten-minute walk home many times before. They waved to some friends as they passed the window of one of the small bars in the town center.

"I didn't see Bill and Jean at the concert," said the man.

"They were there, a few rows behind us."

"Pity. I would've asked them to join us for dinner."

They made their way down Sea Street. Their house was lit up by the security lighting.

"That raccoon is back," said the woman.

"So I see."

"You're going to have to get rid of it. It's becoming a pest."

"He's harmless enough."

"Easy for you to say. I'm always the one picking up the garbage."

"All part of the charm of living away from the city," said the man, putting his arm around his wife's shoulder. "It's getting a little chilly."

They unlocked the front door and walked in. As the man reached out to hit the light switch, they were suddenly pushed from behind. Two masked men rushed through the door, knocking the couple off their feet.

The attackers didn't say a word as they dragged their victims through to the living room. They used ropes to tie their hands behind their backs and made them lie face down on the floor. One of the men held a pistol to the woman's head.

"Please don't hurt my wife," said the man. The intruder did not reply.

"There's money in the kitchen. Please take it," said the woman.

Again, there was no reply. The other assailant darted around the house, checking each room and turning off the lights, before returning to the living room. He shook his head at his accomplice.

"If you're looking for the safe, let me up and I'll open it for you. You can take everything, but please don't harm us," said the man.

The masked men looked at each other.

"Try to stay calm, Tom. Remember your heart," said the woman.

"Please—let me show you the safe." The man tried to stand.

The intruder with the pistol cuffed the man across the side of his face with the gun. He picked up a cushion, put it to the man's head first and then the woman's, and shot them in the back of their heads. His accomplice dipped his gloved fingers in the pool of blood and wrote on the white wall of the living room: *FOR RAUL.*

The intruders left the house from the back door and jumped aboard a small motorboat waiting for them at the edge of the water. The boat was out of the harbor five minutes later, disappearing into the darkness of the bay.

CHAPTER 32

Merriman received the phone call from his sister, Jo, the next morning.

"I just can't believe it," he said. "Murdered."

"I need you here, Mark," said Jo. "I can't face this on my own."

"Of course. I want to be there."

"I was talking to them on the phone yesterday morning. It's just so..."

"Did the police say anything at all?"

"They won't let us into Mom and Dad's house. They say they need to preserve the crime scene."

"Did they say anything else? Was there a break-in?"

"All they said was that they were treating their deaths as murder, but nothing more. It's all so frightening. It just doesn't feel real."

"I'll be there this afternoon, Jo. Don't worry."

"I'll pick you up from Portland airport if you let me have your flight details."

Merriman canceled his meetings for the next few days. He explained to his team what he knew, then took the first flight to Maine, where Jo collected him. Throughout the hour's drive to Camden, Merriman asked her to retell what she knew, every detail she could remember hearing from the police, so he could try to piece together what had happened.

The police had been called at eight that morning. Their father's golf partner was due to collect him from Sea Street at seven-thirty. When he arrived at the house, all of the curtains were drawn closed and there was no answer at the door, even though the car was parked on the drive. He tried phoning the house several times, but it kept cutting to the answering machine, so he called the police. An hour later, the police broke in and discovered the bodies in the lounge. They'd found Jo's phone number in their father's diary and called her with the news.

"Did they tell you anything about what actually happened to Mom and Dad?" asked Merriman.

"Nothing at all. They just said they'd been killed. I can't believe this. How could anyone do this to an elderly couple? They weren't a threat to anyone. These things just don't happen in Camden. They were supposed to be safe there."

"When we get to Mom and Dad's, I'll make sure the police let me in so I can find out what happened."

"I'm glad you're here, Mark," she said, no longer able to hold back her tears.

They sat in silence for the remainder of the drive, and Merriman gazed out of the window. *I hope to God this has nothing to do with my work.*

When they pulled onto Sea Street, the road was blocked with police tape, so Jo parked outside the library and they walked over.

"You can't come through here, sir," said the swaggering police officer manning the perimeter.

"That house belongs to our parents. I need to get through," Merriman replied, already lifting up the tape. The policeman waved over a senior officer.

"He says he's family," he said, still blocking Merriman's path.

"Get out of my way," said Merriman.

"This is a crime scene, sir. We can't let you through," said the senior officer.

Merriman took out his DEA badge and flashed it at the officers. "I'm not taking no for an answer."

The senior officer looked at the badge and tapped his colleague on the shoulder. "I'm sorry, Mr. Merriman. If you don't mind wearing protective clothing, I guess we could let you in. We need to preserve any forensic evidence," he said, lifting the tape. "I hope you understand."

"That's okay. Jo, I think you'd best wait in the car for me." Jo walked back to the car. She'd already made it clear to her brother she didn't want to go in there.

The junior officer brought Merriman a forensic suit, and he slipped it on before following the senior officer into his parents' home. When they reached the lounge, the senior officer stopped and put his hand on Merriman's shoulder.

"I'm afraid it ain't pretty. There's a lot of blood in the room, sir."

Merriman took in a lungful of air. "I can handle it."

He followed the officer into the lounge, where the smell of blood hit him first. His eyes darted around the floor. Very little disturbance to the furniture and no evidence of a struggle. He took a step back when he saw the police outlines of where the bodies had been found. He'd seen these many times before, but this was different. This time, it was personal. He struggled to hold back the vomit, steadying himself against the door.

"Are you okay, sir?" asked the police officer.

"I think so. Is there anything you can tell me about the attack?" asked Merriman, fighting back the tears.

"What I can share with you is that your parents were shot in the back of the head from close range as they were lying on the floor. There's no obvious forced entry so we may be dealing with someone they knew."

Merriman already knew the evidence pointed to a professional execution. He recognized the signs but said nothing.

"Does this mean anything to you?" The officer was pointing across the room over Merriman's shoulder.

Merriman turned around and had to prop himself against the side unit when he saw the words painted in blood on the wall. "FOR RAUL" At that moment, he knew exactly who was behind the execution of his parents.

Oh, Lord, no.

He raced out of the house to get some air. Jo jumped out of the car and ran over to her brother.

"Mark, are you all right? It must have been awful in there."

"I'm okay."

"You don't look okay."

"They were both shot in the head. Our parents were executed. Killed in cold blood."

"Oh my G—"

"I'm to blame, Jo." He fought to hold back the tears. "I've been so stupid. It's all my fault."

"How could you be? You're not making any sense, Mark."

"This has to do with my work. Please forgive me." Merriman covered his face with both hands. Jo hugged him, and he finally let the tears flow. "I'm so sorry."

CHAPTER 33

It was a warm, sunny Sunday morning, and Kent was having breakfast with Sarah in their conservatory. He'd often sit and enjoy the view across the Welland valley from that room and, because of its good light level, he'd use it for reading the weekend newspapers.

"Why the long face?" asked Sarah.

"I'm fine."

"It's just you seem very quiet."

"I'm okay."

"Something's troubling you. You've been like this for a while."

Kent knew she was right, but he couldn't tell her the ugly truth. *Your husband's been unfaithful, he's being blackmailed, probably being followed by dangerous criminals, and our lives may well be in danger.*

"Things are difficult at work at the moment."

"I thought the business was going well. You're always going on about the deals you've been doing with Tritona."

"A couple of deals are going wrong and they could impact on our fund's performance. That's all it is."

I hate lying to Sarah, but what choice do I have? he thought. *When I've figured a way out of this mess, I'll tell her.*

"It's the nature of what you do, John. Not even you can succeed in every deal."

"I know. You're right." He pushed his half-finished breakfast away and stood. "Do you fancy going out for a walk? It seems a shame sitting indoors on such a wonderful day."

"Great idea. Where shall we go to walk off some of that stress? How about Rutland Water."

The next morning, Kent was in his office when his phone rang. "I have Mr. Baumgart for you," said Tara.

"Hello, Dieter. What can I do for you?"

Kent still hadn't worked out whether Baumgart was an innocent in all of this. It was very unlikely, but until he was certain, he'd decided to play things straight and to act as normally as possible; whatever normal was in these circumstances.

"Some good news. We have another transaction we'd like you to handle for us," said Baumgart. "It's a big one."

Kent had no choice but to go along with Tritona's wishes, even if each additional transaction was getting him more deeply involved. Each deal would count further against him if it was subsequently discovered by the authorities that Tritona was backed by criminals, and he hadn't reported his suspicions. It would look as though he'd been complicit in the whole thing. But Tritona, or the people behind them, had him over a barrel.

"Great. What is it?" He tried hard to sound enthusiastic.

"We've heard the UK government is planning to sell off the high-speed electric train line between London and the Channel Tunnel. It's called 'High Speed 1,' I believe."

"That's right. In order to reduce the level of government debt, there are plans to sell off a number of nationally-owned assets. To be honest, we haven't considered bidding for them as the returns from such deals are far lower than our normal target range. The other thing is that there are a large number of infrastructure funds chasing these assets, and they just bid up the price. We prefer deals that aren't auctioned this way, so we can negotiate better terms." When Kent sensed he was trying too hard to dissuade Baumgart from making this investment, he stopped talking.

"I understand all that. However, our investors have just

given us a lot more capital to deploy. The returns on cash are poor at the moment, so we're prepared to accept lower returns if we can put the capital into high-quality assets such as this."

Kent did not know what else to say. Now he was being asked to be the front for Tritona in the purchase of an asset from the UK government. *How bad can this get?* He made one more attempt to dissuade Baumgart by pointing out the poor returns, but the man seemed prepared to accept them.

What the hell. "We'd be delighted to handle the negotiations for you, Dieter. We'll flag your interest in the asset with the advisers handling the auction for the government and take it from there."

"Many thanks. Keep us informed of your progress. Remember, we have no objection to paying a full price for this asset."

"I'll let you know how we get on. 'Bye for now."

Resting his head in his hands, Kent exhaled loudly. How could he represent Tritona as a reputable buyer with the UK government? He knew they were anything but reputable and, if this all came out, the authorities were bound to say CBC was doing it for the money. If that happened, Kent and his partners would be facing a long prison sentence.

He asked Kirkland to handle the day-to-day aspects of the deal. While he had no appetite for the transaction, he needed to be seen taking all of the right steps. He did his best to sound keen on the deal when he briefed her, always conscious of the microphones listening to them. They spent an hour in his office discussing the deal and how to approach the auction.

"Are they crazy?" asked Kirkland, shaking her head. "Tritona does understand the poor returns they're likely to receive from this?" She was raising precisely the right investment issue, as usual. *Sometimes, she's too damn bright.*

"They do. I've explained all that to Dieter, but he's prepared to accept lower returns in exchange for the certainty of the yield from this high-quality asset."

"Is the deal going into the fund or will it be held by Tritona?"

"It'll be held by Tritona."

"Thank God for that. At least it won't dilute our overall fund returns."

"Dead right. It wouldn't be a suitable investment for our fund in any event. This is not a distressed deal."

"I'll need to make it clear to the government's advisers we're not the principal in this and that we act for Tritona."

"I agree," said Kent.

He knew the process involved in bidding for government assets only too well. It would mean CBC vouching for the identity and good standing of Tritona. And the government's advisers would simply accept the word of CBC as a regulated and reputable firm. Each step down this path would take Kent and his firm nearer to the cliff edge.

CHAPTER 34

The funeral service for Merriman's parents was more difficult than he'd expected. Knowing he was responsible for their deaths had deprived him of sleep, and the guilt was eating up his insides. While he was exhausted, he was comforted by the large turnout of friends and family. There were many DEA staff members at the service. Merriman's own team was represented, and there were many former colleagues of his father from his years in the service. It soothed Merriman a little to be reminded of the affection and respect these people held for his parents. *They were good people who'd made a difference with their lives*, he thought. *That should be celebrated.*

As he stood above his parents' grave, Merriman vowed he'd never rest until Felix Safuentes was brought down, and every penny of his seized. *I'll make it my life's work to capture that animal and put him down. Whatever it takes. I owe it to you, Mom and Dad, and to the agents who lost their lives through my stupidity and impatience.*

He was back at his desk a week later. On his third morning back, he was summoned to Robert Butler's office. Although Butler was the most senior member of the DEA's leadership team, like Merriman, he'd come up the hard way, rising through the ranks on merit and years spent in the field. He was a career DEA man in his late fifties, with a reputation for taking no prisoners and not suffering fools lightly. He'd told Merriman many times how much he respected his work and the progress he was making in the war against the cartels.

"Come on in, Mark," said Butler when Merriman tapped on

his open office door.

"You wanted to see me?"

"Yeah. Grab a seat. Can't tell you how sorry I was to hear about your parents. It must've been tough for you. Your father was a good man."

"Thanks."

"How are you coping?"

Merriman bit on his upper lip. "What makes it so hard to accept is that I was the one who authorized the attempted capture of Safuentes. If only I'd..."

Butler shook his head. "You can't blame yourself. The work we do is fraught with risk and, sometimes, we make mistakes. It goes with the territory. Come on, you know that."

"I guess so." Merriman had spent the last three weeks beating himself up. It helped to know Butler, at least, understood what he'd been trying to do. "I'm trying to channel my energy into our work on the Caruana assets. I plan to hit those bastards hard."

"We can do more than that." Butler got up from his desk and closed his office door.

Merriman frowned. "What do you have in mind?"

"We take attacks on our people on U.S. soil as nothing short of an act of war. These idiots have no idea what they've unleashed."

"What do you mean, Bob?"

"The murder of your parents is a provocative act. They invaded our country and attacked our citizens. If they think they can do this and get away with it, there'll be no stopping them. We've gotta send the cartel a clear message they've crossed the line."

Merriman sat forward in his chair. "You have something in mind?"

"This is in strict confidence, Mark, okay?"

"Sure. What is it?"

"You need to keep this to your senior team members only."

"Understood."

Butler leaned forward and lowered his voice. "The Secretary of State has cleared this at the highest level of government. She's authorized a black ops team to attack the Caruana headquarters in Mexico."

"You mean Isla Tiburon?"

"You bet I do. The operation is not official and will remain secret. You know as well as I do what this means." Butler leaned further forward, leaning his elbows onto his desk. "It represents an armed incursion on a sovereign state."

"This is unprecedented."

"It is, but this is war. The U.S. must defend itself. The Secretary of State cannot allow the cartel's actions to go unpunished, but she knows we'd never get the Mexican government to sanction an assault on their soil. Besides, we're not entirely sure who we can trust over there."

"I hear you on that, Bob. Obviously, I'll do everything I can to help."

"That's why I asked you to come and see me. Your team has most of the current intel on the Caruana headquarters. I need you to share what you know with the people heading up the black ops team. I'll get them to contact you."

"We'll give them everything we have. If we pull this off, Felix Safuentes will be no more than a footnote in history."

CHAPTER 35

The distinctive roar of the Sikorsky Super Stallion's seven-blade rotor could be heard from miles away. They came in from the east so the prevailing wind would carry the sound away from the cartel's headquarters. Each one of the eight helicopters carried fifty-five heavily armed U.S. Navy SEALs. It was still dark as they approached Isla Tiburon at 4 a.m.

Special operations snipers had been dropped onto the island an hour before the attack. They'd been ready to take out any guards patrolling the outside, but that wasn't necessary; there was no one around. Consequently, as the aircraft came in to land, the SEALs were confident that no one inside the building would be aware of the impending attack. Surprise was on their side.

Merriman was with Bob Butler and senior defense staff in a special war room at the Pentagon. They sat along one side of a conference table watching a live video feed of the impending attack from helmet cameras worn by many of the SEALs.

"It feels like we're with them," said Merriman close to Butler's ear.

Butler nodded. "It's clever technology."

Merriman's heart was thumping in his chest at the thought of the attack. He could feel the adrenaline racing through him. This was the moment they would turn the war by wiping Safuentes off the face of the earth. *This is for you, Mom and Dad.*

The helicopters landed four hundred yards away, and the troops jumped from the aircraft four at a time and ran toward the building. After disabling the CCTV cameras, they placed explosive charges against the large metal doors and blew them open. Half of the men rushed into the stairwell and down to the first floor, where intelligence reports had indicated they'd find the sleeping quarters and most of the cartel's personnel.

There was no one there.

"What the fuck is this?" said Butler.

"Absolute silence, please," barked the senior defense officer at the head of the conference table.

When the SEALs turned to run back to the stairwell, they were met by a hail of bullets from the cartel's enforcers; they'd walked into a trap. Somehow, the operation had been compromised.

Blood suddenly filled the lens of the helmet camera linked to the war room. The operator in the war room switched to another camera. Men were falling to the ground, torn apart by the bullets.

"My God," said Merriman under his breath. *This is a bloodbath.*

Butler held his head in his hands, unable to watch the carnage.

By the time the other half of the U.S. personnel reached the first floor, the enforcers had disappeared. The first group of U.S. personnel had suffered massive injuries and many fatalities.

Moments later, the video screen filled with bright light as the remaining SEALs threw explosives down the stairwell to clear the area beneath them. They followed up with grenades thrown into the second-floor entrance. When they entered the space, they were sprayed with bullets from enforcers lined along the back of the room. It took fifteen minutes and seven casualties to eliminate the enemy on that floor before the SEALs could make their way down to the next level.

A shard of shrapnel hit the helmet lens as explosive charges lit up the accounting floor. The place had been booby-trapped. The senior officer in the war room nodded to the video operator. The view switched to another camera as a door ricocheted off the wall, narrowly missing the camera. Merriman flinched. When the room came back into focus, it was obvious from the blood on the walls that many of the troops in there had been killed by the explosions.

A fire took hold of the building, filling the space with smoke. Flames licked at the heels of the retreating SEALs. They regrouped at the helicopters to put on breathing masks before making their way back down the stairwell. The thick smoke made progress difficult and slow. Visibility back at the Pentagon was poor, but the sound recorded the continuing slaughter. Merriman could only imagine the horror of fighting an invisible enemy in the dark.

Gradually, the SEALs made their way to the lowest levels and to Jivaro's suite. The smoke thinned and visibility was restored, as the SEALs were now below the fire at this level. In the minutes that followed, they found no cartel personnel left in the building. The enemy had simply vanished. They'd later discover an elevator from Jivaro's suite to the sea, providing an escape route for any remaining enforcers.

An hour and a half after landing, the Americans had captured none of the fifteen lieutenants and there was no sign of Felix Safuentes. The SEALs loaded up the helicopters with their wounded and the handful of remaining injured enforcers and returned to their aircraft carrier.

"Gentlemen, we have just witnessed an unmitigated disaster," said the defense officer after the live feed was terminated. "The cartel must have known we were coming. This was a turkey shoot."

"We have to find the leak. All of our operations will be at risk until we do," said Merriman. "This could put us back years."

"When we find him, I'll personally string him up," said Butler. He had the stoop of a defeated man.

The subsequent debriefing was sober listening for Merriman. The SEALs had lost almost a third of their men in the firefight, with many more badly injured. His hopes of capturing Safuentes, discovering promising intelligence from the cartel's IT systems, and avenging the death of his parents had come to nothing. Instead, they had suffered a massive setback and, to make things worse, now they knew the cartel must have an informer on the inside at the DEA.

CHAPTER 36

A month later, Kent was returning to his office after the usual Tuesday morning investment committee meeting when Tara handed him a note.

"It's a telephone message from a Mr. Cartwright from a firm called Adderley Dickins," she said. "He wants to speak to you about a new deal opportunity."

Kent walked to his desk and threw the message on top of all the others next to his phone. He'd make the call later, if he felt like it. In normal circumstances, he'd deal with a new investment inquiry immediately. In the past, there was nothing quite like the excitement of a new deal, but these were far from normal times. He'd lost most of his appetite for new business. Another transaction was just one more reason for the authorities to throw the book at him, if it was ever discovered he was investing criminal money.

Kirkland stood at Kent's door. "Do you have a moment, John?" she asked.

"Sure, come on in."

"I'm not sure about this high-speed rail deal. We're beyond the first auction with our opening bid, and the final bids are due in by the end of next week."

"What's the problem? Sounds like you're making good progress."

"I've been liaising with the Tritona team, and they've told me to make sure we win the bid by paying whatever it takes."

Is she becoming suspicious? Kent thought. *She realizes paying too high a price for this asset is economic madness.* He had to make sure Tritona got what it wanted, no matter how poor the prospective investment returns might be. If necessary, he resolved he would take over the running of the rail deal himself.

"I raised the issue of returns with Dieter a few days back. He's still comfortable paying a very high price for this quality of asset. His plan is to raise the end customer pricing on the rail line if they need to." Kent was still playing to the hidden microphones, so he did his best to rationalize Tritona's actions, but he was dealing with his most intelligent partner.

"It's a big risk, though. He may not be able to raise prices with the political flak that would create. I can't see this one ever paying."

"Believe me, they're aware of the risks. Besides, the poorer returns will not sit inside our fund, remember. The company will be held directly by Tritona. We'll just manage it for them."

"Okay," Kirkland said, looking less than convinced. "I just needed to make sure they understand the implications of paying to win this thing."

"They do. We've done our job by pointing out the reduced investment returns. In spite of that, Tritona wants to acquire the asset. Now we have to win it for them." Kent picked up his phone as though he needed to make a call. *Got to get rid of her.* "Is there anything else?"

Kirkland took the hint. "No. Thanks for your help." She looked confused as she stood up to leave.

After Kirkland left Kent's office, Tara came in. "That Mr. Cartwright has been on again. He says he must speak to you about his deal today as it's time sensitive. He was quite pushy, almost rude," she said.

Kent held up his left palm. "Okay. Okay. I'm doing it now." He picked up the message from the pile and punched in the numbers as Tara left.

"Can I speak to Mr. Cartwright, please? This is John Kent from CBC returning his call."

"Mr. Kent, thanks for coming back to me," said Cartwright.

"Sorry about the urgency. We have a deal which I think is just right for CBC, but there's not much time to do it, if you're interested."

"Can you give me an outline of the deal on the phone? I want to be sure it meets our investment criteria." Kent smirked as he said those words. Since acting for Tritona, CBC had completed many deals way off CBC's investment strategy. They did whatever Tritona wanted these days.

"Of course. Adderley Dickins is a London-based corporate finance boutique advisory firm. We only do a couple of deals a year as we have a very small team. Consequently, we're very selective over which deals we take on. We only take on winners."

Kent had heard all this before. Most advisors would take on any client if they were prepared to pay a fee. He'd make his own mind up if the deal was worth pursuing or not. "That's comforting to hear. Tell me a little about the opportunity," he said.

"We're advising the management team of Europe's largest independent insurance broking business. I'd prefer not to say the name without a confidentiality agreement in place, but I can tell you the business is very profitable and always has been."

"Why do they need our money?"

"Unfortunately, their bank is one of the many that have run into trouble during the financial crisis and it's reducing all non-committed lines of credit."

"I recognize that story."

"I'm sure you do. We're seeing a lot of bad behavior by the banks at the moment. They're running around like headless chickens. Unfortunately, my client has no committed term facilities—"

"Let me guess. The bank has pulled the overdraft facilities."

"Got it in one. They need the overdraft to meet the usual seasonal peak. Bluntly, my client needs access to cash, and quickly, or else it will fail."

This was exactly the sort of distressed deal Kent had set up CBC to do. Although he had recently been trying to find credible reasons to reject new investment opportunities, he knew he had to walk a fine line. His phone was bugged, so he could hardly kill off a good one like this without arousing suspicion.

"How much do they need?"

"Two hundred million pounds within a month. The requirement is only for three months, though. After that, they'll have cash on deposit again once the premium income starts to come in."

"That sounds like a CBC deal. I'd like to hear more." *Shit!*

"That was our judgment, too. In the short time available, I hope you'll understand we've not been able to prepare a formal fundraising document."

"That shouldn't be a problem." Kent thought for a moment about using the absence of a business plan to kick the deal into the long grass, but many deals came in without one, so that wouldn't be a credible reason. "We can learn what we need from a meeting with the management team."

"Can I suggest we arrange for you to meet the team here, at our London offices, early next week?"

"Yes, that would work well for me. I'll get my PA to arrange a date for me to come down. In the meantime, if there's any background reading you can send me, I'd appreciate it by email ahead of the meeting."

"Of course. I'll also send over a confidentiality agreement, too. I look forward to meeting you."

"'Bye for now."

Kent asked Tara to make the meeting and travel arrangements. Rather than risk another Kirkland situation—having to deal with too many awkward questions—he decided he'd handle this deal personally. Besides, it would be nice to get out of the office for a while and find something distracting.

CHAPTER 37

The following Tuesday, Kent caught the 7:30 a.m. London train from Peterborough. Parking the BMW in the station parking lot reminded him of the frightening experience some weeks earlier. He hadn't seen those men since, but he was convinced they were around somewhere. They'd made their point; they'd let him know he was being monitored.

He unfolded his *Financial Daily* and sat back in his first-class seat to enjoy a quiet read. Rarely during the week did he have an opportunity to read the whole newspaper without interruption. Train journeys were an exception, and he even managed to get as far as the foreign news at the back of the paper. There was a long story about another earthquake in Japan and then an article on America's war on drugs. *It's all so bloody depresssing*, he thought as the train reached King's Cross.

He walked over to the taxi rank, just beating a crowd of tourists to the front of the line. He took a cab to Paternoster Square, some fifteen minutes away. Since he had an hour to kill before meeting the Adderley Dickins people, he'd arranged to meet Jonathan Gateley for a coffee at the Caffé Zero near his offices. Whenever Kent had spare time in London, he'd try to meet up with Gateley to get an update on Oakham Fiduciary Services. After all, following Baumgart's prompt, it was now a subsidiary of CBC, so Kent was ultimately responsible for it nowadays. Besides, Gateley always welcomed a coffee break out of the office.

"How's it going, Jonathan?" Kent asked, shaking hands. Gateley had already grabbed two leather chairs near the window overlooking Cheapside. He had two coffees ready and waiting.

"Pretty hectic, actually. Tritona keeps us busy." Gateley rolled his eyes. "They keep acquiring companies and asking us to set up all sorts of esoteric structures for them. They're a very demanding client." He broke into a smile. "They pay well, though."

Kent was convinced Gateley knew nothing sinister about Tritona. He would have received the same compliance information as CBC did about the three families. Unless they'd heard from Henning's Swedish contact, which was unlikely, there's no way they'd have any suspicion.

"They've kept us busy, too." Kent sipped his skinny latte. "Do you see Baumgart much?"

"Not often. Mostly, we deal with him over the phone. There's not really much reason for him to visit us in London. All we hold here are the original records on the various corporate and trust structures we've set up for them. The real decisions are still taken by them in Geneva."

As they spoke, Kent was decided. *Oakham's just a pawn, being used as much as CBC.*

Half an hour later, Kent stood up to leave. "Well, I must be going. I have another meeting at ten."

It was only a ten-minute walk from Cheapside to the offices of Adderley Dickins at Tower Fifty-Four on Old Broad Street, so Kent decided to walk it. He arrived five minutes before his appointment.

The building was one of those tall, modern office towers that Kent really couldn't stand. Soulless places full of corporate drones. He pushed by the obligatory huddle of smokers outside the building and, as soon as he walked through the automatic doors, spotted the long line backed up at the security scanner. Wayne, the outsourced security operator, whose badge said "Here to Serve," was milking his five minutes of power over the executives entering the tower. He kept asking inane questions and took ages to pass briefcases and laptops through his machine.

Every now and then he'd even look in the direction of his screen to see what was being scanned. That delay, and the hassle of obtaining his visitor badge from a separate reception, meant Kent arrived at the thirty-second-floor offices of Adderley Dickins at 10:08 a.m. Arriving late made him appear sloppy and inefficient, which was the last impression he'd want to create; he was a professional.

He stepped out of the elevator and, immediately, was struck by the bright marble and sheet glass reception area. Adderley Dickins appeared to occupy the whole of the thirty-second floor, and it seemed no money had been spared on their surroundings. Expensive pieces of modern art hung on pale walls, and what looked like individually commissioned pieces of furniture were arranged around the waiting area. Kent thought Cartwright had said Adderley Dickins was a small corporate finance house doing only a couple of deals a year. *Those deals must pay really well.*

"I'm from Cambridge Buy-Out Capital. Here to see Mr. Cartwright," Kent said with a smile to the pretty receptionist. She smiled back at him. *Nice teeth.*

"You must be Mr. Kent. Please take a seat, and I'll let him know you've arrived."

Kent sat on the sofa at the back of the vast space, furthest away from the noisy sixty-inch flat-screen Panasonic. He shook his head; yet another TV blaring out at visitors, broadcasting mindless drivel.

"Do you think you could turn that thing down?" he shouted across to the receptionist while pointing to the TV.

"I'm so sorry, Mr. Kent," she said as she walked over and turned it off.

He immediately felt guilty for causing such a fuss. He'd always been impatient, but lately, with all the strain he'd been under, he was increasingly quick-tempered and critical. There was a time when he would have been ecstatic about the money he was now making, but not any longer. The nightmare of the past few months had changed everything for him. Kent felt dirty and used.

"Thanks," he said, smiling at the young woman, hoping she'd forgive him.

He took a scribbled file note from his briefcase and scanned it to remind himself of the key aspects of the investment opportunity: Adderley Dickins' client was a profitable insurance broking group in urgent need of two hundred million pounds, or else it would fail; the bank was about to withdraw the company's short-term overdraft facilities; the cash was needed for three months only; and a large equity stake was up for grabs for CBC if it could move quickly. In Kent's old life, this would have been a good one—a great company at death's door, desperate for rescue finance. Back then, he would have been salivating over the enormous return on the transaction if it all stacked up, though that would depend on the caliber of the management team he was about to meet.

"I can take you through now," said the receptionist as she came to collect him.

Kent combed his fingers through his hair, smiled at her again, and then picked up his briefcase. He followed her shapely figure, her tight, short skirt revealing long, attractive legs. Suddenly, he felt a pang of guilt. *You bloody fool. That's what got you in trouble in the first place.*

They walked along a wide, glass corridor past several empty rooms. It seemed strange there was no one else in any of the offices; no telephones ringing, no tapping of keyboards, none of the regular sounds of a busy work environment. The only sound was the echoing of the young woman's high heels as they clicked against the white marble floor.

At the end of the corridor was a large meeting room with a view over the London skyline. Kent took his eyes off the woman's rear and looked through the glass paneling. Three men were sitting at a boardroom table. He assumed two of them were members of the management team and one must be Cartwright.

"Mr. Kent, thanks for coming," said the man in the dark blue suit as he stood up, power-shook Kent's hand, and then closed the meeting room door.

The man was a good five inches shorter than Kent's six foot. *No doubt the viselike grip is to make up for his lack of height,* Kent thought. He had an American accent too. Cartwright didn't have an accent when he called about the deal last week. The other two men didn't bother to stand or introduce themselves, hardly the best way to impress a prospective investor here to rescue their business. *The price of the deal just went up.*

"Good to meet you," said Kent, looking at his host and deliberately avoiding eye contact with the bad-mannered peasants.

"Can I get you a coffee?"

"No. Thank you. I've just had one. Water would be fine." Kent walked to the far side of the room and placed his briefcase on the mahogany table. "Which one of you is Mr. Cartwright?" The three men looked at each other as though Kent had asked a difficult question. "They get harder from here, guys." There were no smiles; the wit seemed lost on all of them.

"The thing is, we've brought you here on a false pretext," said the American.

"I don't understand."

Kent looked across the table and scrutinized them. The three men were wearing almost identical white shirts and dark blue suits. Something was wrong, but Kent couldn't quite put his finger on it. The one doing the talking had a military-style buzz cut, a style that struck Kent as hardly corporate professional. He looked like he was in his mid-thirties, very lean, and clearly worked out. He had an intense frown and kept glancing at the smartphone in his left hand, as though he was expecting an important call, or needed to be somewhere else soon. The man appeared in a desperate hurry to get down to business.

"Is the deal off?" Kent said.

"There is no deal," said the American. "Take a seat."

Kent remained standing. He didn't appreciate the aggressive tone. "Then what am I doing here?"

"Please, sit down and I'll explain." The American poured

Kent a glass of water.

Kent sat, but left his unopened briefcase on the table; he wasn't planning on staying long. "Which one of you is Mr. Cartwright?"

"None of us."

Kent bolted upright. "So who—"

"Cartwright doesn't exist." The American looked like he wanted to fight.

Kent forced a laugh. "I must be in the wrong office."

"That's funny. If you just give me a moment, I'll explain."

"You've got thirty seconds before I'm out of here."

The American put down his phone, leaned forward on his elbows, and clasped his hands together. He glanced at his colleagues before staring at Kent.

"My name is Mark Merriman." He paused. "I'm the Head of Intelligence at the DEA."

CHAPTER 38

Kent went cold inside. "The DEA?" he said, deep furrows forming across his brow. He knew something was wrong from the moment he'd set foot in reception. Was this how it all ended?

Merriman nodded. "The U.S. Drug Enforcement Administration."

"I know what it means." Kent paused, then said, "You people must have me mixed up with someone else."

"There's no mistake."

"There has to—"

Merriman raised his right hand. "Just hear me out."

"What's the DEA got to do with me?"

Merriman ignored the question. "These gentlemen here are Special Agents Whitlock and Young." The others lowered their heads a little as their names were mentioned.

Kent gave them a condescending once-over. That's why they'd never bothered to introduce themselves earlier. They looked like a couple of well-dressed bruisers, nowhere near as polished as the one doing all the talking.

"I don't care who you are. I came here to discuss a deal. Now, is someone going to tell me what the hell's going on?"

"There never was a deal. The firm of Adderley Dickins doesn't exist. We're the only ones here." Merriman pointed to the offices. "All this you see around us is made up."

Kent stood. "I'm leaving. I don't know who you people think I am."

"Sit down, John. You're gonna hear this." Merriman's tone made it clear it wasn't a request.

Kent sat. He looked at his watch, shook his head, and exhaled loudly through his nose. "This had better be good."

Merriman paced the room. "What we're about to share with you is confidential. You can't speak to anyone about it, not even your wife, Sarah. Understood?"

Kent flinched and uncrossed his arms. *Jesus, these people must have been monitoring me as well.* "How do you know my wife's name?"

"We know everything about you," said Special Agent Whitlock with a self-satisfied smirk.

Kent instantly disliked him and the way he kept cracking his fingers and playing with the oversize silver fraternity ring on his right hand, as though he wouldn't think twice about using it as a knuckle-duster.

Special Agent Young jumped in with his two cents' worth. "Where you live, your family, everywhere you worked before you started CBC. We know you're a bright boy, a first at Cambridge and an MBA from Harvard."

Kent didn't think much of him, either. *Another muscle-head.*

"Okay." Kent's mouth was dry as he spoke. "You have my attention, now get to the point; I haven't got all day." He gulped down some water.

"The reason we brought you here under the pretext of a new deal was to avoid any awkward questions from your team at CBC," said Merriman. He stopped pacing. "Or from the people at Tritona."

These guys have done their homework, thought Kent. "I'm listening." A bead of sweat ran down his brow. He wiped it by pretending to smooth back his hair.

"We know all your investment funds come from Tritona in Geneva. Without them, you don't have a business."

"And that's your business because?"

"Because, wise guy, the people at Tritona don't get their money from where they say they do."

"You don't know what you're talking about."

"I'll spell it out for you." Merriman walked over to Kent's side of the table and pulled up a chair next to him. He sat facing Kent, leaning forward, with his elbows resting on his knees. "Tritona isn't what it appears to be. It's a front for the Mexican Caruana drug cartel, the most powerful organized crime group on the planet." He paused and stared right into Kent's eyes.

Kent maintained eye contact and tried not to blink, his heart pounding in his chest as the news began to sink in. *Fuck! This is far worse than I'd imagined. There's no backing out now. I'm in too deep. They definitely killed Anton, so they'd think nothing of killing me or Sarah.*

Kent lowered his gaze. "That makes no sense."

"All of Tritona's money comes from the Caruana cartel. None of it is legit, in spite of what they may have told you."

"That's impossible." *Where the hell was this conversation going? Was he about to be arrested? Did they think he'd been colluding with these gangsters all along? Would they even care he was being blackmailed?* Every impulse in Kent's body told him to get out of there.

Merriman remained silent.

"Do you think we're a bunch of amateurs?" asked Kent, his face full of incredulity. "We carried out comprehensive compliance checks before we took Tritona on as an investor, and they all came out clean." They did everything by the book when Tritona first emerged as a potential investor. Kent didn't know about their criminal backers back then. He wanted, no needed, to get this on the record. He was not a criminal.

Merriman stood and walked over to the large window, with his back to Kent. "I'm sure you checked them out, John. We know you're a professional. We know you've nothing to do with their illicit activities." Whitlock and Young shook their heads no, as if to confirm he couldn't possibly be involved.

Kent couldn't tell whether or not they were mocking him, so said nothing.

Merriman turned to face Kent. "But we need your help."

"I can't see how I can help you. I don't know anything about this."

"We know where the cartel's money comes from. We even know how it ends up in Geneva under Tritona's control. From there, however, the trail goes cold. We know who the key players are, which is how we found you. You're in a great position to provide the documentary evidence we need."

"You think I'm a key player? You guys need to do your homework."

"CBC manages most of Tritona's investment assets." Merriman pointed his right index finger at Kent. "That makes you a key player as far as we're concerned."

"You're wasting your time with me. I can't tell you anything."

"Don't play games with us. We need evidence linking those investments back to Tritona. You can access the documents we need. We both know that."

"I can't help you."

"You've gotta be shitting me, right? You can't believe you can continue to operate as usual? I've just told you where your investment funds are coming from and that your investors are the biggest source of illicit narcotics entering the U.S. market. CBC no longer has a business. It's finished."

Kent had known his business was finished the moment he'd discovered Tritona's criminal involvement. That was not news to him. "Of course, you can prove all of this?"

Merriman looked over to his colleagues. "Is this guy serious?" Whitlock and Young laughed and shook their heads.

"How do I even know you're who you say you are?"

"College boy here thinks we're the amateurs." Merriman took out his DEA badge, walked over to Kent, and thrust it under his nose. "Does this make you feel any better?"

Kent didn't bother to look at it.

"I didn't think so," said Merriman, with increasing venom. "Don't fucking pretend you think we're making this all up," he shouted. "We've been tracking the cartel for years. This is a massive investigation. We haven't come all this way to play games with you. We're here to finish the job, and you're going to help us."

"I can't help you. I'm sorry." *Go find some other idiot to put his life on the line.*

Merriman sat next to Kent again. This time, he pulled his chair closer, his face just a few inches from Kent's. He lowered his voice. "John, if you don't help us, then we'll have to assume you're part of Caruana's criminal network. We'll assume you're in it for the money, because that's how it looks. You see where this is going, don't you? Losing your business is not the worst it gets. Think it through for a moment."

"I have nothing to fear. I've done nothing wrong."

For a split second, Kent thought about cooperating with the DEA, but it made no sense. It was clear they'd done a lot of work on this, but without access to CBC's files they didn't have enough to put him away. Not yet, at least. He was certain the Caruana cartel would think nothing of killing anyone found helping Merriman. Right now, there was no contest.

Merriman thumped the table hard. Kent jolted back in his seat. "When we get the evidence we need, and make no mistake, sooner or later, we'll get it, you'll go down with everyone else. We're offering you the chance to walk away from this, in exchange for saving us a lot of time and unnecessary effort."

"If you want to be difficult," added Whitlock, "we'll have your ass extradited to the U.S. Forget the fourteen-year sentence for money laundering here in the UK. Conspiracy, wire fraud, tax evasion, you name it. We'll have you locked up for the rest of your life."

"Have you finished?" Kent wanted to tell them all to go to hell.

"You're making a very big mistake," said Merriman. "This is the biggest decision you're ever going to make. Don't get it wrong. Think of Sarah and what this means for her. How will she cope on her own if you're growing old in some U.S. prison?"

"Growing old will be a luxury," said Young. "The cartel's likely to get to you first. We got plenty of their boys behind bars." "Someone like you'd fit in real well."

"I assume I'm free to go?" Kent stood, grabbed his briefcase, and started making his way to the door.

Merriman got off his chair and blocked Kent's path.

Kent stopped. *Move out of my way, little man.* If it wasn't for the two bouncers, he would have pushed his way past. "I'm leaving."

"For the moment, you're okay to leave, but you need to think this through, John." Merriman handed Kent a card. "Contact me on that number when you see sense." He stood aside and opened the door.

Kent breathed in the rush of fresh air as he left the room.

"But don't leave it too long," shouted Merriman as Kent hurried along the corridor. "Pretty soon, we'll find the evidence we need elsewhere, and then you won't have a choice."

Kent raced out of the building and made his way back along Old Broad Street, looking for a cab. He had no idea what his next move would be, but he was certain Merriman was not the type to give up.

CHAPTER 39

The fast catamaran took just over an hour and a half to make the crossing from Naples to the island of Capri. The water-level views of Mount Vesuvius across the Bay of Naples were a magnet for the tourists aboard the vessel.

Kent and his wife first visited the island as university students. Back then, all they could afford was a week's camping under canvas, living off beer and pizza and falling in love. Since that time, they'd returned to the island too many times to remember. It was their favorite getaway in the Mediterranean.

When he suggested to Sarah that they spend a few days on Capri, she didn't need persuading. She needed only a couple of days to make arrangements for colleagues to cover her patient workload at the hospital, and they were off. They booked themselves into the best hotel on the island, in a suite overlooking Tragara Point, a rocky outcrop just off the coast. Most days, they spent their time relaxing at the hotel then, around 6 p.m., they'd take a walk into the main square to mingle with the locals. They liked the quieter feel of the island in the evenings, when all the day-trip tourists had returned to the mainland. Each night they chose another of their regular restaurants for dinner, but always after enjoying apple martini cocktails at their favorite bar on Via Certosa.

It had been a week since Kent's shock meeting with Merriman in London, and he was in need of a break. The last few months had been chaotic, and he was still struggling to comprehend how things had ended up in such a mess. However it happened, he only had himself to blame—his stupid, overarching ambition had blinded him to the risk he'd been running. Now, his life was a disaster; he was alone, in a dangerous trap with no obvious way out.

After three or four days, Kent began to release some of the pressure. He'd even enjoyed a couple of good nights' sleep. If he could have given it all up, and gone back to his simpler student days with Sarah, he'd have done so. They were broke back then, but no less happy.

On the fourth evening, the Kents had dinner on the terrace at La Capannina.

"It's good to see you relaxing for a change," Sarah said. "I've been worried about you, John."

Kent feigned surprise. "Worried?"

"You haven't been yourself for weeks."

"I'm fine. I'm under a lot of pressure at the office. That's all."

"You need to learn how to switch off more. Push some of the workload onto your partners."

"I delegate as much as I can."

"You don't know the meaning of the word. You're such a control freak."

The wine waiter brought over a bottle of Brunello. Kent welcomed the interruption while he poured them both a large glass.

"I love you, Sarah," he said as they clinked glasses.

"So are you going to tell me what's wrong?"

"Nothing's wrong."

"Something's bothering you. I can see it in your face." She reached out to touch his hand.

Kent thought for a moment. Sarah was in almost as much danger as he was, so he had to tell her something. But how, without frightening her?

"It's complicated."

"We have all evening."

They were briefly interrupted by the waiter as he brought over their starter of grilled gamberoni—Sarah's favorite. Kent waited until he had gone to speak again.

"I don't really know how to tell you this." He reached across and squeezed her hand.

"It can't be that bad."

"You know we signed up Tritona a while back?"

"Yes. The people in Geneva?"

Kent nodded. "They were keen to back us and, after Grampian failed, we were desperate to find new investment capital."

"Don't tell me Tritona is about to fail."

"No. It's much worse than that."

Sarah shot him a concerned look, and Kent wondered whether or not to continue.

"You have me worried now." She put down her wine glass. "What is it?"

"I'm sorry, Sarah, but there's no way to dress this up."

"Go on."

Kent looked into her large brown eyes. She had such an angelic face. One of the reasons he loved Sarah so much was because she always saw the best in people. He'd always done his best to shield her from the hard realities of his business life. This was way beyond that. What he was about to tell her would change their lives forever, and it would certainly terrify her. He wanted to stop right there and rewind the conversation. *I can't do this to her.*

"Come on, John."

"I feel so bloody stupid." He paused, searching for the right words. He cleared his throat and looked back into her eyes again. "Tritona is a front for organized crime, and the money we've been investing on their behalf is all illegal drug money."

"Oh my God!" she said, clasping her hands to her mouth. "Oh my God!"

There was no going back now. "I'm so sorry. We were deceived into thinking they were a legitimate organization. They told us a pack of lies and, in my desperation to replace Grampian, I failed to ask enough questions. By the time I found out, it was too late."

"You've got to give the money back. Just give it back."

"It's not that simple. The money has been invested."

"Drugs! Have you reported all this to the police?"

"No." Kent recognized the incredulity in Sarah's eyes. How could he tell her he was being blackmailed, without telling her the reason why?

"Why not? You've got to speak to them. You've no idea what the hell you're dealing with."

"I don't believe Anton's death was an accident."

"What do you mean? What's Anton got to do with this?"

"He and I were discussing Tritona in my office. He was raising questions about where their money came from and telling me how he'd discovered something about their backers. The next morning he was dead."

"But that could be a coincidence. He was killed riding his bike on his way to the office."

Kent knew Sarah needed to believe his business partner's death was a straightforward road accident, but he had to be honest with her. "I don't think so. I think he was murdered."

"This can't be happening. You've got to be wrong."

"Somehow, they knew Anton and I were concerned. They must have thought we were onto them or something."

"But how could they know?"

"I think they were listening to our conversations."

The waiter came over to ask if they were enjoying their meal, and Kent waved him away.

"You think they're monitoring your offices?" Sarah's hands were trembling, and all color had drained from her face.

"That's exactly what I think." Kent knew from the timing of the blackmail note that his offices were bugged, but he couldn't share that with her.

Sarah stared at the table in silence for a few seconds. "Are we safe?"

"I think CBC still has a great deal of value to Tritona. We

move a lot of their illegal money into legitimate assets. They need us. I think we're safe for as long as we cooperate with their money laundering. But if we go to the authorities, if we stop complying..."

"My God! What are we going to do?" Sarah's eyes were welling up.

"I'm sorry, Sarah." Kent reached across the table and held both of her hands. They sat in silence for a while.

"You still have to go to the authorities."

"Don't underestimate the threat if these people discover I've talked. I'm certain Anton was killed as a deterrent. The last thing I'm going to do is put your life at risk."

The waiter came back to clear their plates and asked if they'd like to order dessert, but they'd both lost their appetites. They paid for the meal and left. As they drew near to the hotel, Sarah said, "Promise me something."

"What's that?"

"You'll not keep all this to yourself from now on. Share everything with me, even if you think I won't want to hear it. I can't believe you've been holding on to all this for months and you kept it to yourself."

"I promise. I didn't want to frighten you. I wanted to protect you, but once I found out who we were dealing with, you had to know." He hugged her. "I've been so bloody stupid."

Kent decided not to share with Sarah the conversation with the DEA. He'd already scared the life out of her. What good would it do to heap on more pressure?

CHAPTER 40

Kent had been back from vacation only a few days when his compliance partner, Adrian Johnson, asked to meet with him.

"What's up?" asked Kent, recognizing the familiar look on Johnson's face.

He looked as though his world had come to an end. Johnson was the firm's worrier, which is why Kent had made him the compliance partner in the first place. Compliance partners are paid to worry about the rules and regulations, acting as counterweights to the risk-taking activities of the deal-doers. Kent needed someone in the team to control the worst excesses of his other partners and to keep them out of trouble.

Johnson sighed. "We've been selected for an FCA active review."

"Is that a problem? We've had them in the past. Our records are always in good shape, so what's there to worry about?"

"This is different. We're the first private equity firm in the country selected for this particular type of review."

"What do they involve?"

"Active reviews have only recently been introduced by the FCA's new investigations department. They're part of the regulator's response to not having been sufficiently prepared when the financial crisis hit. They took a lot of bad press for being behind the curve when problems first surfaced among supposedly healthy banks and other institutions."

"I can't see why we should be concerned about this."

"When I took the call from the FCA this morning, the chap from the new unit said we ought to set aside at least two weeks for their visit, and that it would not just be about us providing evidence we've followed our own internal systems and controls."

Kent angled his head. "What else do they expect?"

"He said they'll be checking a number of matters back to source documents, and they want to speak to a number of our investment clients. As we only have one main client, this will involve troubling Tritona with a lot of admin."

Kent now understood why Johnson was troubled. Sure, the work would cause an admin headache for Tritona but, much worse, there was also a real risk the review would uncover the problem with Tritona's documentation. What if the FCA people decided they wanted to speak to Tritona's own investors as part of their work? As they didn't exist, that would be a complete disaster.

Kent stood, walked over to his window, and looked toward Cambridge, deep in thought. Someone was bound to be listening to this conversation. By now, they'd know there was a potential problem if the FCA came crawling over Tritona's records.

"When did they say the review will take place?" Kent asked.

"Four weeks from today. They wanted to come in earlier, but I knew you'd want time to make sure all of our files are in order and to lay the groundwork with Tritona. I pushed them back as long as I could."

Four weeks is nothing. "Do you think they would allow us any more time?"

"I doubt it. They seemed keen to start."

Kent shook his head then turned to face Johnson. "Okay. I'll speak to Baumgart and settle things with Tritona."

"Thanks. That would help."

Johnson still looked as if his life was over. Did he know more than he was letting on? Had he been examining Tritona's files?

"Is there anything else?"

"Just one more thing."

"Fire away."

"It's more bad news, I'm afraid."

"What is it?" *If you've discovered the fake passport, for God's sake don't blurt it out. They're listening to us.*

"You'll never guess who's heading up the new investigations team at the FCA."

A wave of relief washed over Kent as he realized his partner was not about to put their heads in a noose. "Some idiot who couldn't cut it on our side of the industry, no doubt. Who is it?"

"Your best friend, Doug Wright."

Kent slumped into his chair, flooded with panic. *Fuck, fuck, fuck!* That's why CBC had been chosen as the first private equity firm to undergo an active review. It all made sense. It was no coincidence. That bastard, Wright, was out to make trouble for them. He was bound to dig deep into the files at CBC and would go out of his way to disrupt Kent's business. What if Tara mentioned the suspicious activity report she thought Kent had filed with the NCA? As it was never sent, Wright would assume he was trying to hide something and would then involve the authorities. When that happened, the whole shitty mess would be discovered. *Christ, what if the cartel think I've tipped off the authorities to cause this?*

"Then you'd better make sure our files are in good shape, Adrian. We can't afford to give him anything to go on. He'll go for the jugular."

CHAPTER 41

That night, Kent took Sarah out for dinner in Stamford. He rarely had time to eat out, other than with clients, during the week. Only when they were in the noisy Italian restaurant was he confident their conversation was not being heard. When they were in Capri, he'd told her they couldn't discuss Tritona in the house or car in case they were being monitored.

Over their bowls of penne arrabbiata, he explained what had happened earlier in the day and what it all meant if Wright dug too deep into CBC's affairs.

"I'm certain Wright will probe until he finds something. He won't stop until he does."

"How long have you got before his people come in?" asked Sarah.

"Only four weeks."

"You can't delay any longer, John. You have no choice now. You must go to the authorities."

Kent pushed his half-eaten dish to one side.

"The alternative is you lose control of the whole situation and it becomes really ugly," Sarah continued.

"I know. I'm already there. It's the only choice I have left."

Sarah was right; there was nothing else he could do. At least if he went back to Merriman, he stood a chance of laying down some conditions so he could protect himself. After all, Merriman wanted something from him, so there would be room to negotiate.

"I'm just going to use the bathroom," Kent said, rising from the table.

He made his way to the back of the restaurant. In the corridor just outside the men's room was a payphone stuck to the wall. He stopped at it, retrieved a business card from his wallet, and punched in the number. When it connected, he recognized the U.S. ringtone and, immediately, his stomach muscles tightened.

"Merriman," said the voice from the other end of the line.

"It's John Kent. I've decided to help."

"Okay. We'll be in touch." The call ended.

Kent shook the handset to check the phone was still working properly. *That's it?* Here he was, putting his life on the line, and that's all the man had to say? Was this some kind of game to Merriman? He took a few deep breaths, forcing himself to calm down. Maybe the American was just being cautious, avoiding a long conversation over an unsecured phone line. How long would he leave it before he made contact again? They only had four weeks, so it needed to be very soon.

"You were a long time," said Sarah when Kent returned to the table. She was already halfway through her coffee.

He whispered in her ear before he sat. "I've done it. I've taken the first step. I just used the payphone in the corridor."

Sarah squeezed his hand and managed a thin smile. "You're doing the right thing, John."

He hoped she was right. He'd never been more frightened in his life.

Three days later, Kent was on his way to the office, driving down the A1M motorway, when a police car raced by, lights flashing. Instinctively, he hit the brakes. He hadn't seen the car in his rearview mirror; he'd been in a world of his own, thinking about Merriman and whether he ought to call him again. He was certain he'd been speeding, but no more than eighty miles per hour, surely?

As the police car passed him, its rear lights lit up the words Pull Over.

"That's all I need," said Kent, under his breath. "A bloody

speeding ticket."

He slowed down behind the patrol car and came to a stop on the hard shoulder of the motorway. The police officer sauntered up to Kent's car window. Before he could say anything, Kent said, "I'm really sorry, officer. It's not like me to be racing along the motorway. How fast was I going?"

"Too fast, I'm afraid, sir."

"I'm sorry."

"Can I see your driving license?"

Kent reached into his briefcase and handed his license to the police officer. The officer examined the document carefully then compared the photo on the license with Kent. *He's making a meal of this.*

"Mr. Kent, I'd like you to follow my vehicle as we cannot deal with this safely while we're on the motorway. It's too dangerous here."

"I hope this won't take too long, officer. I have a meeting at the office shortly."

Kent did not have any meetings that morning, but he wanted the policeman to know he was dealing with a busy executive who didn't have time to waste.

"Just follow me in your car, sir."

The officer jumped into the patrol car and drove off the motorway and onto the A14. Kent followed at a safe distance behind, wondering why the police didn't focus their efforts on catching real criminals like Tritona.

After half a mile, the patrol car took the first exit. "Where's this bloody idiot taking me?" Kent grumbled.

When both vehicles approached the crossroads at the end of the exit, the patrol car went straight across the junction and toward a large set of metal gates. Kent read the sign to the right of the gates. It said: "USAF Alconbury."

Now he understood. They were taking him to a safe location for a meeting with Merriman. What would be safer than a U.S. air force base?

Kent followed the patrol car for a few hundred yards until it stopped outside an old redbrick building. The police officer led him inside.

"Please wait here, sir," he said, pointing Kent to a small waiting area with two worn-out leather chairs.

Kent did what he was told and took a seat. A few minutes later, he heard footsteps coming down the corridor.

"John, please forgive the cloak and dagger arrangements," said Merriman as he shook Kent's hand. "It was necessary to protect you, just in case. I don't think you were followed. Our instructions were to hold you for long enough on the motorway to ensure no other car slowed down behind you. If the police officer was less than certain, he wouldn't have led you here."

"Don't worry. I understand the need for precautions more than anyone," replied Kent.

"Follow me."

Merriman took him to a small, windowless meeting room. The place looked shabby. Special Agents Whitlock and Young were already sitting at the folding wooden table in the middle of the room.

"Nice place," said Kent.

"Take a seat." Merriman pointed Kent to the seat at the head of the table so they could all see him.

"I need to call the office to let them know I'll be late."

"My guess is we'll need a couple of hours," Merriman said.

Kent took his mobile phone from his suit pocket and rang Tara. He said he'd be coming in midmorning. He gave no reason and ended the call before she could ask any awkward questions.

Merriman waited for Kent to put his phone away. "So, you've decided to help us, John. What changed your mind?"

Kent had already decided not to share his concerns over Wright's impending FCA investigation. He wanted Merriman to believe he was doing this because it was the right thing to do. That way, he'd be able to extract certain commitments from him in return.

"On reflection, I just thought it was the right thing to do. I realized I needed to put aside my professional concerns as there was more at stake. That wasn't entirely clear to me when I first learned about all of this in London. It was a lot to take in."

Merriman smiled skeptically at his two colleagues. "It is the right thing, and I understand the risk this represents for you personally."

"Do you?"

"You'll be helping us bring down some of the most dangerous criminals in the world. Only a fool would think that would be risk-free."

Special Agent Whitlock poured them all a coffee. Merriman checked the emails on his phone one more time then took off his jacket and slung it over the back of his chair. He stayed on his feet and started pacing the room.

"We need quite specific help from you, John. I won't sugar-coat this. Obtaining the information we need is going to put you at some considerable risk. We'll try to minimize that risk, but we can't eliminate it entirely."

At least he's not feeding me bullshit. "What do you need me to do, exactly?"

"As we said to you in London, we've good evidence to link Tritona to the drug proceeds coming from the Caruana cartel through the Mexican banking system."

"I know nothing about that." Kent wanted to remind Merriman of his innocence in all this.

"We understand that. You've been duped by the cartel into helping them. We know that."

"Make sure you remember it."

Merriman raised his open palms. "Hey, we're on the same side."

"That's not how it felt in London."

"But you've come to the right conclusion now. Let's move on."

"Okay."

"Only you can provide the last link in the evidence we need.

Once the monies leave Tritona, our documentary trail runs cold. We know from our intelligence reports that CBC plays a key role in acquiring assets for the cartel, but we lack hard evidence. Without that proof, we can't seize these assets and neither can we make money laundering charges stick against the senior cartel members."

Kent wriggled about in his chair. The use of the words "only you" worried him. If he really was the only person able to provide this evidence, then it would be obvious to the cartel he was the one who talked. This was getting worse.

"Exactly what do you need me to do?"

Merriman nodded to Special Agent Young as he sat.

Young pulled his chair closer to the table and retrieved a note from his jacket pocket. "We need original signed documents establishing the SPVs being used by Tritona to acquire the assets you manage for them. We need the constitutional and title documents to the corporations and trusts which have been set up by Oakham Fiduciary Services. Finally, we need the stock certificates linking those entities to the investee companies you've been acquiring at CBC," he said, reading from his list.

Kent sat upright. *These guys are not mindless muscle-heads, after all. They know what they're talking about.* "Is that all? Sure you don't want a signed photo of all the people at Tritona while I'm at it?"

"I know. It's a big ask, John," said Merriman.

"Copies won't do?"

"No. They must be original signed documents," said Young. "Otherwise, they won't stand up in court. Copies could be dismissed as fakes."

"How am I going to extract original documents without being noticed? This isn't going to work. You'll have to think of something else." There was panic in Kent's voice.

"Calm down, John. We've thought this through," said Merriman. He poured them all a refill. "When you deliver the original documents to us, we'll prepare and return to you fake replacements within forty-eight hours. You'll be able to replace the originals with the fake ones on each file. Your exposure is just forty-eight hours at a time. These files can't be in constant use."

"The files you need are not in regular use, which is precisely why I'll struggle to access them without raising questions."

"You'll think of something," said Whitlock.

Merriman nodded to Young, who continued, "Once you've extracted the documents we need, we'll arrange a safe location for you to drop them ready for our collection. You'll be able to collect the replacements from the same place."

"Where is that location?"

"We'll get to that. How long will it take you to get hold of the original documents?" asked Young.

"It's not a simple matter. I'll need some files from Oakham's offices as well as CBC's. My guess is a couple of weeks, at least."

"Take as much time as you need," said Merriman. "We're in no hurry. We want to get this right."

"My accessing these files is going to raise a lot of awkward questions."

"You're the CEO. You can demand to see any file you want," said Young.

"It's not that simple. It would look unusual for me to request so many files myself."

Merriman screwed his face. "You must do this yourself, John. We cannot risk involving anyone else."

"I need to think about this."

Kent stood and walked around the room as he chewed it all over.

This would represent an enormous personal risk. It would take just one person to see him extracting files to be exposed. But Wright's visit was imminent, and he was bound to find out about the letter to the NCA. If Kent didn't go along with this plan, Merriman wouldn't hesitate to use the buried letter as a reason to have him extradited to the U.S. How long would he last in prison? The cartel wouldn't take any chances. They'd certainly have him killed in prison to prevent him from making any deals. There was no choice. Kent would have to cooperate with Merriman, in spite of the risk.

"Okay. I'll do it."

"That's the right decision," said Merriman.

"But there are conditions."

"What do you mean—conditions?"

"When all this is over, I want complete immunity from prosecution."

"No problem. You've done nothing wrong. Remember?"

"I want it in writing before I release any documents."

"You'll have it. What else?"

"I need you to find a way to draw the cartel's attention away from me as the source of the evidence. Without this, there's no deal."

Merriman thought for a moment. "We could always put you in our witness-protection scheme."

"That won't work. I want a life after this. The evidence can't be seen to have come from me. If you can't find a way to fix this, then we don't have a deal."

"I can understand that, John. We need to think this through a little more to get it right." He paused while he thought some more. "What if we deliberately leaked a message out, after we've seized the assets? Something along the lines that the key evidence came from one of the cartel's own senior lieutenants. That way, they'll think one of their own talked. That'll help deflect attention away from you."

"Something like that might work. Whatever happens, I can't ever be called as a witness and can never be attributed as the source. Is that agreed?"

"You have my word. I'll do whatever it takes to draw attention away from you. If you get hold of the documents we need, there'll be no need for you to become a witness. They'll stand up as evidence on their own."

Kent realized that was probably the best he could do in the

circumstances. At least now there was plan of action which might just work. It wasn't risk-free, but it was a way forward, a chance to take some control back over his life.

"I have one more question."

"Not another condition, I hope."

Kent glared at Merriman. "Does Dieter Baumgart know about all this? I assume he knows he's working for a drug cartel?"

Merriman laughed. "Of course. He's been working for the cartel for years. They're all involved."

"I thought as much."

"Why are you asking about Baumgart and not Kulpman?"

"Because Baumgart's the main man."

"Wrong. Kulpman's on the cartel's direct payroll. He's Caruana's man on the ground at Tritona. Nothing happens without his say so. He's the one who runs the show in Geneva. Baumgart's just the front man."

Now it all made sense to Kent. There had always been something weird about Kulpman. *I bet that animal organized the DVD and Anton's hit and run.*

The rest of the meeting was taken up with a detailed discussion about the specific documents Kent needed to obtain. They agreed on a safe place for him to drop the documents and to collect the fake substitutes.

As Kent drove to his office, he called Sarah. "I've finally been in to see the dentist about that pain."

"You've done the right thing, John. That was never going to get better on its own."

Both of them knew not to say anything more on an open line.

"I love you," Kent said before hanging up.

While he was worried about the threat to his own life, he was much more concerned about the risk for Sarah. She hadn't caused any of this—he had. Now all he wanted was to make sure his wife was safe. But he knew she was still at risk, and that fact was eating away at him.

CHAPTER 42

Kent managed very little sleep over the next few days. The worst thoughts came to him in the middle of the night when Sarah was asleep. He'd wake up and stare at the ceiling for hours. How was he going to access both the CBC and Oakham files without raising awkward questions? He imagined being caught with sensitive files in his briefcase and having to explain why he was taking them home. Worse still, what if the cartel's people following him or bugging his offices picked up his unusual activity and realized he was gathering evidence? He envisaged all manner of torture and violent threats to him and Sarah. The plan had sounded quite logical in the meeting with Merriman and his colleagues but, in the cold, dark loneliness of the early hours, it seemed like a certain route to a shortened life. It was now far from clear this was the right thing to do.

Exactly one week after his meeting at USAF Alconbury, the solution came to him. He was driving to work when he realized Wright's imminent FCA investigation was not only a threat, but also a way through. He could use the investigation as cover for why he, as CEO, had to take a fresh look at key files. In that capacity, he had to make sure CBC and Oakham were properly prepared for the FCA's visit. After all, Johnson had said the investigation was a completely new type of review and that CBC was the first firm in the private equity sector to go through one. It would be wrong for the CEO not to be closely involved in a high-level investigation into his own firm, particularly one being headed up by Wright. The more he thought it through, the more the plan came together. He decided to implement the plan that day. Since there were only three weeks until the inspection visit, there was no time to delay the process.

When Kent arrived at the office, he called a meeting of the partners, at which he asked Johnson to explain the significance of the FCA's upcoming investigation. With Kent's encouragement, Johnson played up the reputational risks to the firm and Tritona if all of the files were not in perfect shape. Johnson laid it on thick, as if the very survival of the firm was at risk. After all, it was unusual for his compliance function to play a central role in the activities of the firm. Normally, he'd quietly get on with his back-office compliance work while the other partners got to do all the exciting deal activity. This was Johnson's moment in the limelight, and Kent did all he could to egg him on.

Kent emphasized to the partners that the head of the new investigations team at the FCA was none other than Doug Wright. He reminded them Wright was far from being a friend of the firm, having been removed from his CEO position at Henderson Wright by CBC. He was telling them what they already knew, of course, but he wanted the hidden microphones to pick up his reasons for being closely involved with reviewing the sensitive files. He was doing his best to protect CBC and Tritona, by making sure everything was in good order for the regulator's visit.

"Here are the first few files," said Johnson as he delivered some of the documents to Kent's office right after the meeting.

Kent enjoyed the moment of relief now he had complete access to the files without raising questions. He pointed to the corner of his room. "Great. Leave them over there, and I'll bring them back to you in a few days once I've finished with them. Don't worry. I'll make sure my office door is kept locked when I'm not here."

Johnson looked relieved; his compliance files would normally be locked away as they contained sensitive personal information on investors. As compliance officer, his neck was on the line if personal client data was not protected. "Do you want me to stay and help? I'd be happy to."

"No thanks, Adrian. I'm happy doing this alone. I'd prefer you to concentrate on helping the other partners finish reviewing their own deal files before I see them. We can't afford not to be ready on all fronts once Wright's team arrives. We don't know where they'll choose to start their work."

"Okay. That sounds sensible to me."

Kent spent the remainder of the day leafing through the files. He knew exactly what to look for: any direct evidence linking the investments made by CBC back to Tritona via the multitude of SPVs arranged by Oakham Fiduciary Services. By six that evening, his briefcase was crammed full with original signed documents he'd lifted from the files.

He sent a special text message to the agreed number, locked his office door, and then left the building and jumped into the BMW. Thirty minutes later, he pulled into a large service station on the dual carriageway about a mile from the exit for USAF Alconbury. He filled his car up with gas and took his briefcase in with him to the cashier's desk. There were a couple of people in the line in front of him, so Kent took the opportunity to scan the room. CCTV cameras were positioned in every corner, and the sign for the toilets pointed to the back of the building, away from the fuel pumps.

He paid for his fuel and walked into the toilet block, where he went to the end one of six cubicles and closed the door behind him. The place smelled badly. He didn't want to touch anything; it was filthy. He stood in silence and listened for movement, occasionally glancing at his watch. *Come on.*

Moments later, there was a tap on the small outside window. Kent slid it open, and Special Agent Whitlock appeared at the opening. Although Whitlock was hidden from anyone else's view by a thick bank of bushes, as previously agreed, no words were spoken by the two men.

Just as Kent opened his briefcase, he heard someone else walking into the toilets. The footsteps grew louder. Whoever it was chose the cubicle next to Kent's and closed the door. Kent's heart was pounding in his chest. He froze. Why had the person chosen that particular cubicle when all of the others were still empty? Had he been followed here? Was he about to be discovered red-handed passing over evidence to the authorities?

Kent kept absolutely still while Whitlock tapped his watch as though he was impatient to get on with things.

"Wait a minute, will you?" Kent mouthed to the agent.

The person in the adjacent cubicle made no noise. What the hell was going on? He waited a few seconds before carefully removing the documents from his briefcase and handing them to Whitlock. As he did so, Kent dropped a handful of papers onto the wet floor. He bent down to pick them up, and it turned his stomach to think of what was now soaking into the papers. Whitlock looked furious as he grabbed the wet documents, shaking his head and pursing his lips.

By the time Kent had closed his briefcase, Whitlock was gone. Kent slid open the door bolt, left his cubicle, and ran past the one still occupied. He was about ten feet from the exit, when someone shouted, "John."

Kent gripped the briefcase hard, lowered his head in a charging motion, and raced for the door handle. Someone grabbed his shoulder from behind, and Kent braced himself for an attack, swinging the briefcase around as a weapon.

"John. It's me, Michael." The man held his hands up to protect his head from being struck by the briefcase.

Immediately, Kent recognized one of his neighbors from their village in Rutland. "Michael, I'm so sorry, I didn't recognize your voice when you called out."

"You look as though you've seen a ghost. Are you okay? I didn't mean to frighten you."

"Yes, I'm fine. I was just surprised to hear my name called out in here. That's all."

"You don't look okay. Are you sure you're all right?"

Kent turned. "Great to see you, Michael. I'm sorry, but I have to run. I'm already late for an appointment." He walked quickly to his car and sped out of the forecourt to avoid having to explain his irrational behavior.

When Kent looked at his watch, driving away, he calculated the whole thing had taken less than ten minutes, but it had felt more like an hour. The adrenaline was still coursing through him, and sweat ran down his face, as he checked his rearview mirror. While it had been a terrifying experience, some part of him felt a sense of exhilaration and excitement, knowing he'd won the first battle in the war against his tormentors. Hopefully, it would get a little easier from here.

Two days later, Kent made the same stop on the way home. This time, as well as handing over a thick bunch of new papers to Whitlock, he collected the fake substitute documents. The forgeries would be placed into the original files the next morning. They were good-quality copies, and Kent found it difficult to tell them apart from the originals. Merriman's people clearly knew what they were doing.

It took a week and a half to complete the extraction and substitution of the key evidence on CBC's files. The process was over without a hitch, and Kent's confidence was slowly increasing. The plan was working, the hardest steps had been taken, and he was on the way to getting his life back.

CHAPTER 43

One week before the scheduled start of the CBC investigation, Wright arrived for work at the FCA's Canary Wharf offices. Swaggering past the front desk, he flashed his ID to the security guard without stopping. He didn't acknowledge any of the staff as he made his way to the fast elevator for the executive suite. Wright had never had time for the little people. He was not paid to be liked; he had an important job to do.

In the short time since joining the FCA as head of the high-profile investigations unit, Wright had rapidly become the public face of the new proactive regulator. He'd been on the BBC and several cable channels and had appeared in many of the newspapers, setting out how he was going to be using his position to keep the financial services sector in check. He'd make sure they didn't break the rules, and if they did, he'd be over them like a rash.

Walking by the lines of employees waiting for the staff elevators, an arrogant smirk filled Wright's face. The main elevators stopped at every floor, but the executive one was much faster. It served only the executive suite so there was no line. He pressed the call button, and the doors opened immediately. When he walked in and hit the only button for the twenty-second floor, nothing happened. He punched it several times, but still there was no response. Shaking his head and cursing, he walked over to join the crowd at the other elevators. No one let him jump the line; he could wait his turn like everyone else. While he collected the that-showed-him stares, Wright vowed heads would roll for the indignity he was now suffering.

After stopping on every floor, Wright arrived at the top of

the building six minutes later; he'd timed it. A complete waste of his valuable time. Outside his own corner office, he barked an order at his PA to "get someone to fix that bloody elevator and fast" then walked into his room, slamming the door behind him.

At ten o'clock, Wright welcomed a journalist from the *Sunday Post* into his office. In previous interviews, he'd set out what his priorities were going to be and what style he would adopt in carrying out his department's new investigations. Today's interview was an in-depth session to get to know the man who was Doug Wright. The article allowed him to remind the world how he'd built one of the world's powerhouse accounting firms almost single-handedly. Of course, he chose not to dwell on the fact that Henderson Wright was almost brought to its knees by his aggressive deal-making, or the fact that he was fired as a condition of the rescue financing deal. According to Wright, he had finished what he set out to achieve at Henderson Wright and was looking for his next challenge. He'd received many lucrative offers but had only accepted the FCA executive position so far.

The journalist asked what appealed to him about his new role.

Wright thought carefully. "When you've reached the top, it can be hard to find another challenge commensurate with one's skills. The FCA role offered me the opportunity to give something back to the financial services market. After all, the market has been good to me." He spoke each patronizing word slowly so the journalist could capture every pearl of wisdom in his prepared answer.

The journalist didn't seem entirely convinced, but she made a few scribbles on her pad. He waited until he judged she'd captured his all sage pronouncements before continuing.

"Too many financial services firms made a killing in the boom markets without properly recognizing the risks they were building up. My role will be to use my considerable experience and skills to investigate firms before they run into trouble, before it's too late. My aim will be to ensure financial services firms properly recognize and address risk. This will be achieved through a series of proactive and intense investigations before things go wrong."

During the rest of the interview, he didn't once mention his team of fifty staff. He acted like this was a one-man investigations department. A modern-day Eliot Ness.

Wright power-posed for a couple of photos before escorting the journalist to the elevator lobby. Ordinarily, his visitors would be left to find their own way out, but Wright always found time for journalists. They were useful to him. They helped maintain his high profile and so had something he wanted. As they approached, a sign in front of the executive elevator doors read: Out of Order. He apologized and called one of the others, but didn't wait for it to arrive; he was too important to waste more of his valuable time standing in the corridor.

When he returned to his office, he instructed his PA to call the offices of CBC and put Mr. Kent on to him. A call Wright had been dreaming about for days.

"John Kent speaking."

"This is Doug Wright." Wright left an awkward pause. He'd once been on the other end of Kent's silent pauses. It felt good to be giving some back.

Kent wasn't going to play the game and quickly filled the silence. "How can I help you, Mr. Wright?"

"I wanted to make sure you're going to be ready for our visit next week."

"Yes. We'll be ready. Is there anything else?"

"Nothing for the moment, but you ought to allow plenty of time for our investigation. It will be thorough and unrelenting." A self-satisfied grin spread across Wright's face.

"We're always happy to make time for visits from the regulator, Mr. Wright. We've nothing to fear from administrators and bureaucrats. Cheerio." Kent terminated the call.

Wright stared at the handset then slammed down the phone. He'd just been getting started, but it would look weak to call back, as much as he wanted to. He'd extract his pound of flesh the following week when he'd make sure Kent would forever regret removing him from Henderson Wright. He would not be satisfied until he had ruined CBC one way or another.

By twelve-thirty, Wright wanted some fresh air. He'd developed a habit of taking a short walk at lunchtime before having a lavish, full-service, three-course meal in the executive dining room. When he walked toward the executive elevator, a man in blue overalls was just removing the Out of Order sign as he approached.

Wright peered at the engineer. "I assume that bloody thing's fixed? I can't believe it has taken you so long."

"Yes, sir. It's now working perfectly. I'm really sorry for the inconvenience. Let me call it for you." The engineer punched the switch and stood back.

Wright didn't bother to acknowledge him. He stepped forward and waited for the bell to indicate the arrival of the elevator. When the doors opened, instinctively, Wright inched toward the unit. Before he realized the elevator was not actually there, it was too late. He fell forward then felt a lunge in his back as the engineer shoved him. Wright plunged twenty-two floors down the dark shaft.

The engineer closed the doors and positioned the Out of Order sign back in place. By the time Wright's dead body was discovered, the man in the blue overalls was long gone.

CHAPTER 44

Kent caught the seven-thirty commuter train to London. The extraction of evidentiary documents from CBC's deal and compliance files had gone better than he could have hoped; there'd been no awkward questions, and the substitutes provided by Merriman's people looked convincing. However, he was less confident about the plan working as well at Oakham Fiduciary Services. He'd hardly spent more than an hour at their offices during his previous visits. They were bound to be curious about his inquiries. He'd used the same cover story—he needed to ensure the files were in good shape ahead of the FCA's visit the following week. Jonathan Gateley, Oakham's CEO, hadn't questioned the arrangements when Kent called him to set up his visit. He accepted the reason Kent gave him and appeared to understand the rationale behind it. Kent had emphasized that he was subjecting his own firm's files to the same high-level review, which seemed to go down well. But the fact that Kent was not going to be working in his own office environment made him nervous. He wouldn't be in control. Something could easily go wrong.

Twenty minutes into the train journey, the steward came along the first-class carriage pouring out hot drinks and handing out complimentary newspapers. Kent ordered a coffee and took the *Financial Daily*. He'd just settled back into his seat to read the paper when his mobile phone rang.

"John. It's Joanna."

"Hi, Joanna. I can't talk much as I'm on a train, and the mobile reception isn't great."

"Okay. I'll keep it brief," said Kirkland. "We've just

completed the HS1 rail deal. Tritona's winning bid was seventy-six billion pounds. Can you believe that?"

"Well done. Geneva will be pleased. That's a hell of a price. I'm just glad it's not in our fund."

"It's a wacky price, and I did tell you it would take a very high bid to win the auction. There was a lot of interest in it."

"So it seems. If they plan to keep the asset for the very long term and just collect the yield, then the price is a little more credible. That's what they say they'll do. It certainly won't sell on at a profit if they wanted to flip it quickly."

"By the way, I've put you and me down as CBC's directors on the board of the SPV that was used for the acquisition. I hope that's okay?"

"No problem. Thanks for letting me know about the deal. See you back at the office in a few days."

"Good luck with your file review. Rather you than me."

Kent finished the call. He could only fake his excitement for so long. The High Speed 1 deal was another potential nail in his coffin if his and Merriman's plans went horribly wrong. He'd just knowingly assisted a criminal organization launder seventy-six billion pounds. The UK authorities would throw the book at him if they ever found out. He'd never be able to explain it away. Merriman's little scheme had better work.

With the hot coffee in one hand and the newspaper in the other, Kent scanned the front page. "Ugh?" he shouted, spilling his drink down the front of his shirt and tie. The hot liquid burned his skin as one of the train stewards rushed over to help him mop up the mess.

Kent held his shirt away from his chest. "It's okay, I'll do it," he said as the steward began to wipe up the coffee on the table. "Really, I'm okay. I'll take care of it."

Kent ignored the onlookers and picked up his paper the moment the steward left. A photograph of Doug Wright was in the middle of the front page. The headline read: "FCA Investigations Head Dies in Freak Accident." The article started by describing the circumstances of Wright's death. Apparently, he'd stepped into the executive elevator on the twenty-second floor of the FCA's building only to find that the elevator was not there. His badly mangled body had fallen the full height of the tower. He wasn't discovered for two hours as he'd gone missing over lunchtime. Expert commentators were quoted, postulating that Mr. Wright would have died instantly. No doubt about it. He would not have suffered. The article went on to describe how the police were treating the circumstances of his death as highly suspicious; there was early evidence to suggest the elevator control unit had been tampered with. The remainder of the piece gave a summary of Wright's recent appointment as the head of the regulator's new investigations team following a successful career building up Henderson Wright as a global firm of accountants.

Kent could feel his heart racing while his mind did overtime. Evidence of tampering. Suspicious death. Then the chilling thought hit him. Had the recent CBC partners' meeting led directly to Wright's death? At that meeting, the partners had discussed Wright's imminent visit. If, as Kent suspected, CBC's offices were bugged, then Tritona and/or the cartel would know Wright was a threat to them if he came digging too deeply.

The more he thought about the circumstances of Wright's death, the more he was certain he'd been murdered. His death was not an accident at all. The cartel wouldn't hesitate to wipe out any perceived threat. Anton was murdered on his way to work and now Wright. Kent was lucky to be alive. *If they find out about Merriman, I'm a dead man.*

Still in a world of his own when the train arrived at King's Cross station, Kent remained in his seat as the other passengers left the train. Could he really go on with this? Suddenly, the stakes seemed higher and more real.

Kent needed space and time to think this through, so he called Gateley to say his train had been delayed by a power failure on the electric rail line, and he was still stuck on it. He'd be there as soon as he could, but it might be some time.

He gathered his things off the sticky table in front of him and folded the newspaper under his arm. When he walked out of the front entrance of the station, he turned right along Euston Road. Where could he find a quiet space to sit and think? As he headed west along the busy street, he kept looking around to see if anyone was following him. A few minutes later, he reached the British Library. There had to be somewhere quiet in there he could sit and gather his thoughts.

He found a deserted reading area on the second floor, where he read the *Financial Daily* article again and again. His hands were trembling and he felt cold. The risk of continuing with Merriman's plan was simply too high. He couldn't do it any longer. Who would be next? Sarah? Another one of his partners?

On the ground floor, at the rear of the building, was a row of payphones. Kent retrieved Merriman's card from his wallet and punched in the number.

After several rings, a very drowsy-sounding Merriman answered the call. "This had better be good."

"It's Kent. We need to talk."

"Do you know what time it is over here? Can't it wait?"

Kent was risking his life, and the man he was risking it for couldn't be bothered to speak to him because it was in the middle of the night.

"Fuck you. I'm not going through with the plan."

An elderly man, standing at another payphone, threw Kent a look as if to say: don't you know this is a library?

Kent no longer cared. "You can find some other idiot to help you. I've had enough of all this. I'm out."

"I'm sorry. Relax, okay? I was woken up by your call," said Merriman.

"I'm putting my life on the line for you. It's not worth it."

"What's happened?"

"Hold on." Kent waited for the man to finish on the other payphone and watched him leave. Then he explained the circumstances of Wright's death and how he was all set to lead an investigation into CBC's files the following week.

"And you didn't think to tell us about the FCA? Big mistake."

"I've had a million and one things to think about with all this going on. I've not had time to give you a running commentary."

"I don't give a squat. Don't tell me you've been busy, like that's some excuse. You know full well an investigation by the FCA could wreck all of our plans. You should've told me."

"What do you want from me? I've told you now, haven't I? That will have to do."

"This changes everything. We need to finish this process faster than we thought. We can't allow a visit from the regulator to fuck up our plans."

"Are you listening to me? I told you I'm not doing this anymore. Wright's death was no accident. I don't intend to be the next victim. I'm out. Finished." Kent was shaking as he shouted down the phone. People walking by were beginning to stare at him, but he didn't care.

"Calm down, John."

"Don't tell me to bloody well calm down. It's not you in the firing line. I'm not doing it. Go find some other mug."

"Look, we already have all we need from the CBC files. All we need now are the Oakham documents and we're done. It's only a couple of days' work. You can't pull out at this point. You have to finish this thing."

"You're still not listening to me. It's over."

There was a long pause. "I'm going to level with you, John. If you pull out now, we'll still seize the assets we know about, then we'll quietly let Caruana know you helped us. Do you understand me? We are that close to breaking the cartel. Do you really think we're going to let you fuck this up for us? That ain't gonna happen."

Kent felt like head-butting the wall. "You wouldn't dare do that. We have a deal. Remember?"

"Try me, John. We have nothing to lose. You do. The deal was we protect you as our source, but only if you see the whole thing through."

"That's not how I saw it."

"I'm telling you as it is. Your call."

This duplicitous bastard has got me in a corner. I'm a dead man if I don't help him. As a shrewd negotiator, Kent recognized that Merriman had the upper hand. He'd already provided enough help to guarantee his own death should the cartel find out. He realized he had no choice but to see through the end of the process. Merriman had now shown his true colors; the man had no real interest in anything other than bringing down the Caruana cartel and he'd stop at nothing to get what he wanted. That much was clear. *He'd happily feed me to the cartel if it suited him.*

"Okay. I'll finish it. You'd better keep to your side of the bargain when all this is over."

"We'll keep to our side of the deal. Provided, of course, you meet all of your obligations." Merriman's tone sounded menacing rather than reassuring.

Kent slammed down the phone. Merriman was no longer an ally; he was an adversary. Kent would have to take as many precautions as possible to protect his own interests from now on. He couldn't rely on Merriman to have his back. The American couldn't be trusted, and Kent owed him no favors.

It was just after 11 a.m. when Kent arrived at Oakham Fiduciary Services. He made his apologies, blaming the train for his long delay. Gateley set him up in a large meeting room where he had a whole bunch of files already waiting for Kent's review.

"Did you see today's *Financial Daily* piece on Doug Wright?" asked Gateley as they sat down for a chat over coffee before Kent started his work.

"I did. What a dreadful accident," replied Kent.

"An awful way to go. Can you imagine falling twenty-two floors to your death?"

"I can't even begin. At least it would have been quick."

"Do you think our investigation will still go ahead?"

"It's hard to say. We ought to assume it's still on, but we shouldn't be surprised if they postpone it. I'm down here now so I might as well complete the file review as planned, just in case."

"That sounds right. I'll leave you to it, John. Let me know if you need any drinks or whatever bringing in. If there's anything you don't follow, just let me know. Some of the corporate structures are a little esoteric, shall we say."

"Thanks. I will do."

When Gateley left, Kent closed the door behind him and started wading through the files. Most of them contained original documents which were signed by Baumgart. The documents were those needed to establish offshore holding companies and trusts which were then used to hold both the direct investments made by Tritona and those made through CBC and its funds. They would definitely provide the evidence Merriman needed to tie Tritona to the underlying assets. He looked around the room, checking for CCTV cameras before dropping the relevant original documents into his briefcase. The main risk now was if Gateley checked the files before Kent could replace the missing papers with fake substitutes, but there was no choice.

At the end of the day, Kent took a cab over to the Marriott Hotel on the south bank of the Thames, overlooking the Houses of Parliament. Tara had booked him in there for the few nights he estimated it would take to complete his review. After checking in, he made his way to the top floor where there was a large gym facing out over the river. He left his briefcase in one of the secure lockers in the changing room and went for a run on one of the many treadmills. He built his pace up quickly while he stared down at the commuters making their way back and forth across Westminster Bridge. He envied them for their mundane, predictable lives. At least they were safe and could sleep at night.

Kent was a few minutes into his run when Special Agent Whitlock finished his workout on an adjacent treadmill and left the gym. There was no eye contact between the two men; they were two strangers, exercising after work. Whitlock returned to the changing room to get dressed, using the locker next to Kent's. When it was clear that he was not being watched, he used a special key to open Kent's locker and removed the contents of the briefcase, slipping them into his holdall. He was gone before Kent was halfway through his routine.

CHAPTER 45

Kent sat in the bar of the Marriott Hotel having a quiet drink after dinner. He stared out of the window as he ran over recent events in his mind. The city lights were reflecting off the Thames, and late-night revelers were making their way across Westminster Bridge to the tube station on the opposite bank.

So far, Merriman's plan appeared to be working and the dangerous part would soon be over. Even the initial shock of Wright's murder was beginning to fade. Now, Kent felt more angry than fearful—angry he was being used by Merriman as a pawn in his vendetta against the cartel, angry he'd been duped by the cartel into their money laundering scam, and angry about the future that had been stolen from him. What lay ahead now was uncertainty and pain. Once the publicity came out about Tritona and the cartel, there would be no future for CBC. The whole market knew Kent's firm handled all of Tritona's investment activity. Even if it was made clear that CBC was a victim in the whole affair, no sane investor would commit new investment funds to the firm. The reputational risk would be simply too high for them. And once Merriman had seized the cartel's assets, there'd be nothing left, not even a portfolio management role to play. Where once Kent had been counting on the management fees and carried interest on Tritona's vast portfolio to make his fortune, there would be zilch. His dreams of becoming private equity's first European billionaire would be ruined. It would never happen, and he'd have no opportunity to make it all again. How could he when his personal reputation was about to be put through the shredder?

Kent ordered another glass of wine—a large one—and thought about what he might do with his life if and when he could ever put the Tritona mess behind him. He really wanted to continue investing. It had been his life, and he was good at it. He didn't have any hobbies or passions outside of work. *My whole life's a fuck up.*

Staring out of the window, in the distance, a train ran across Waterloo Bridge. Then, a minute later, another passed in the opposite direction. *That's it!* The solution had been staring Kent in the face—the HS1 rail investment CBC had just closed. Merriman's team didn't yet have the original documents in relation to this new deal. It hadn't even been completed when Kent was pulling the documents together for Whitlock. Why let that ungrateful bastard, Merriman, grab the asset? What value was it to him? Already, he had enough evidence against the cartel with the files Kent had given him. What difference would one more asset make? *None.*

He swirled the last of the wine around his glass as his mind wandered. Kirkland had mentioned earlier in the day that Kent had been appointed a director of the holding company used to acquire HS1. Maybe he could use that position to transfer ownership from Tritona's SPV to one of his own family trusts. Certainly, he had the power to sign it over under the investment management agreement. Once the cartel's people noticed it was missing, they'd assume Merriman had seized the asset along with all the others. And as for Merriman, he would know nothing about the deal, anyway; he'd never been given the documents. There was no way for him to pick up it was missing, not unless Kent told him. *It's ingenious. The perfect, victimless crime.* He gulped down his drink and ordered another to lubricate his thinking.

The following morning, Kent was back at Oakham's offices to continue the file review. He spent a few hours collecting documents for Merriman then asked for the HS1 file. On it was a record of the cash transfers from Tritona's various offshore accounts and a thick section on the ownership structure, including an intermediate Tritona holding company, the SPV on whose board Kent was now a director. That company was held by a new Tritona trust. Several corporate layers below the holding company was the actual HS1 rail operating company. There were enough layers of impenetrable corporate fog to throw off any prying eyes.

Kent examined the investment paper setting out the acquisition's financial structure. There was debt financing from a syndicate of lenders amounting to thirty-six billion pounds. The loans sat in an intermediate holding company, below the vehicle on whose board Kent was a director. Tritona had provided equity financing of forty billion pounds, taking the total financing to seventy-six billion pounds.

He looked up at the door to make sure no one was there then quickly filled in the necessary transfer paperwork. It only required the signature of a properly authorized director, of which he was one, to put Kent's scheme into action. At the stroke of a pen, one hundred percent of Tritona's forty billion pound equity capital investment in HS1 passed from the SPV to Sarah's offshore trust in Guernsey. Kent had long kept most of his wealth in Sarah's name in case he was ever sued; at least they could protect their assets that way.

When he was finished with his review work tonight, he decided he'd take the whole HS1 file away with him and keep it with him at the hotel. With a bit of luck, it wouldn't be missed for some time—hopefully, not until long after the seizure of the cartel's assets, when Oakham's team would assume it was taken by the DEA. If it was noticed before, then he'd simply say he was still reviewing it. Whatever happened, no one from Oakham could be allowed to see the transfer he'd just made.

Kent didn't do much work for the rest of the day; he was too busy perfecting his plan. He calculated that the forty billion pound equity investment would generate income of three point two billion pounds each year, as the financing structure stipulated an eight percent running yield. He planned to set up the payment details for this once he was back at CBC. Normally, during the first few days following completion of a new investment, the CBC team would need to set up payment arrangements with the management team at the investee company. That way, the operating company would know where to transfer interest and dividend payments as they became due. The HS1 management team would have no idea in this case that the recipient bank account was the one used by Sarah's trust in Guernsey. The team would have no reason to doubt the payee information provided by CBC. They'd do as they were told. One day, the investment might even be sold. Kent would be happy if all it did was repay the forty billion pound original investment cost, but it was likely to do better than that in the long run.

Kent had just ripped off both the cartel and Merriman, and neither of them would be any the wiser. The moment Kent had put his signature to the transfer document, he'd become one of the ten richest people on the planet, at least on paper.

The next few days were spent going back and forth to the Marriott's gym, dropping off documents and collecting the fake substitutes to put onto Oakham's files. The whole process was finished just four days before the FCA's scheduled visit. When he returned to Cambridge on Thursday afternoon, Tara told him she'd just received a telephone call from the regulator's office canceling their visit and apologizing for any inconvenience.

Inconvenience. The threat of their visit had allowed unfettered access to the HS1 file. *Thank God for Doug Wright.*

CHAPTER 46

It was 8 p.m. in Washington D.C. when Merriman drove up to the entrance gates and let down his driver window. The armed guard asked him for details of whom he'd come to see and for two forms of photo ID before scanning his car for explosives. Nothing was taken for granted. All visitors to the Department of Homeland Security's D.C. headquarters were carefully screened before being allowed through the security gates. Merriman was allowed through and instructed to park his vehicle in a specified space. When he entered the building, he had to show his ID once again before being escorted to a monitored waiting area, where he took a seat.

There, he faced a blank wall. The only things breaking up the monotony of the decoration were a photo of the sitting president and the American flag. As he sat, he thought about the significance of the next hour or so. This would be the making of his career, the moment he entered the big leagues. If only his parents were alive to witness this moment. His father, in particular, would have been so proud.

"Madam Secretary is now ready to see you, Mr. Merriman," said a smartly dressed intern as she collected him. He followed her along the corridor, staring at the walls. Hanging on them were portraits of all former presidents. At the end of the passageway, he entered a spacious, bright office with a large mahogany desk next to a French window. On one side of the room were two sofas. He sat on one of them and waited. One day, not so far into the future, he'd hold a similarly powerful position in central government and would enjoy an office like this.

"Sorry to have kept you waiting, Mark," Ann Laudel said as she returned to her office. Secretary Laudel was only the second person to head up the Department of Homeland Security. Like Merriman, still in her thirties, she was young to hold such a senior position in a key government department. She was also ambitious and was never one to miss a moment of success in front of television cameras. "I was being prepped for the press conference."

Merriman stood and thrust out his hand. "Good to see you again, Madam Secretary."

"Are you all set for the conference?"

"Yes. Ready to go. I sent over my presentation this afternoon. Were you happy with it?"

"Yes. It reads well. Obviously, I'll introduce the session and round up at the end, but the meat of this evening's press conference is your presentation. Shall we go up?"

"I'm all set." Merriman tightened the knot in his tie.

Laudel led Merriman from her office, up a flight of stairs and through to a large conference room. It was packed with journalists and TV camera crew. The room grew quiet as Laudel and Merriman walked out and approached the podium.

Laudel was smiling from ear to ear. "Good evening, everyone. Welcome to the Department of Homeland Security and to our press conference." Cameras flashed and the live television broadcast started. "I've said it many times before, one of the most significant threats to the U.S. and the American way of life is the proliferation of illicit drugs and the associated violence. In recent years, the vast majority of drugs on our streets have entered the U.S. across the southern border with Mexico. Today, one massive drug cartel, the Caruana cartel, controls an estimated ninety percent of organized drug activity in this country. It's the most successful and most threatening organized crime group ever faced by the U.S. Tonight, we are announcing a significant success in our fight against this evil organization. As a result of what we are about to announce, all Americans will be much safer from the threat posed by the illegal narcotics trade. I'd now like to hand over to Mark Merriman, who is the Head of Intelligence at the Drug Enforcement Administration."

Merriman stepped forward to the microphone. "Thank you, Madam Secretary. Good evening, everyone." The cameras flashed as he launched into his presentation. This was his moment. He inhaled deeply, puffing out his chest and holding in his stomach muscles. "Secretary Laudel has already stressed the magnitude of the threat to the U.S. represented by the Caruana cartel. To give you some idea of the size and strength of this criminal organization, if it was listed on the New York Stock Exchange it would figure in the top-five public companies in this country." He looked around the room as he paused for effect. Journalists scribbled furiously while others relayed the information quietly over their cell phones.

He continued, "Historically, we've focused our activities on securing the physical border to the south and confiscating drug shipments when we've identified them. Unfortunately, this had only limited success. The plain truth is we can't monitor the whole of the border all of the time. There will always be shipments that escape our net, no matter how much resource we devote to this problem. In recent months, we shifted the emphasis of our intelligence activities, devoting more attention to the proceeds of illicit drug sales. We started by seizing physical shipments of cash crossing the border back into Mexico and escalating our electronic surveillance, so as to trace the movement of the cartel's funds once they entered the international banking system. Today, we are able to announce a major breakthrough." He paused to drink some water, but his real objective was to raise the level of anticipation in the audience.

"In the last few hours, we have seized cartel assets with an estimated value of four hundred billion dollars." He paused again to allow his audience to absorb the figure. "We believe this represents some ninety percent of the Caruana cartel's assets. In effect, we've killed off this threat to our nation's security by chopping off its head. Without access to its massive financial resources, the cartel is no longer able to acquire and distribute illicit drugs, nor is it able to control its vast network. We've seized the rewards of the last ten years' work by this criminal organization. It has been emasculated, if you will."

The press pack applauded. Laudel joined Merriman at the microphone in order to share in the glory of the moment in front of the live TV cameras. "We're happy to take any questions," she said. Twenty hands went up at once. Laudel pointed at one of them.

"Can you say anything about the nature of the assets which have been seized?"

Laudel nodded to Merriman. "More information will be made available tomorrow, but the assets comprise mainly shareholdings in quoted and unquoted companies and some real estate holdings," replied Merriman. "To many, these assets would've appeared completely legitimate, having been laundered through a complex network of corporate structures by the cartel and its advisers. The cartel's leadership would've assumed these assets were beyond our reach and completely at their disposal."

Laudel pointed at another journalist. "How were you able to identify these assets if they appeared completely legitimate?"

Merriman continued, "Through tireless intelligence gathering. A major breakthrough occurred when we were able to obtain critical information from a member of the cartel's own senior leadership team. I'd prefer not to say any more about this, for obvious reasons."

"What will happen to these assets now?" asked another journalist.

"They'll first be recorded and over time they'll be sold. The proceeds will be retained as federal revenue for the benefit of the American people," replied Laudel.

Three and a half thousand miles away, Kent was watching the live broadcast on a satellite news channel at home with Sarah. Merriman had called him earlier in the day to let him know the announcement was imminent. At least Merriman had kept his word and had pointed to a senior cartel insider as the source of the information leading to the seizure of the assets. The cartel's attention would be focused inward when looking for clues as to who'd talked. There'd be no reason to suspect CBC or Kent.

Kent began to think through what he would say to his partners once he'd received the all-clear from Merriman to discuss it with them. Right now, none of them would know anything about the cartel or the significance of the press conference currently being held in Washington. Kent dreaded having to tell his partners that the assets managed by CBC were now the property of the U.S. government. How was he going to break it to them that CBC was now dead, and they'd all soon be out of work?

Baumgart arrived at Tritona's offices at his usual time. He hadn't heard about the broadcast from Washington which had gone out long after he'd gone to bed, and he'd yet to check his messages. As he drove into the parking lot, a small convoy of police cars drove in behind, blocking the exit. Baumgart opened his car door then fell back into his seat when he saw the squad of armed police surrounding him.

"Get out of the car and down on the floor!" shouted the senior officer in charge.

Baumgart, his face paling by the second, put up no resistance and did what he was told, lying face down on the parking lot. "What's this about? I have done nothing wrong."

One of the officers put his knee between Baumgart's shoulders, pulled both arms round behind his back, and strapped on handcuffs. It took three officers to haul his large frame from the tarmac and push him in to a waiting police van.

Other armed officers began to file into the Tritona building. Kulpman was watching the whole thing from a second-floor window. The moment he saw Baumgart being forced to the floor, calmly he walked down the emergency staircase at the back of the building and left from a rear door. He disappeared into the woods nearby.

Jivaro was enjoying a few days at his summerhouse in Mazatlan. He'd been entertaining potential new suppliers when he heard the news of the press conference. He missed the conference himself but was given a blow-by-blow account by one of his lieutenants. In his rage, he vowed he would have Merriman's head and those of all his family for this.

"He's no idea what he's started," he shouted. "If he wants a war, he'll have one."

Jivaro had to move rapidly. His enemies would exploit this setback unless he responded quickly and dramatically. He ordered his people to obtain a complete list of the assets seized by the DEA. No details had been released at the news conference, so he needed to establish how much of the cartel's wealth was still safe before deciding how to respond to the Americans' attack.

Next, he instructed his chief enforcer, Miguel Rios, to do whatever was needed to find out which of his lieutenants had collaborated with Merriman.

"Suspect everyone and spare no one until you find out who has done this," he barked down the phone to Rios. "I want the traitor's head."

Rios couldn't wait to get started. He'd find the collaborator and personally deliver his head to Jivaro. Already, he had his suspicions as to which of the lieutenants might have talked. He told his henchmen to grab three of the most likely candidates and to take them to the cartel's offices in Tijuana for interrogation. He ordered them to be held until his arrival, as he would take personal charge of the interrogation process.

Later that day, under the cover of darkness, Kulpman returned to Tritona's offices as instructed by Jivaro. A police patrol car sat in the front parking lot. Two officers were in the car, monitoring the building. Kulpman crept closer to the car, keeping to the shadows. He crouched down next to the rear fender and took out a silenced pistol from his jacket pocket. He jumped to his feet and fired two bullets each into the heads of the police officers.

Kulpman waited a few moments to make sure there were no other patrol cars watching the building. Once he was certain he was alone, he let himself into the offices where he used a flashlight as he walked around the dark rooms. No files had yet been taken; everything appeared to be in its place. No doubt the offices would be emptied by the authorities over the next few days. Behind the office block, he walked across to the storage unit used by the groundsmen to keep their lawnmowers and gardening equipment. He picked up two large cans of gasoline, took them back to the offices, and poured the fuel over the filing cabinets. Standing back, he lit a cigarette and threw it onto the liquid before disappearing into the woods. Walking away, he could feel the warmth of the flames at his back.

CHAPTER 47

Kent called his partners together for the dreaded meeting first thing Monday morning. From their conversations, he could tell they thought the meeting was about the recently canceled FCA visit and, maybe, to discuss the feedback from his detailed file reviews.

Kent looked at Tara as he struggled to choose his opening words. "Tara, there's no need to take any minutes, but you're welcome to stay. This affects you as much as everyone."

Those few words, and Kent's somber tone, caught the attention of everyone in the room. Immediately, they quieted down and turned to him, anxious to learn more.

"This is a very difficult and shocking matter," he said, looking around the conference table. He cleared his throat. "There's no easy way to put this."

"Don't worry," said Johnson. "We know all about Doug Wright. No doubt the FCA will send someone else to audit us once they've replaced him."

Kent wished this was just about Wright's death. "Sadly, it's something much worse than that, I'm afraid." Johnson looked confused, but before he could say anything, Kent continued. "CBC is finished." There was absolute silence in the room as Kent paused. He collected the penetrating stares of his partners. "Over the weekend, I received a call from the Drug Enforcement Administration in the U.S."

"Why on earth would the DEA call you?" asked Johnson.

Kent held up his right palm. "I'm trying to explain."

"Sorry."

"The DEA informed me they'd seized, with immediate effect, all of the assets managed by CBC."

Kent took a sip of his coffee, buying enough time to choose the right words. By the look of the stunned faces around the boardroom table, he wasn't sure it mattered much to them how he explained things. What did matter, however, was how this played out to anyone still listening in to this conversation. They had to hear how Kent and his team were shocked by news of the DEA's seizure.

"I know it's hard to believe," Kent continued. "It sounds incredible, but it transpires the funds we've been investing on behalf of Tritona are actually criminal proceeds from the sale of illicit drugs in the U.S."

Johnson looked ready to explode. "What? That makes no sense at all."

"You're saying Tritona is involved in the drug trade? That can't be right," said Kirkland while the others shook their heads in disbelief.

"My reaction was the same, Joanna. I'm still shocked," replied Kent, convincingly. "The DEA explained that Tritona has always been a corporate front for a Mexican drug cartel called Caruana. Apparently, this cartel is the most powerful organized crime group in the world. Much of their wealth was channeled through Tritona and, from there, into legitimate investments, most of which have been acquired and managed by us. We have, unknowingly, become a critical part of their money-laundering activities."

Long looked as if he was about to have a nervous breakdown. "I did the compliance checks, and they all came out fine. We would have picked up anything suspicious. We're talking about some of the best-known families in Europe behind Tritona, for goodness sake."

"I said the same thing, Kevin. But the truth is the families don't exist, at least not as investors in Tritona."

Long looked beaten. "That's impossible. How can—"

"We were duped. The DEA said anything we received from Tritona, verifying their identity and those of their so-called investor families, would've been a forgery."

Kent was bombarded with questions as the implications of what he'd just shared became clear. Were they all about to be arrested? What would now happen to the assets which had been managed by CBC? Would this story be all over the press in the morning? Would they be sued?

Kent waited for a break in the questioning. "All I know at this moment is the DEA has seized the assets. Legally, they're no longer under our control. We shouldn't deal with them in any way or else it would appear as though we are trying to interfere with the legal process."

"So, what do we do, sit on our hands?" asked Johnson. "There must be something we can do."

"The DEA may want some assistance from us going forward, but our involvement will be purely administrative, helping them to understand the files we have and assisting in the handover. That's all."

"This is bound to be all over the press," said Long. "We'll be torn to pieces by the media."

"The only official PR they're putting out concerns the cartel and Tritona. But, you're right, Kevin. It's likely the press will pick up on the story since it's well known Tritona is our most important investor."

Johnson buried his head in his hands. "This is a complete disaster." Then he looked at Long. "How the hell did we let this happen?"

Kent could not allow Long to take the heat for this. "We're all responsible for this nightmare. I've been assured by the DEA that CBC is under no suspicion. They regard us as a victim in all of this, which is exactly what we are. It's important we get that message out there when we're speaking to the press."

Kent's performance was convincing. It had to be for the cartel. He had to assume they were monitoring everything. CBC was definitely not the source of information for the DEA.

"The UK authorities will be all over us," Kirkland said. "We thought the FCA's investigation was going to be tough. That would be a walk in the park compared to what they'll hit us with now."

"The FCA and the police will want to crawl all over this, Joanna, and rightly so. We've nothing to hide. Remember, we're victims in this."

"That doesn't make it feel any better," she said.

"You're right. The truth is we've lost everything. Our business will fail."

"Dead right," said Johnson. "This has killed our business and shredded our reputation. We've been working for a drug cartel for Christ's sake. It doesn't get any worse."

The remainder of the meeting focused on how to handle the expected press inquiries, how the staff would be informed, and agreeing what legal advice ought to be taken by CBC in order to deal with the whole thing properly. The FCA would expect no less. The partners concluded they'd be tied up for weeks winding down the firm and handing over the management of the assets to the DEA, so they could be sold by the U.S. government. All for no reward and for the pleasure of being mauled by the press.

Kent could do nothing to change the reality of the situation for his colleagues. There were no words or hope to offer them to soften the blow. He, at least, had the comfort of knowing he'd tucked away the investment in HS1. All of the necessary documentation was now in place, and it was beyond the reach of Merriman and the cartel. When the dust settled on all this, he'd still be a very rich man.

CHAPTER 48

Rios took one of the private jets to Mazatlan so he could report personally to Jivaro on the progress of his investigation. He'd spent four bloody days looking into who had collaborated with the DEA. So far he'd interrogated three cartel lieutenants at the Tijuana sawmill, but he was no closer to finding out who had betrayed them. None of those questioned had survived the ordeal.

"The important thing is to find the traitor and quickly. I understand there'll be casualties. No one can be trusted," said Jivaro.

"In time, I'm confident I'll find who talked and I'll deliver him to you," said Rios.

"Continue with your work, Miguel. We cannot show any weakness. We must send our enemies a clear signal. They must know I'm still in command of this organization, and that we've not been weakened by the Americans."

Rios needed no encouragement. He already had his next list of victims lined up. While the interrogation process was a convenient excuse to remove some of his high-ranking competitors within the cartel, he wasn't sure it was going to help find their traitor. He was more hopeful he'd learn something from a meeting with one of his important contacts he had coming up in a few days. One way or another, he'd find answers for his boss.

"I do have some news," Rios said.

"What is it?"

"I've heard from Kulpman. It seems all the assets managed by Tritona were seized by the DEA."

"Everything?"

"That's what he said."

"That's much worse than I'd assumed."

"It's a massive blow."

"The American has made this personal. He will regret what he has done."

"What can I do to help?"

"Nothing yet. I'll tell you what I have in mind for Mr. Merriman later. Did Kulpman say who might have talked?"

"He said Baumgart's been arrested."

"Baumgart would not do this. He's too weak. But we cannot let them squeeze him for information."

"I know exactly what to do."

"Good. Once we've dealt with him, we'll move on to Merriman."

CHAPTER 49

Cancun Airport was hot, sticky, and heaving with tourists, with fresh planeloads arriving by the hour. Arguments flared up as people ran into each other or wheeled their suitcases across open-toed sandals. Just inside the entrance to the arrivals hall, illegal cab drivers were touting for fares, adding to the chaos.

Looking like a regular tourist with his designer shades and knee-length shorts, Frank Halloran breezed his way to the taxi rank outside. He'd told his colleagues back at the DEA he was going to Mexico for a few days in the sun.

The cab he climbed into was a death trap—bald tires and the usual spongy brakes—pretty much like all of the others he'd been in when visiting this part of the country. Most visitors didn't think twice about the safety of these vehicles, and yet they wouldn't have gone anywhere near cars like these back home. They all had their brains in vacation mode, but not Halloran.

Unlike most tourists, he wasn't headed for the hotel district to the east of the airport. Instead, he traveled west across the Yucatán Peninsula toward the town of Merida, some two hundred miles away. He could have rented a car, but the roads were bad, and he hated the hassle of arguing over fictitious damage when he came to return the vehicle to the rental office. It was an annoying scam and, besides, rental contracts left a paper trail.

As they drew near to Merida, Halloran gave street-by-street instructions in fluent Spanish. It was just after 4 p.m. when the taxi pulled up outside an ochre-rendered house on a scruffy street about a mile outside the town center. He paid the driver who then released Halloran's bag from the trunk—normal practice with tourists running up a large fare. No payment, no bag.

He walked to the front door of the house and used his own key to let himself in. Once inside, he took his bag upstairs to one of the two bedrooms and threw it on the bed. The place was tidy enough. The only thing disturbing the peace was a barking dog from the property next door.

An hour later, Halloran was enjoying a cold beer from the well-stocked refrigerator when he heard a car pull up right outside. He stood up from the kitchen table and watched as three men got out of a black Mercedes. Two of the men looked like hired gorillas. The third was in a well-cut, light gray suit. They let themselves into the house.

Halloran ignored the muscle-heads but shook hands with the suit. "I made it here before you this time, Miguel."

"Let's go through to the lounge where we can talk," said Rios. "I'm sure we have much to discuss."

Halloran and Rios made their way into the lounge at the back of the house, while the other two men went through to the kitchen, grabbed cold beers, and fired up cigarettes.

Two years ago, Rios had approached Halloran when he was a young agent at the DEA's Mexico division. Rios made it his business to know the backgrounds of all field agents on his patch. He targeted those from poor backgrounds and offered them money beyond their dreams in exchange for information on the DEA's activities.

Halloran had been an easy turn. Raised by a single mother in a poor part of Arkansas, he'd had a difficult childhood. Working to put himself through college, he despised many of his fellow students who seemed to have it all given to them on a plate. They had no idea how tough life could be and what it was like to worry about the next meal. When Rios approached him, Halloran was receptive; he never wanted to face the risk of poverty again. Once he'd made that pivotal decision, all he had to do was continue providing information to the cartel, bank the money for ten years, and he'd be set up for the rest of his life.

Since becoming an informant, Halloran, under close supervision from Rios, had worked diligently, putting in long hours and assisting Merriman's team in whatever way he could. He'd quickly become an exemplary employee at the DEA headquarters, demonstrating an ability to get on with everyone, an ambitious work ethic, and an eagerness to help out. All this meant he was exposed to many of the DEA's activities and plans, even those outside his immediate area of responsibility.

"You're beginning to put on weight now you're back in the U.S.," said Rios, poking Halloran in the ribs.

"Too much food and not enough exercise."

"Now, tell me about Merriman. What did he think of our little birthday gift? I trust it was appreciated?"

"I think it had the desired effect."

"His little mole could have hurt us."

"How did you discover who he was?"

"It was easy once you'd told us about Merriman's increased use of undercover agents. After that, we were more careful with our new recruits at head office. Vargas asked too many questions. He stood out."

"Was that the name he was using?"

"Arturo Vargas. Thought he was clever."

Halloran thought about the memorial service for the undercover agent and how difficult it had been for his parents. He wasn't proud of his betrayal, but he was trapped, and there was no going back. "I'm glad my information was helpful."

"It was very helpful. Once we suspected Vargas, it didn't take too long to get him to speak. He squealed like a little pig."

Halloran faked a laugh and rushed to change the subject. "I see my tip about the raid on Isla Tiburon was well-timed."

"Jivaro was very grateful for that."

"It wasn't easy getting that information."

"I can imagine, but thanks to you we were able to move our key people off the island and destroy sensitive records."

"Good."

"The best part was giving Merriman a bloody nose. I wish I could have been in your offices to witness his reaction. Arrogant bastard."

"Both Merriman and Butler were in a major panic. You sure showed them."

Rios suddenly adopted a serious face. "By now, they must know we have someone on the inside working for us."

"Let's just say they're being extremely careful with sharing information, but I'm sure they don't suspect me."

"Watch your back. We need you in place."

"I'm okay for now."

Rios rubbed his hands together. "What do you have for me today?"

Halloran knew each time he was summoned to Merida he was expected to deliver something of value. Sometimes he rationed the information he had; that way, he'd try to have something ready for his handler. Disappointing him too often was not an option as he knew what Rios was capable of doing if things didn't go his way. He was careful to stay on the right side of the monster.

"I've heard nothing more about undercover agents. As I've said before, this is kept at the highest level, but I'll keep trying."

"You must have something for me. What do you know about our assets at Tritona?"

"Only what was announced at the press conference. I wasn't on that team. But there's a good chance I'll get pulled into dealing with the Tritona seizure as a lot of people are getting sucked into that at the moment."

"It was a setback for us. I need to know who helped Merriman from our side. Someone is feeding him information."

"I'll do everything I can."

"It must be your highest priority, Frank. Find the informant and quickly."

"I'll deal with it."

It would be difficult, if not impossible, to unearth Merriman's informant, but Halloran was not going to share his concerns with Rios. As long as there was a chance Halloran would be called upon to help out on the Tritona case, he had ongoing value to the cartel. That was enough for Rios today.

Rios stood up to leave. "Now, we must leave you. Enjoy your few days in the sun, my friend." He smiled at Halloran. "Jivaro has left a little bonus for you in your account this time. A token of his gratitude for the work you did in helping us with Vargas and the attack on HQ."

"I appreciate that."

By 7 p.m., Halloran's visitors had left. He'd stay in Merida for one night only then finish his vacation in Cancun, mixing with all of the other tourists. Whatever happened, he had to stay long enough to go back with a suntan.

CHAPTER 50

The small, high-security prison on the edge of the village of Mauvoisin was used by the Swiss authorities to house sensitive prisoners. These were men and women who might be at risk from the wider prison population if they were kept in mainstream institutions. They were kept at Mauvoisin for their own protection.

On the third floor of the concrete building, Baumgart had his own cell, a ten foot by eight foot box with a barred window looking out over the Alps. His large frame filled the room. For a man used to luxurious living, this was a massive shock to the system. The food was disgusting, and his cell suffocating, but the worst of all the indignities was his having to mix with the weird array of real criminals. He wasn't like them; they were uncivilized.

He was being held at Mauvoisin pending his extradition hearing in Geneva. The idea of being extradited to the U.S., and being held in a U.S. maximum-security prison for the rest of his life, frightened the hell out of him. He knew it would not be a long life in those conditions. He was not cut out for that sort of existence. If there was a deal on the table that meant he could avoid being sent to the U.S., he'd take it, even if that meant spilling the beans on the cartel.

No such deal came. Two weeks after his arrival, Baumgart was scheduled to appear at the central court in Geneva for the first of three appearances under Swiss extradition proceedings. It was a two and a half hour drive by prison van. His slot in court was scheduled for 11 a.m., so he was up and dressed in his smartest suit and ready to go by eight. He couldn't stomach any breakfast; his lawyer had led him to expect the worst, advising Baumgart he was likely to be unsuccessful in challenging the extradition process. In all probability, he'd be on a plane to the U.S. within the month. The Swiss authorities had no time for those who used the secrecy of its banking laws to assist criminal and terrorist organizations. It damaged the country's reputation, and they would not tolerate it.

Three guards came to collect Baumgart from his cell just after eight. They handcuffed him and led him down three flights of steps into the prison courtyard, where a white, unmarked prison van was waiting. Two of the guards climbed into the front of the van while the other sat in the separate, specially strengthened rear box compartment with Baumgart. He was the only prisoner on that morning's court run to Geneva. Even though he'd lost some fifteen pounds since his arrival, the wooden bench creaked under his weight when he sat on it.

The guard placed cuffs around Baumgart's ankles then shouted the all-clear to his colleagues up front. Shortly before eight-fifteen, the security gates slid open, and the van drove out of the courtyard, heading north on Route de Mauvoisin toward Verbier.

This time of year the snow was thick on the ground, but the main roads were largely clear. The driver still needed to concentrate on the winding route descending two thousand meters down the mountain to the valley floor. The two guards in the front were chatting and listening to the radio while there was no conversation at the back. Baumgart just closed his eyes and thought about the nightmare of the months to come. He had no real defense to his crimes. He'd been greedy and had allowed himself to be seduced by the money and lifestyle. He knew the authorities were going to throw the book at him. No doubt they'd use him to set an example. This thought, and the rolling motion of the van, made him feel nauseous.

Ten minutes into the journey, the vehicle approached a one

hundred and eighty-degree bend on the mountain road. The driver pumped the brakes in plenty of time, anticipating this dangerous stretch and the sharp curve ahead. The shiny new patches of steel barrier provided ample evidence of those who'd underestimated the danger and had careered down the side of the mountain.

About a hundred yards before the bend, the driver lightly touched the brakes again. A large truck careened around the bend from the opposite direction, going far too fast and straddling both lanes. The guard slammed on the brakes and tugged furiously at the steering wheel, trying to avoid a collision. The van skidded to a halt moments before impact with the truck. Baumgart and the guard at the back were thrown against the front of the rear compartment and then hurled back onto the wooden bench.

Two heavily-armed henchmen jumped out of the truck, spraying bullets from their machine guns. The two guards in the front cab were dead within seconds as the van was holed with rapid fire. Baumgart and the remaining guard threw themselves onto the floor. They were not injured due to the heavily strengthened metal cage surrounding the rear compartment of the van.

When the shooting was over, Kulpman stepped out of the black Mercedes which had pulled up behind the truck. He ordered his men to move their truck while he walked over to the rear window of the prison van and looked in. Baumgart and the guard were cowering on the floor. Baumgart lowered his forearms from his face, looked up, and then stumbled to the window once he realized who was out there.

"Franz. Thank God it's you. Get me out of here, quickly," Baumgart shouted.

Kulpman smiled but said nothing.

"The other guards have the keys," continued Baumgart, pointing to the front of the van.

Kulpman walked to the front of the van, dragged out the body of the dead driver, and sat in the driver's seat. He put the gearbox into neutral and released the handbrake. As the vehicle began to roll down the road toward the dangerous bend, Kulpman jumped out. He watched as the van accelerated and hurtled toward the steel barrier. Baumgart was still at the rear window, thumping on the door in desperation. The vehicle smashed through the metal fence and flew three thousand feet to the bottom of the valley, bursting into flames on impact with the ground.

Kulpman and the two henchmen jumped into the Mercedes and sped off in the direction from which they'd come. The whole thing was over in less than five minutes.

CHAPTER 51

Bill Grendon loved everything about his gleaming new Honda CRV all-wheel drive. For years, he'd bought cars made by U.S. manufacturers, refusing to consider any foreign-built vehicle for his private limo business. Mostly, he'd stuck to GM or Chrysler, much the same choices as his father had made. Then, recently, he'd watched a TV documentary on PBS and learned his "American" car was actually made in Mexico. He felt robbed, but it gave him permission to consider the Honda when he came to change his vehicle a couple of months back. He'd always secretly liked the styling. The truth was, but for the "buy American" rhetoric he kept spouting to his friends, he'd have bought one much sooner.

The car was now exactly five weeks old but was still receiving all the tender loving care Grendon could lavish on it, including parking it in his garage overnight rather than leaving it out on the drive where it would attract the dust and bird shit. After maneuvering it into the garage at the end of another long working day, he remained in the car checking his diary and reviewing his bookings for the following day.

In his mid-fifties, Grendon sported a gray mustache, which had become bushier over the years as his hairline had receded. He'd run a limo business for the almost thirty years since he'd left the army. He much preferred the freedom of being his own boss, out and about and answerable to no one, rather than being stuck behind a desk. He was not ambitious. He was his company's only employee, but he'd won a few prestigious long-term driving contracts over the years, mainly on the strength of his strong reputation for reliability and honesty. People trusted

Bill Grendon.

It was 7:30 p.m., and Grendon was hungry. It had been a tough day, with three airport runs back to back and, worse still, no time to stop for lunch. He was looking forward to his wife's homemade dinner. Barbara Grendon was an excellent cook, and preferred to make dinner at home rather than eat out. He was always disappointed with the quality of the fare on the rare occasions they did go out for dinner. Nothing beat Barbara's home cooking, not even close. After thirty-five years of marriage, his expanding waistline was living proof of his appetite for Barbara's cuisine.

He entered the modest ranch-style property from the internal garage door.

"Barb."

As usual, Grendon had called and spoken with his wife about an hour before to let her know when he was likely to arrive. She'd confirmed his dinner would be ready when he got home, but there was no smell of cooking.

"Barb, I'm home." Still no reply.

He walked into the kitchen and had to turn on the light. There was no sign of his wife and no note. Barbara always left him a note to avoid worrying him if she had to go out.

"Barb. Where are you?" There was a hint of concern in Grendon's voice.

When he drove up to the house he'd noticed the light in the living room was not on either, so he knew she couldn't be in there. He ran to the master bedroom, but there was still no sign of her. Sitting on the bed, Grendon called his wife's cell phone, but it went to voicemail.

After changing into some casual clothes, he tried her cell phone again. Straight to voicemail. As he walked into the living room and reached to turn on the light, he thought he heard a moaning sound. Had Barbara fallen and injured herself?

The truth was much worse. When the light went on, facing him in the middle of the room was his wife bound to a dining chair. She'd been gagged and had clearly been struck in the face several times; she had a bleeding nose and badly bruised left eye. Behind her chair, staring at Grendon, were two muscle-heads.

The one with a deep scar on his right cheek spoke first. "Welcome home," he said, tapping his palms on Barbara's shoulders.

Grendon hurled his body at the man. "What have you done to my wife?"

Scar-face punched Grendon to the ground and kicked him hard in the stomach. "Shut the fuck up."

Grendon curled up in pain, and Barbara tried to scream.

"If you do exactly as we say, then your wife won't be harmed."

Grendon crawled over to an armchair and heaved himself into it. He could see the men meant business, and he knew he was no match in any physical fight. They were a good twenty-five years younger than him and much fitter.

"What do you want? We don't have much money," he said, holding his stomach.

Scar-face slapped Barbara hard in the face then glared at Grendon. "I told you to shut up."

Grendon raised both palms in the air. What in God's name did these animals want? "Okay, okay. I'm sorry. Please don't hurt her again—please."

"We'll be staying here tonight."

The other intruder tied Grendon to another dining chair and gagged him. After the men turned off the light and left the room, the Grendons sat trembling in the dark. As their eyes grew accustomed to the poor light, they could see each other. Barbara motioned with her eyes to her husband, drawing his attention to the telephone near his chair. He rocked his seat around, but the phone line had been cut right through.

These people couldn't be thieves. If they were, they'd have taken what they could by now and left. What did they want? As he looked at his trembling wife, Grendon made a poor job of hiding his own terror from her.

CHAPTER 52

After a long, sleepless night for the Grendons, the two intruders came back into the living room.

"Listen to me very carefully," said Scar-face, standing over Grendon, his tone calm and business-like.

Grendon nodded to indicate he was paying attention.

"This morning, you'll pick up your regular client at eight o'clock. The difference is once you've collected her, you won't follow your usual route."

More nodding from Grendon.

"Instead, you'll follow my friend here, in his car." Scar-face pointed in the direction of his accomplice. "Do you understand?" He pulled down the gag from Grendon's mouth so he could respond.

Grendon took a few deep breaths. "I understand, but my first client is a schoolgirl. There must be some kind of mistake?"

"There's no mistake. We know exactly who your client is."

"But how—"

Scar-face slapped Grendon across his cheek. "Just follow our instructions. If you don't, your wife will be killed. Is that clear?"

Barbara moaned through her gag and rocked in her chair.

"I understand. Please. Don't harm my wife. I'll do exactly what you want."

"Now you must get ready for work. We leave at seven-thirty." Scar-face led Grendon to the bedroom to get changed while the other watched his wife.

Shortly before seven-thirty, he pulled Grendon back into the lounge. The other man was no longer there, but Barbara was still bound to the chair.

"I'll be staying here with your wife." Scar-face pointed toward the window. "My friend will be following you in the silver Nissan across the street."

Grendon went pale at the thought of being separated from Barbara. "What do I do when I get there?" He flinched, expecting to be struck again.

"As soon as you pick up your client, you must follow the Nissan and stay closely behind it. If my friend loses sight of you for one moment, he'll call me and your wife will be killed. If you follow our instructions exactly, then I promise your wife will be safe, and you'll both be free later today. Is that clear?"

"I'll do exactly as you wish. Please don't hurt my wife. I beg you."

"Her life is in your hands. Now, you must leave."

Grendon kissed his wife on the cheek and squeezed her hand. "Don't worry, Barb. I'll do exactly as they say. You'll be safe. I promise." He kissed her again. She said something through the tight gag still in her mouth. Grendon didn't catch what she said, but he knew from the look in her eyes what she was trying to convey. "I love you, too," he said.

Once in the garage, Grendon reversed the Honda onto the drive then looked at the silver Nissan across the street in his rearview mirror. When he pulled away, the Nissan followed closely behind. Grendon toyed with the idea of using his car phone to call the police, but when he looked down at the handset, the cable had been cut. His captors must have disabled the phone overnight. Who were these people and what did they want with his client?

Just before eight, Grendon pulled up outside the detached, colonial house in Herdman Park. The Nissan parked fifty yards behind, but Grendon could still see it. He honked his car horn once and, a few moments later, the front door of the house opened. Patti Merriman and her youngest daughter, three-year-old Erin, stood in the driveway, waving good-bye to seven-year-old Emma. She ran down the path and climbed into the Honda.

"Good morning, Mr. Grendon," said Emma as she fastened her seatbelt. "Mom says hello."

"Good morning, Emma. Are you all set for school?" Grendon smiled and waved to Mrs. Merriman as he moved the car away from the curb. She waved back, as she did every weekday.

A knot tightened in his stomach when the Nissan drove in front of his Honda. All he had to do now was follow the vehicle if he was going to keep Barbara safe. But how was he going to go through with this? Were these animals going to harm Emma?

For security reasons, the DEA sometimes arranged for the children of sensitive personnel to be taken to and collected from school by trusted limo companies. As one of the most respected drivers, Grendon had the contract to collect Mark Merriman's eldest daughter. Grendon didn't know what Merriman's work involved exactly, only that he held some senior position working for the government, but he knew enough to realize he was now involved in some sort of kidnap attempt.

He followed the silver Nissan east onto a two-lane highway for a few minutes—the usual route. Then it diverted. Grendon looked at his passenger in his rearview mirror.

Emma wrinkled her nose. "This is a different way to school, isn't it?"

Grendon thought about ramming into the Nissan to force it off the road, but Barbara kept flashing up in his mind. He was powerless to intervene. They wouldn't hesitate to kill his wife.

He turned his body briefly and smiled. "It is, Emma. Unfortunately, there's been an accident on the regular route, so we have to find an alternative."

Although the thought made him sick, Grendon convinced himself the government would pay any ransom demand made by these gangsters, and Emma would soon be released unharmed. She was in no real danger. If he did what he was told, everyone would come out of this safely.

Ten minutes later, the cars left the highway and drove through a set of open steel gates. At the end of the quarter-mile tarmac road was a private airstrip which looked as if it hadn't been used in years.

"What's happening, Mr. Grendon? What are we doing here?" asked Emma, panic in her voice. "Can I please use your phone to call Mom?" She looked down at the handset. "The phone's broken." She began to cry.

Grendon gripped the steering wheel hard and said nothing. What could he say in answer to Emma's questions? He couldn't even bring himself to look at her. He was about to trade a young girl's life to save his wife.

The Nissan accelerated toward the only aircraft in sight, a private jet, and Grendon followed. As soon as the cars came to a halt, the man in the Nissan jumped out, ran to the Honda, and grabbed the girl.

Emma began to scream and kicked out at her abductor.

Grendon froze and stared at the jet as the man carried Emma toward it.

Scar-face appeared at the aircraft's door then stepped off the plane and walked up to the Honda.

Rage boiling inside him, Grendon climbed out of the car. "What have you done to my wife? I'll kill you if you've harmed her."

Scar-face did not reply. He took out a pistol from his suit coat and shot Grendon in the head. Then he returned to the jet, where the girl was already under sedation and strapped into a seat. Five minutes later, they were in the air.

"Good work, gentlemen," said Rios, who was on board and had watched the whole thing through his window. "Very good work."

CHAPTER 53

It was just after ten in the morning when Patti Merriman received the call every mother dreads. The school principal called to inquire why Emma was not in today.

Patti's heart was in her throat. "What do you mean, Emma's not there?"

"Oh." The principal sounded as though she was caught off-guard. "She is coming in today?"

"She should have been there at least an hour and a half ago."

"There's probably a sensible explanation for this, Mrs. Merriman. The driver may be stuck in traffic. However, it's our policy to inform the police as soon as possible in these circumstances." There was a poorly disguised panic in the principal's voice. "I'll contact the police while you call the driver. Let's talk again in a few minutes."

Patti was shaking when she picked up the phone to call Grendon. The phone kept going to voicemail. When she called her husband on his cell phone, it also went to voicemail, so she contacted Gail, his PA, and asked her to track him down urgently.

Five minutes later, Merriman called back. "What's wrong, Patti?"

"Emma didn't arrive at school this morning."

"What?"

"Bill picked her up as usual, but I heard from the school a few minutes ago, and they say they haven't seen her."

"Have you tried calling Bill's cell?"

"Yes, several times, but I keep getting his damn voicemail."

"I'm on my way home. Have you called the police?"

"Yes. The school is contacting them now. I'll speak to the principal again now and let you know what's happening as soon as you get here. Hurry, Mark, please."

Immediately, Merriman sent Halloran to Bill Grendon's house to speak with his wife to see if she'd heard anything from her husband. Then he asked Karen Camplejohn to contact the police to see if they'd heard anything. A call from the DEA's office would command a swifter response and at the right level within the police. They'd know this was not just a call from some overly protective parent.

Merriman jumped into his car and put his foot down. On the drive home, he called Patti to see if she'd learned anything. She hadn't, but she said she might have missed a call as she was continually dialing Grendon's cell phone.

"Okay. Stay off the phone, Patti. People may be trying to contact us. I have someone going over to Bill's house right now. I'm sure everything's going to be all right."

Fifteen minutes later, he arrived home.

"Where's our little girl, Mark?" Patti said, running out to meet him at his car.

He hugged her. "I'm sure she's okay." He didn't know what else to say to comfort his wife. It was always possible she was not okay. Too much time had passed since Emma had been collected by Grendon.

They went into the house, and Merriman's phone rang. It was Halloran.

"Mark. It's not good news."

Merriman felt cold. "What is it, Frank?"

"I've just arrived here. I rang the bell several times, but there was no answer so I went round to the lounge window to see if anyone was in. It looks like Mrs. Grendon has been shot. The police are on their way."

Merriman's breath was knocked out of him. He gripped a chair for balance. "God, no!" *Emma's been taken.* "Stay there, Frank. Find out what you can and keep me briefed. I want to know everything."

"Of course."

When Merriman told Patti, she went limp, and he had to grab her to prevent her falling to the floor.

She started to sob. "This can't be happening, Mark. What's happened to Emma? Where is our little girl?"

Merriman bit his lip; he knew full well what the events meant. Moments later, he took another call. This time it was from a police officer.

"This is Captain Ryan. We've found Mr. Grendon's Honda SUV at Houghton Airfield. It's bad, I'm afraid, sir."

Merriman took a couple of paces away from Patti so she couldn't overhear the conversation. "One of my team just phoned and told me about his wife."

"It gets worse. The driver of the SUV has also been shot. He's dead. We think it's Mr. Grendon, but we've yet to confirm that."

Merriman's breathing was now shallow. "What about Emma?" he asked, bracing himself for a shock.

"There's no sign of your daughter, sir. I'm sorry."

"That means she's been kidnapped. This has all the signs of a professional team."

Across the room, Patti turned white and fell backward into the sofa.

"She must have been put on a plane from Houghton. We're checking flight logs as we speak."

After the call, Merriman was torn. His wife needed him right now, but he knew he'd be more useful working with the police back at his office. There, he'd have access to government security and intelligence systems to assist in the search for his daughter. So he called Patti's sister, who lived thirty miles away, to ask if she'd come over and look after her. He didn't want to leave Patti, but he understood how important quick action could be in these circumstances.

Merriman was in automatic pilot driving back to the office.

He thought about who was likely to be behind his daughter's disappearance. It had to be the work of the Caruana cartel. Although he'd made many enemies in his work, the coincidence of timing, right after the seizure of assets, the recent murder of his parents, and the professional nature of the morning's events all pointed to the cartel.

If Safuentes touches one hair on her head, I'll hunt him down and kill him.

When he arrived at work, most of his team were there waiting to help. Halloran came rushing in and gave a report on what he'd found inside the Grendons' home. The police had allowed him access to the house, where he found Mrs. Grendon bound to a chair and gagged. She'd received a single pistol shot to the back of the head.

A police team joined Merriman's meeting in one of the conference rooms. Captain Ryan briefed everyone on what they knew so far. It was clear the Grendons had been held hostage at home overnight. There was evidence to support this; neighbors had seen the Honda pull into the garage yesterday evening. It was likely that threats to Mrs. Grendon were used to coerce Mr. Grendon into going along with the abductors' plans. Mr. Grendon was found dead next to his car at a small, local, private airstrip. He'd been shot once in the head at close range. Shortly after 8:30 a.m., according to witnesses, a private jet, had taken off and headed south. There was no record of a flight plan.

Merriman looked at his watch. "It's just after one. They'll be in Mexico by now."

Ryan looked confused. "What do you mean, Mr. Merriman? Do you know who these people are?"

"I think we all know this is the work of the Caruana cartel. It's payback," Merriman said, looking round the room at his team. They nodded in agreement.

He spent the next hour briefing the police officers on the DEA's investigations into the cartel and the recent substantial seizure of Caruana's assets. They all agreed it was plenty motive enough for them to abduct his daughter.

When the meeting was over, Merriman walked back to his own office and shut the door. He slumped into his chair, rested his elbows on his desk, closed his eyes and massaged his forehead with his fingers. He exhaled loudly through his nose.

Not our little girl, please.

CHAPTER 54

Sitting almost at the tip of Mexico's one-thousand-mile-long Baja California peninsula is the burgeoning city of La Paz with a population of almost a quarter of a million. Supported by a successful tourist industry, land prices had rocketed in recent years.

Jivaro was one of the first to spot the city's early growth prospects. He bought up huge tracts of land around the city years ago and, gradually, built up a chain of hotels and tourist attractions as part of his expanding real estate empire. Further out from the city, south along the coast, the landscape became more arid. It was characterized by undeveloped land, served only by a few dirt tracks, leading to some of the most spectacularly beautiful coastal views. Jivaro owned much of this too.

Accessible only by boat, and set back about two hundred yards from the coast, was a derelict house on Jivaro's land. Eight hours after the private jet took off from the Virginia airstrip, Rios and his two henchmen carried the sedated young girl from the speedboat, across the deserted beach, and into the house.

Once they had her locked away in a windowless back room, Rios made the call to his boss. "We've got her. Everything went according to plan, and there were no loose ends."

"Fine work, Miguel," replied Jivaro. "She is not to be let out of your sight."

Jivaro allowed twenty-four hours before making contact. Merriman hadn't managed any sleep since Emma had been taken and, by the time the call came in on his direct line, he was expecting to hear the worst. Most ransom demands were made in the first twelve hours, so he was braced to hear his daughter had been found murdered.

He picked up the phone after three rings, delaying answering to give the police team time to start tracing the call, even though he knew this would be futile.

"I have her," Jivaro said. "She's beautiful. Looks just like your wife."

"You do anything to harm her, and I'll kill you." Merriman didn't care about the police team sitting around him.

"You're in no position to issue threats. Just remember what I did to your parents."

"Where is she? I want her back here today. You got that, you fucking animal?"

"You'll have her back, but first you must return something of mine."

Merriman knew full well what Safuentes wanted. "What do you want?"

"You have forty-eight hours to release my assets and to provide a legal waiver to any future claims over them."

"I don't have that kind of power."

"*You* took the assets, so you must find a way of returning them."

"It's just not that easy."

"It's your problem. Once my lawyer is satisfied with the waiver, you'll have your daughter."

Jivaro finished the call.

Merriman turned to the police. They shook their heads, confirming they hadn't been able to trace the call.

"She's alive," said one of the officers. "At least she's alive."

Merriman looked at him. "If you believe anything that madman says."

He rose to his feet and left the room. He searched for a quiet office, somewhere he could call Ann Laudel without being overheard. The U.S. administration's policy was not to negotiate with criminals and terrorists. There was no way he could return the cartel's assets, even if he'd wanted to. But maybe with his strong professional relationship with Laudel, and their recent successful press conference, she'd be motivated to help. Laudel had very good senior connections in the government. It was worth a try.

When Merriman called her direct line, Laudel answered immediately. "I can't imagine how difficult this must be for you and Patti."

"Patti's distraught. I know how this is likely to end, but I can't bring myself to tell her. I can't take her hope away."

"I can understand that."

"I need your help."

"I'll do whatever I can."

"Is there any way we can make an exception here? Maybe release some of the cartel's assets in exchange for my daughter. I know it's a lot to ask."

"Let me make some calls and see what I can do. I'm sorry, Mark, but I don't need to tell you what the answer's likely to be."

"I understand, Ann. I'd never forgive myself if I didn't try."

A few hours later, the kidnapping was leaked to the media. Merriman was certain the leak had come from the cartel as it would send a clear message to Jivaro's enemies that he'd not been weakened by the DEA's actions. No one was beyond his reach.

Then the major U.S. networks picked it up and kept showing the recent press conference, with TV footage of Merriman and Laudel describing the record seizure of cartel assets. At that point, Merriman knew it was over, and that his last hope had vanished. Even if the administration had been minded to make an exception, in light of the high profile now being given to the case, it could not afford to be seen breaching established policy.

The following morning, he took a call from Laudel. She'd made several calls, as she said she would, but she'd been unsuccessful. She told him what he already knew. While he had great sympathy from inside the government, the publicity on this one was simply too high; no senior politician would want to be seen arguing for a change in U.S. policy.

An hour later, another call came in on Merriman's direct line.

"You have only twenty-four hours left and yet we've heard nothing from you," said Jivaro.

"I'm still working on it. I'm going to need more time," replied Merriman.

"Twenty-four hours." The line went dead.

Merriman put his head in his hands. There had to be something else he could do.

CHAPTER 55

Realizing he was out of options, Merriman drove home to be with his wife. After explaining to Patti his failed attempt to release some of the assets in exchange for Emma, he began to steer her expectations toward the awful prospect of losing their daughter. Patti broke down in tears and held their youngest daughter close to her.

An hour later, someone knocked on their front door. Merriman opened it then took a step back when he saw Kerry Donohue standing in front of him. "Hello, Kerry. What are you doing here?"

"I'm really sorry to intrude at a time like this," she said.

"Come in." Merriman led her into the lounge and introduced his team member to Patti and her sister.

Donohue apologized again for coming over to the house then took a seat on the sofa next to her boss. "I looked for you at the office and was told you'd come home," she said. "Something really strange has come up. I thought you ought to hear about it as it could be important."

Merriman quickly glanced at his wife then looked at Donohue. "What is it?"

"Since we seized the cartel's assets, I've been recording the details of each investment so we have a complete inventory."

"Go on."

"Well, for my own curiosity, one of the things I've also been doing is cross-checking the assets we're recording against a press search."

"What kind of press search?"

"I put the phrase 'CBC deal completion' into my Internet search engine then printed off the results. This gave me the press coverage of all of CBC's deals in the last couple of years."

Merriman noticed his wife tearing up. "Where's this going, Kerry?"

Donohue was the most intelligent member of his team. She was thirty-one and had been with the DEA since graduating from MIT in computer science. The problem was she could never just cut to the chase. She had a habit of verbalizing her logic in front of people. It was just the way her mind worked, and it seemed to help her think, but sometimes Merriman found this frustrating.

"Sorry. I eliminated those deals before Tritona started to use CBC. Then I compared the remaining list of transactions to my record of seized assets." Donohue shifted her weight on the sofa. "The strange thing is the two should agree, but they don't."

"Maybe not all deals were publicized." There was a hint of irritation in his tone.

"I agree, but that's not how my lists differ."

Merriman sensed Donohue might be onto something, so he cut her some slack. "Go on."

"There's one very large deal which is actually covered in the press, but it's missing from our list."

"The list of assets came from CBC, so how can we have a deal announcement but no record of the investment?"

Donohue smiled. "Same question I had."

"What do you know about the deal?"

"Well, the missing investment is something called HS1. As a matter of fact, it was the very last deal completed by CBC using Tritona's money. The article I found in the *London Evening Tribune* mentioned CBC's investors paid seventy-six billion British pounds for it. That's over one hundred billion dollars, and yet we've no record of it at all."

"So where is it?"

Donohue shrugged her shoulders. "All I know is CBC didn't

provide us with the documentation for it. They must still have it."

Merriman froze. "Which means—"

"Which means, at the moment, it's not been seized by the U.S. government."

Merriman jumped up and kissed Donohue on the cheek. "You're a genius."

"What is it, Mark?" asked Patti, her face a picture of confusion.

"Kerry has discovered a valuable asset which was bought using the cartel's money, but it hasn't yet been seized. If we can locate the documentation for it, then maybe we could offer this to the cartel as a ransom payment."

Pattie held her fingers to her mouth. "Oh my God! We have less than twenty-four hours. There's no time to lose." She smiled for the first time since their daughter was taken.

Merriman and Donohue left for the office in his car so they could continue the conversation. He wasn't certain he'd done the right thing raising Patti's hopes. The idea was still a long shot, and he was still not convinced the cartel hadn't killed Emma soon after taking her. But the more Donohue explained the anomalies in her research, the more he was certain CBC was holding something back.

As they approached their office building, Merriman turned to Donohue. "Who else knows about this, Kerry?"

"You're the only person I've shared it with."

"Let's keep it that way."

"What still confuses me is how such a massive investment could've been missed from CBC's list of assets. It makes no sense."

"It's certainly suspicious."

What was Kent up to? He certainly had some explaining to do if he still wanted to avoid prosecution. The deal was he had to be cooperative and completely transparent.

As soon as they returned to the office, Merriman checked the details of Donohue's research. No surprise. She was absolutely right. There was, indeed, a substantial missing asset. Twice, he read the printout of the article by the *London Evening Tribune*. Apparently, HS1 had been a UK government-owned, high-speed, electric rail line leading from London to the Channel Tunnel. Recently, it had been auctioned off in order to raise money to reduce the level of government borrowings. The article went on to say the rail line was a goldmine, enjoying highly predictable revenues for many decades to come.

Wasting no time, Merriman found a quiet office and shut the door. He picked up the phone and punched in the number for CBC.

"How can I help you?" said Kent when Tara put through the call.

"I want you to call me back from a public phone in five minutes." He gave no further explanation.

"I'm about to start a meeting. Can I call you later today?"

"Cancel the meeting. This won't wait. I need to talk to you now." Merriman terminated the call.

Kent put down his phone. What was Merriman doing calling on an open line? Who did the man think he was? Kent had delivered his part of the bargain. CBC was supposed to have nothing more to do with the DEA or Merriman now he had his evidence. Kent considered not calling back, but soon thought better of that idea. He didn't trust Merriman, so there was no point aggravating him.

He walked out of CBC's building and across Science Park to a bank of public payphones and made the call.

"It's Kent."

"Where are the HS1 documents?" asked Merriman.

Shit! Kent's throat constricted. How did Merriman know about that? Did he suspect Kent was deliberately holding it back? Even worse, was it possible the man already knew he'd taken the asset? What the hell could he say? Whatever Kent came up with, it had better be convincing if he was going to avoid prosecution.

"I gave the documents to you along with all the others." It was the best response Kent could come up with in a few seconds. There was no point denying the existence of the asset. Merriman clearly knew about it.

"Don't fuck about with me. I don't know why, but we both know you didn't give us that file. You paid seventy-six billion pounds for the company, so where is it? You don't just lose an asset of that size."

"Then there must be some clerical error. I thought I gave you all of the relevant files but, clearly, I didn't. I can only apologize. I'll look into it and call you back as soon as I can."

"Let me explain this carefully, so there can be no misunderstanding. For reasons I can't share with you, my child's life is at risk. If I don't have the HS1 documents within the hour, then you'll be arrested and shipped to prison in the U.S."

"Your child—"

"I haven't finished."

"I'm sorry."

"You won't live long enough to get out of prison, because my next call will be to the cartel. I'll tell them you still have their asset because you decided to keep it for yourself. You'll end up the same way as Baumgart."

"Baumgart's dead? How? When did—"

"Call me when you have the file. You have less than an hour." Merriman finished the call.

Baumgart's dead. The cartel must have wiped him out to guarantee his silence. *Jesus!* Kent would be next if he didn't give Merriman what he wanted. In that fleeting moment, Kent had gone from being one of the world's ten richest individuals to having nothing. No business, no reputation, no prospects—nothing.

He smashed his head hard against the phone box. "Fuck, fuck, fuck!" *What if the cartel is already wiping out everyone involved?*

When Kent recovered his composure, he called Sarah. "Just checking you're okay."

"I'm fine, John, but I can't talk. I'm about to see another patient."

"I just wanted to make sure you're all right."

"Has something happened?"

"No. Nothing."

CHAPTER 56

Kent moped about Science Park, his head throbbing. What was all that about Merriman's child being unwell? Why mention it, unless it was his half-arsed way of excusing his aggressive behavior? The man had always been hostile, so what was different now?

Kent closed his eyes and leaned against a wall. There was no alternative; now the DEA knew about it, he had to give up HS1. Merriman had too much on him, and he wouldn't hesitate to inform the cartel about his cooperation, if it suited him. He rubbed his temples. The documents transferring the asset to Sarah's trust were still in his briefcase. He'd have to bury them as though that transfer never existed. As far as the outside world was concerned, CBC still had legal control of HS1.

What was the point in delaying the inevitable? Kent walked back to the payphone and called Merriman. "Good news. I've located the missing file."

"Oh yeah?" Merriman's tone made it clear he knew Kent was up to something.

"Yes. It wasn't where it should have been. It was our most recent deal completion, and the file hadn't yet been placed in the usual cabinet for completed deals. It was an oversight, and I apologize." Kent knew his words sounded hollow, but he didn't want to go to jail, nor did he want the cartel to learn he'd kept their investment. "I will need something from you first, though."

"Like what?"

"A letter. Making it clear I'm immune from prosecution."

The HS1 asset was Kent's last chip in the game. Now it was

obvious he couldn't trust Merriman, he needed a written guarantee Merriman wouldn't come after him later.

"Scan the HS1 documents and email them to me now. We'll talk about immunity later."

"No. Our deal was I'm kept out of all this. I want your written undertaking before I sign anything."

"For pity's sake."

"No immunity. No HS1."

"Okay, I'll email something over. Don't lose that file."

"Once I have your letter, I'll release it."

Two hours later, Kent had his immunity letter and had scanned all the documents the DEA needed and emailed them. Half an hour after that, Merriman sent one of his agents from USAF Alconbury to collect the originals.

That was it; the asset was gone, but at least Kent was free of the worry Merriman would come after him down the road.

Jivaro called Merriman exactly forty-eight hours after issuing his initial ransom demand. "You think you can call my bluff and play games with your daughter's life?"

"I'm not playing any games. I've done all I can to persuade the U.S. authorities to release your assets, but it's just not possible," replied Merriman, seated in his office surrounded by police officers. He'd been waiting hours for the call to come in.

"Then you know the consequences of your failure to meet my demands. We've nothing more to discuss."

"Wait, wait," Merriman said, anxious to avoid the call coming to an abrupt end. "I do have something to offer you."

"I'm listening."

Merriman hadn't discussed the HS1 asset with anyone else in his department, besides Donohue, nor had he sought the government's consent to handing it over to the cartel. He knew what the answer would be if he'd tried. He'd take his chances and live with the consequences.

"We've located a major asset which hasn't yet been seized. It's the investment in HS1, worth in excess of one hundred billion dollars. If you release my daughter, I'll release that asset to you." Merriman collected all the confused stares from around his office, but he didn't care.

"You don't have to tell me what it's worth. Release it immediately. I'll have my lawyers check the paperwork. When they're completely satisfied, we'll talk."

Jivaro ended the call.

Merriman didn't want to let go of the asset without his daughter's prior release, assuming she was still alive, but what choice did he have? He had nothing to lose and everything to gain by handing over the asset now.

He left his room in order to avoid any awkward questions from the police, and then locked himself away in one of the empty offices. His first call was to Kent to tell him what additional paperwork they would need him to sign to transfer the investment from CBC. He explained it would be different to the method they'd been following in connection with all the other seized assets. This time, it wasn't being transferred to the U.S. Treasury. Kent was confused and raised a few difficult questions, but was otherwise compliant.

Then Merriman called Patti to update her. He wanted to give her something to hold on to, but he took great care to avoid raising too much false hope. Even if Emma was still alive, he had to be realistic about their chances of getting her back.

An hour later, he called Kent again to check the transfer paperwork was complete. Kent told him a courier had already been to CBC to collect the signed documentation and a scan of it was being emailed immediately.

"Why exactly was the transfer document silent on the transferee?" asked Kent.

"It's got nothing to do with you," spat back Merriman.

"I would have expected it mention another U.S. department if—"

"I haven't got time for this."

Merriman ended the call then looked for Kent's email before forwarding it to the Mexican law firm Safuentes had given them. No doubt, they'd fill in the blank transferee box with the name of one of the cartel's corporate vehicles. Minutes later, he was called in to see Bob Butler. Word about his trade with the cartel had already reached his boss.

"This is gonna create a shit-storm, Mark."

Merriman kept a poker face. "Only if it's found out."

"Look. I'm on your side here, but if this gets out, you know you'll lose your job over it."

"What was I supposed to do? If I asked for government consent to use the asset as a ransom, you know what the answer would've been."

"I'd do the same in your shoes. But if the shit hits the fan, I didn't know about any of this."

"I hear you."

Merriman waited in his office all afternoon, expecting a call from the cartel or its lawyers, confirming receipt of the signed transfer Kent had supplied.

He heard nothing.

At 8 p.m., he set off for home, leaving clear instructions he was to be contacted the moment the call came in.

There was no call.

CHAPTER 57

Four long days had passed since the last communication from Safuentes. By now, Patti was frantic and had to be put on tranquilizers. Merriman took no comfort in having always known in his heart their daughter had been killed soon after she was taken. He didn't care that his last-minute attempt to trade HS1 for his daughter's life would probably cost him his career. Given a second chance, he'd do the same thing again for the slim chance of saving Emma.

In the long, sleepless early hours, Merriman had had time to think over the events of the past few days. In that time, he'd grown increasingly suspicious of Kent. Why exactly had he held on to HS1? Merriman had never really bought the pathetic story about a filing error. And why had Kent asked so many awkward questions about the transfer when it didn't matter to him? The man was too smart by half. Was it possible Kent had frustrated the transfer to the cartel in some way?

Back in his office, Merriman called some of his team together. Maybe one of them could spot a flaw in the transfer documents. He explained to his team how Kent, as the CEO of CBC, had supplied the information and original documents to enable the DEA to seize the cartel's assets. Up to now, he'd kept Kent's identity as the source to himself and the DEA leadership team as he'd been trying to protect him. He owed him nothing now, not since he'd tried to hide the HS1 file.

After two hours poring over copies of the transfer paperwork Kent had supplied, everything appeared to be in order. Just before 2 p.m., Merriman stood up as he had to attend a regular

DEA leadership meeting that afternoon.

Once Merriman left the room, Halloran put on his suit jacket, explaining to his colleagues he had arranged to meet an old college friend for lunch and was now running very late. He sprinted to his car and put his foot down when he was on the Capital Beltway heading east. Once across the Potomac River, he headed south on Route 210 then took the exit for Franklin Square Park.

On the edge of the park was a rest area where he pulled in behind a pickup truck. He jumped out of his car and ran over to the truck.

"Where the fuck have you been?" shouted the driver of the pickup. "I've been waiting here for over an hour. I was about to leave."

Halloran raised his palms. "I'm really sorry. I know we said one o'clock, but I was called into a meeting at short notice by my boss. It was impossible for me to let you know."

"If we tell you to be somewhere at a certain time, then you're there at that time. Is that understood? Do you think Rios will understand when I tell him you were late?"

"I'm sorry. Please explain the circumstances to Miguel. I won't let it happen again."

The driver looked like he wanted to spit. "I've got another package for you." He reached behind his seat and picked up a small courier box. He handed it to Halloran, who placed it into his briefcase.

"Before you go, I need you to pass on some important information to Miguel."

"What is it?"

"Tell him the name he is looking for is John Kent of CBC in the UK. That will mean something to him."

The driver gave Halloran a blank look then wrote down his exact words as they clearly meant nothing to him. "I'll make sure he receives the message. Not sure he'll forgive you being late, though."

"He'll forgive me. That message is something Jivaro himself will want to know as soon as possible."

Halloran got out of the truck and jumped back into his own car. He waited for the truck to pull away before taking the package out of his briefcase. He stared at it for a couple of minutes before placing it back into his case. He waited in the rest area for half an hour before making his way back to the office.

Merriman was returning to his office after the three-hour leadership meeting when he was stopped in the corridor by Halloran. "Mark, a delivery came for you while you were in your meeting. I signed for it and left it on your desk."

"Thanks," replied Merriman, who didn't stop.

When he reached his desk, he picked up the small package. His heart started thumping in his chest. Something about it reminded him of the package which had arrived on his birthday. He opened it carefully, his fingers trembling. The dried blood on the inside wrapper was the first thing he noticed. Then he stopped breathing.

"Oh God, no," he said, falling back into his chair. The open box still cupped in his hands, he sat staring at the small, severed left hand of his daughter. How was he ever going to tell Patti about this? *It will kill her.*

When his brain began to function, Merriman noticed a note tucked inside the package. He unfolded it.

It said: "I would have traded your daughter for the asset. You tried to be too clever."

CHAPTER 58

A week later, Merriman was still off work, looking after Patti. While he was beginning to come to terms with events, she wouldn't accept the death of their daughter in the absence of a body. Something inside her needed to keep alive the small hope that Emma would be back any day soon.

Tuesday afternoon, Donohue stopped by the house to speak to her boss.

Merriman opened the door to her then stood back. "Not now, Kerry, please. This is a difficult time for us. It can wait."

Donohue looked embarrassed but stood her ground. "I wasn't sure I should come over, but I thought you'd want to know something."

He exhaled loudly then opened the door wide. "You'd better come in."

"The last thing I want to do is intrude at this sensitive time. It won't take long. I promise."

Merriman led Donohue into his study and closed the door so they wouldn't disturb Patti. They sat on opposite sides of his desk.

"What is it?" he said.

"When we all met last week to review the transfer documents for HS1, none of us spotted anything wrong with them. They appeared to be okay."

"I've thought a lot about this over the last few days. I think the documents were fine." He shook his head. "I'm sure they killed Emma soon after they took her."

"But that doesn't explain the note from Safuentes."

"He's an evil bastard. Probably sent it to get inside my head."

"I'm not so sure."

Merriman knew Donohue well enough to realize she was onto something. "What makes you say that?"

"Because the transfer document wasn't valid. The cartel never got their asset back."

"But we all checked—"

"Superficially, everything appeared to be in order, but it wasn't."

"How?"

"I took copies home last night and read them over. They were properly completed, all right, but the signature on the stock transfer is not John Kent's."

Merriman narrowed his eyes. "Not his signature?"

"It's his handwriting, for sure, but not his usual signature."

"That doesn't make sense."

"It actually reads 'John Fortnam' on the signature line."

"Who the hell is John Fortnam?"

"I don't have a clue. There's no one with that name at CBC."

"Have you searched the Oakham files?"

"I've searched everywhere for the name." Donohue paused. "I don't think he's real."

"Are you thinking what I'm thinking?" he asked, gripping his fingers together tightly.

"I think this was Kent's deliberate attempt to undermine the transfer."

"So do I." Merriman closed his eyes and shook his head. "I don't believe it."

"My guess is the cartel's lawyers picked up Kent's little ploy and thought it was us being smart. That would explain why we didn't hear from them again."

"I want Kent brought to the U.S. I don't care what it takes. Better still, I'll throw him to the savages at the cartel and let them deal with him. His greed may have cost Emma her life."

CHAPTER 59

CBC was like a funeral home in the days following the DEA's asset seizure. Kent's partners spent their time resigning from the boards of portfolio companies and helping the U.S. authorities with their admin as they took over responsibility for the investments. Various U.S. government agencies were involved, but there was no longer a role for CBC. It was depressing work, and all for no reward. Gradually, as the portfolio disappeared, there was less and less to do.

Kent started turning up at the office around midmorning. He hated witnessing the slow death of his creation and spent as little time at CBC as he could. It was not the successful end of the firm he'd once hoped for. He'd always imagined handing over an investment powerhouse upon his eventual retirement, but now his firm was coming to a sad, ignominious end.

What's more, he had the difficult task of making staff redundant as the workload diminished. Many of them had been with him since he'd founded the firm. They were friends as much as colleagues, and he'd let them all down. He knew how hard it would be for them to find work in the private equity industry again now that CBC's reputation was in tatters. In recent days, the newspapers had been filled with stories of CBC's connection to organized crime. Most of them didn't care the firm had been deceived into dealing with the cartel. It made a more interesting story, and sold more papers, spelling out in lurid detail how one of the world's leading private equity firms had become a front for drug money. It would be impossible for anyone at CBC to maintain a professional reputation after all this.

Kent was planning to leave the industry altogether when the firm was wound up. Like the others, he had no choice; he'd be unable to work in financial services again. The FCA would never give him license to operate in another regulated firm. They'd look pretty stupid authorizing the CEO of a firm with proven links to the biggest organized crime outfit in the world. He had no idea what he was going to do with his time. Now almost fifty, he'd gone from being a master of the universe to nothing in a matter of months.

Whatever it was he decided to do, he could never let it show that he remained one of the wealthiest people on the planet. When he'd received the HS1 transfer documents from Merriman and saw a blank space where the transferee should have been named, Kent soon worked out that Merriman planned to siphon off the asset for himself. Why else would it not go to the U.S. Treasury like all the others they'd seized? Kent was having none of it, so he'd deliberately invalidated the transfer documentation with a fictitious signature. That left the asset still in Sarah's name. The cartel would simply assume the DEA had taken it along with all the others. And now Kent had his immunity letter from the DEA, Merriman could go swing. What could he do about it? Merriman could hardly let on he was planning to steal the asset for himself. Still, Kent would have to be vigilant, taking care to hide the income coming from the investment, at least in the early years.

Two weeks after the asset seizure, Kent was at home reading his Sunday newspaper. He picked up the international section and began to read an article about rising Mexican drug cartel violence. It went on to describe the recent kidnap and murder of the daughter of a senior DEA official by the Caruana cartel. He stopped breathing. The official named was a Mark Merriman, the DEA's Head of Intelligence. It was not clear as to whether or not there had been any ransom demands. A few days after the kidnapping, a body part from the young girl had been sent by the cartel, indicating she'd been killed.

Kent's heart felt as though it was about to explode in his chest. That's what Merriman must have meant when he said his child's life was at risk. Had the cartel demanded the return of HS1 as a ransom? Maybe Merriman hadn't been trying to steal the asset for himself. That would explain why he'd sounded so desperate. *Jesus!* Had Kent caused the murder of this young girl? He dropped the newspaper and stared into the middle of the room.

"Are you okay, John?" asked Sarah. He didn't answer. "John?"

"I don't feel well," he said as he stood up and ran to the bathroom.

He threw up into the toilet and then sat on the bathroom floor, leaning against the radiator. How long would it take Merriman to discover what he'd done to the transfer document and to work out he still had the asset? He was bound to hold Kent responsible for his daughter's death. Now he'd issued an immunity letter, and so couldn't come after him using the law, Merriman would think nothing of telling the cartel Kent had stolen the investment. *What a fucking mess.*

Sarah knocked on the bathroom door. "Are you all right in there, John?"

"I'm okay. I think I ate something that didn't agree with me. Give me a few minutes."

Kent stayed seated on the floor, trying to work out what he should do. One thing was crystal clear: he and Sarah had to disappear and quickly. He couldn't have more than a few days before Merriman discovered what he'd done. Maybe he was onto him already.

Later that afternoon, Kent drove to his squash club for a scheduled league match. He didn't feel like playing much, but he needed something to take his mind away from the horrific situation he was in.

While he was out, Sarah heard Kent's cell phone ringing; he'd forgotten to take it with him. The phone rang several times, but she couldn't find it. Eventually, she heard the ringing coming from his briefcase in the study. She opened it and grabbed the phone, just missing the call. As she placed the phone back in the briefcase, she saw a DVD tucked into the same side-pocket. She took it out and inspected it. No label. *Can't do any harm to look.*

She placed the disc into the drive of the iMac on the study desk and waited for it to start. Complete with sound, the video played out in high resolution on the wide screen, showing Kent and Tara in the Geneva hotel suite. Sarah took a step back and held her hand to her mouth.

The bastard!

CHAPTER 60

Two days later, Kent had to let go ten more staff and three partners. They all knew it was coming, but it still didn't soften the blow. By late afternoon, he was shattered having had to deal with the emotion of the redundancies while knowing the cartel would be coming for him anytime soon. There were only days, maybe hours, to figure out what to do.

How was he ever going to persuade Sarah to disappear and leave behind all their family, friends, work, everything? How could he tell her he stole the cartel's investment and that stupid act had, in all probability, led to the murder of an innocent young girl? She'd have to know they'd be on the run for the rest of their lives, pursued by the most brutal drug cartel in the world. Could he really do this to her? Maybe handing himself in was a better option for both of them.

A new email popped up on Kent's screen, shaking him from his self-pity. By coincidence, it was from Sarah, so he opened it immediately.

John,

I know about you and that bitch. Saw the video and every ugly detail.

I told you what would happen if you ever did this again. I said there would be no second chances. I've moved out. Don't bother to come looking for me.

In your briefcase, I found a set of documents relating to something called HS1. For some reason, they were in the name of my trust, so I've taken them.

Good-bye

Kent stopped breathing, then closed his eyes. *I've lost everything.*

"Can I ask you a favor, John?" asked Tara from outside his open office door.

Kent bolted upright in his chair. "I'm sorry. I didn't see you standing there."

"You seemed lost in your own world."

"What is it?"

"Would you mind dropping me off on your way home? My car's in for a service and they've just called to say they need to keep it in overnight."

Tara lived near the village of Oundle, which was not much of a detour for Kent on his regular route home.

He looked at his watch. "Okay, but I'm leaving now. Something urgent has just cropped up."

"Great. Thanks. Sorry to be a pain."

Kent quickly closed the email, powered down his PC, stood, and grabbed his briefcase. He hovered around Tara's desk while she packed her things. "We really need to get going," he said.

He raced along the A14 to Thrapston then headed north on the A605. On their way back, Tara tried to make small-talk about the events of the past year and how sad it was that the firm had been brought to its knees. Kent wasn't really listening, his mind dominated by Sarah's email and where she might be.

"I've lined up another position with an insurance company in Peterborough," said Tara.

"I'm pleased for you."

"It's pretty dull work, but it'll pay the bills."

"I'm sorry we won't be working together."

"Take a left here. It's much quicker," she said as they drove past Oundle Golf Club.

Kent turned left onto a single-lane road called Harley Way. They drove about a mile along the quiet country lane.

Tara pointed to their left. "Pull in here, John."

"Here? Why here?" he asked, slowing down the BMW near

a gated entrance to a wood. The footpath sign next to the gate said: "Lyveden New Bield."

"Just do as I say." Tara had taken out a pistol from her handbag and had it pointed at him.

"What the hell are you doing? Are you mad?"

"Shut up and get out of the car."

"What?"

She released the safety and moved her finger over the trigger. "Get out of the fucking car."

Kent climbed out of the vehicle. Tara did the same, keeping the gun pointed at him.

"Throw me the keys," she said, closing the gap between them.

"Have you lost your mind? What are you playing at?"

Tara shot at the ground close to Kent's feet.

He jumped out of the way. "Okay, okay," he said, holding up his hands.

"The next one won't miss. Now throw me the keys."

He threw them to her.

She pointed with the pistol to the gate leading to the wood. "Follow the footpath."

Kent did what he was told while Tara followed him with the gun pointing at his back. After five hundred yards, they reached the Elizabethan ruin of Lyveden New Bield, a dilapidated aristocratic manor house. Tara ordered Kent into the building. It was getting dark, and no one was about.

"Get on your knees."

Kent knelt on the ground. "Tara, please, what's going on?"

She walked around to face him, holding the pistol two feet away from his head. "This is about the documents you provided to the DEA."

"What documents? I don't know what you're talking about."

"Don't play games with me, John. I know all about the files you gave to Mark Merriman."

"I swear, Tara, I don't know what you're talking about. I had no contact with the DEA before they called me to say they'd seized Tritona's assets. I haven't given them any documents."

"There's no point denying it. The cartel has a mole inside the DEA."

Kent flinched. "What do you know about the cartel?"

"Everything."

"I don't understand."

"I work for the cartel. I always have."

"That's not possible."

"Do you really think Tritona just stumbled across CBC?"

"What do you mean?"

"I knew how desperate you were to find another investor to replace Grampian Capital. That's when I introduced Tritona."

Kent lowered his head. "You're making this up."

"The cartel has a number of people, like me, who've been placed in key financial firms."

"Why?"

"Our job is to introduce them when a firm like CBC is desperate for money and isn't likely to ask too many questions."

"I don't believe you, Tara. What are you really up to?"

Somehow, she must have found out about HS1, Kent thought. She always had access to his private files. Now CBC was over, she was looking to be cut into the deal. That's what this was all about—money.

Kent made eye contact with Tara. "You know about High Speed 1, don't you?"

"This has nothing to do with HS1."

"You want a slice of it. Am I right?"

"A slice of what?"

"Drop the pretense. You know I've stolen that investment and you want in on it. Don't treat me like a fool."

"You're more stupid than I thought."

"I know what you're after. I get it; I'll cut you in. It's big enough for both of us."

Tara shook her head. "I've just told you I work for the cartel, and now you tell me you've stolen one of our assets."

"I don't believe you."

"How do you think Tritona knew to step into CBC's shoes on the Henderson Wright deal?"

"Coincidence."

"Don't be an idiot. Do you really think it was a coincidence the DVD of us in the hotel room in Geneva turned up just as you were planning to write to the NCA?"

"You knew about the DVD?"

Tara laughed. "We set you up. The whole time in Geneva was planned. We had the DVD ready in case we needed leverage over you, in case you failed to cooperate."

"I thought it meant something to you."

Tara raised an eyebrow and snorted. "You can't really believe I found you attractive? You're pathetic."

The woman had played him from the start. "You bitch."

"Finally, you're getting it. Now you must realize Anton's death was no cycling accident?"

"You didn't kill him. Please, tell me that you had nothing to do with that."

"He was in our way, asking too many questions, so I had to deal with him. Doug Wright was another one."

"Oh, Jesus!"

Tara walked closer to Kent, holding the pistol only six inches from his head.

"Tara, please. I beg you. Your mother. What would she think if she saw you now?"

She smiled. "My mother's been dead for years. You still don't get it, do you?"

A chill coursed through Kent's veins. "You evil—"

"You should've stuck to investing, John. If you'd played the game, you'd have been rich. The moment you agreed to help the DEA, your future was written."

She moved her finger over the trigger.

Kent closed his eyes. He thought of his wife and of the life they would never live together. He thought how much he loved her. *I'm so sorry, Sarah. Forgive me, my darling.*

He braced himself. "Tara, please."

The sound of a single shot reverberated around the old ruin as Tara fell to the floor. She was dead before she hit the ground.

Slowly, Kent opened his eyes. *Am I still alive?*

He jumped to his feet and looked around. Tara's contorted body was face down, blood spurting from the bullet wound in her head. "How did it all come to this?" he mumbled.

There was movement in the shadows some fifty feet away. The light was fading fast; it was difficult to see anything. Kent narrowed his eyes. "Who's there?"

The red dot of a rifle's laser sight appeared in the middle of Kent's chest. The round ripped through his heart before the sound of the shot reached his ears.

Merriman was seated behind his desk when his cell phone rang.

"Merriman," he said, answering the call.

"It's done."

GLOSSARY OF TERMS

DEA: Drug Enforcement Administration. This U.S. government agency is responsible for investigating and assisting in the prosecution of criminals involved in the illegal narcotics trade.

FCA: The Financial Conduct Authority. This is the government body responsible for the regulation of financial services firms in the UK.

Leveraged buyout: The acquisition of a company assisted by debt finance. A leveraged buyout firm is a private equity company that specializes in undertaking leveraged buyouts.

SEC: The Securities and Exchange Commission. Among other things, this is the body responsible for the regulation of public companies in the U.S.

NCA: The National Crime Agency. This UK law enforcement body, known as the "British FBI," is responsible for tackling serious organized crime, including class A drugs, people smuggling, fraud and major gun crime.

SPV: Special purpose vehicle. These are corporate and other legal structures used to acquire investments and other assets.

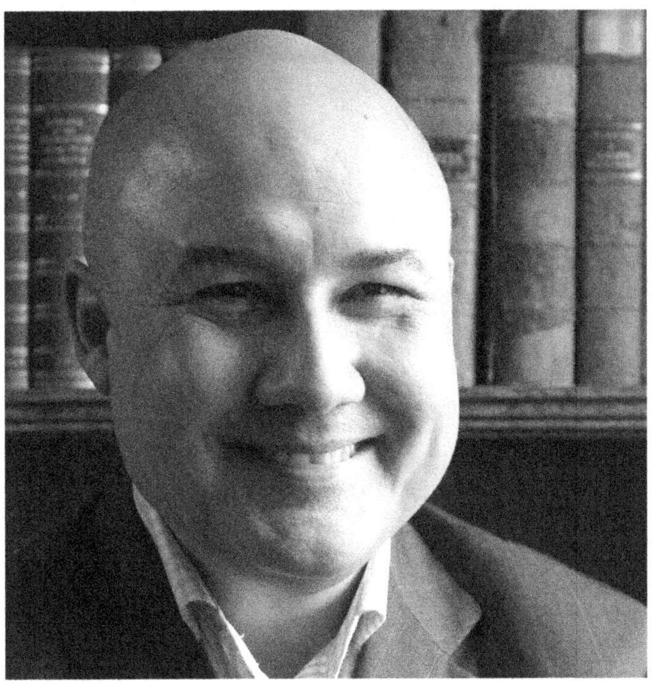

Martin Bodenham was born in the UK. He is the author of the financial thrillers *The Geneva Connection*, *Once a Killer*, and *Shakedown.*

After a thirty-year career in private equity and corporate finance, Martin moved to the west coast of Canada, where he writes full-time. He held corporate finance partner positions at both KPMG and Ernst & Young as well as senior roles at a number of private equity firms before founding his own private equity company in 2001. Much of the tension in his thrillers is based on the greed and fear he witnessed first-hand while working in international finance.

http://www.martinbodenham.com/

On the following pages are a few
more great titles from the
Down & Out Books publishing family.

For a complete list of books and to
sign up for our newsletter,
go to DownAndOutBooks.com.

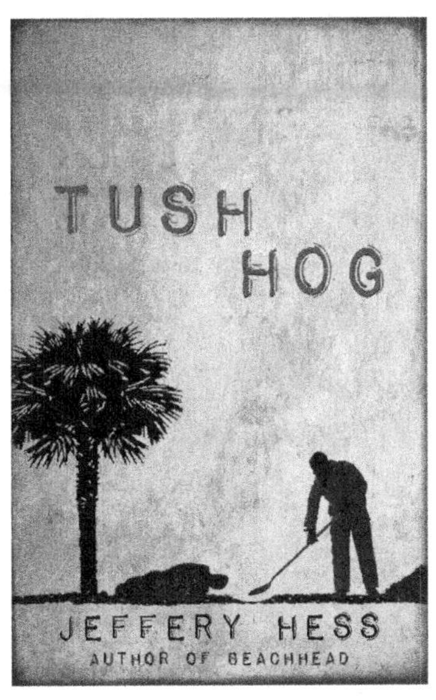

Tushhog
A Scotland Ross Novel
Jeffery Hess

Down & Out Books
May 2018
978-1-946502-60-5

It's 1981 in Fort Myers, Florida, where Scotland Ross squares off with a redneck clan, a Cuban gang, a connected crew from New York, and one friend who does him wrong.

Crimes of violence, drugs, and theft pale in comparison to the failure of self-restraint.

Tushhog is a story of compulsion, the types of people who take what isn't theirs, and the repercussions that follow.

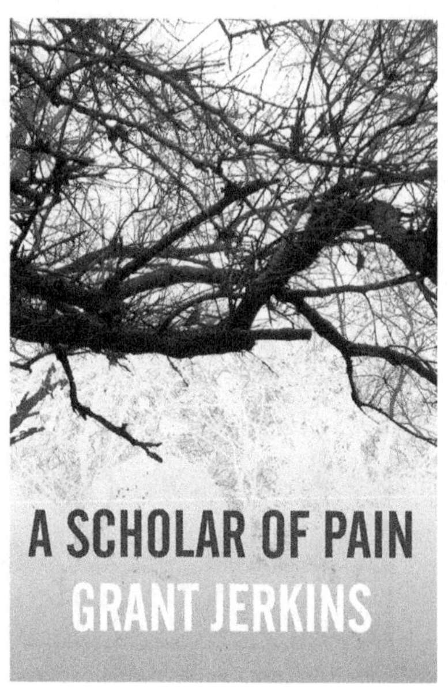

A Scholar of Pain
Grant Jerkins

ABC Group Documentation
an imprint of Down & Out Books
March 2018
978-1-946502-15-5

In his debut short fiction collection, Grant Jerkins remains—as the *Washington Post* put it—"Determined to peer into the darkness and tell us exactly what he sees." Here, the depth of that darkness is on evident, oftentimes poetic, display. Read all sixteen of these deviant diversions. Peer into the darkness.

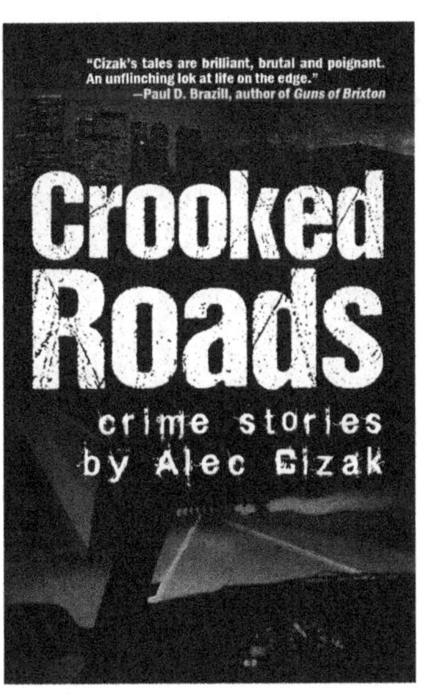

Crooked Roads: Crime Stories
Alec Cizak

All Due Respect, an imprint of
Down & Out Books
978-1-946502-97-1

You want heartfelt sensitive stories about the mid-life crisis of a middle-class white guy? How about ironic tales of suburban marriages where the love has faded? Yeah, if that's what you want, pick up some other book, because this short story collection, is not for you. This book is about real humans in the real streets of cities and small towns. People who are messed up, people at the edge of things—at the edge of sanity, at the edge of morality, at the edge of legality. Criminals, the homeless, the depraved, the perverted, and just normal folk at the end of their rope. Go ahead, pick it up, give it a read. We dare you.

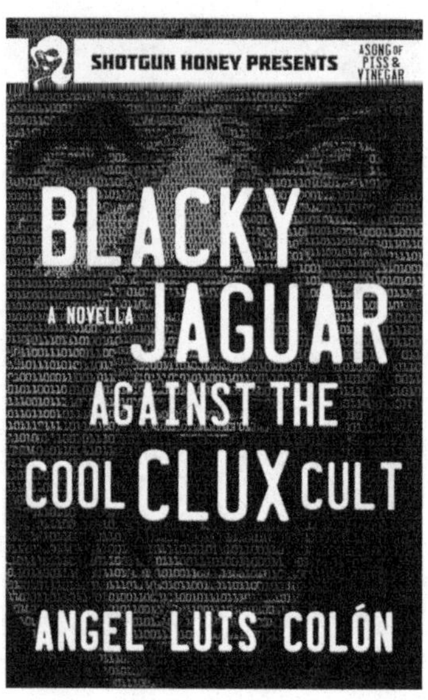

Blacky Jaguar Against the Cool Clux Cult
Angel Luis Colón

Shotgun Honey, an imprint of
Down & Out Books
978-1-943402-86-1

After painting the Cross Bronx Expressway red—literally—and losing his beloved car Polly to his ex, Linda Chen (who isn't returning his calls because she's not a complete idiot), Blacky decides his time is running short and has tasked himself with one last stop before tossing hands up and surrendering: Graceland.

Of course, nothing Blacky Jaguar sets his mind to ends up being simple. Contacted by an old frenemy, Blacky finds himself strong-armed into an online cabal known as The Cool Clux Cult and their shadowy internet tough-guy leader, neilDATASS-tyson.

Made in the USA
Las Vegas, NV
13 January 2025